Aqueduct To Nowhere

The sequel to "No Roads Lead to Rome"

R.S. Gompertz

"I would rather be first in a little Iberian village than second in Rome"
Epicurus
341-271 BCE

ISBN 978-0-9825829-5-4
V-111213

www.noroadsleadtorome.com
Vía del Prat

Also by R.S. Gompertz
NO ROADS LEAD TO ROME

Spain 123 AD. On the edge of the Roman Empire, a poisoned governor leaves behind the opportunity of a lifetime.

Mysteriously promoted, a senator's inept son finds himself in an ancient world of trouble. Within days of taking office, Hispania's taxpayers are in open revolt, all legionaries depart to build Hadrian's Wall, and the once-sleepy province is rocked by slave revolts, bread riots, and fad religions.

A quixotic saga steeped in humor and history, No Roads Lead to Rome chronicles the clumsy schemes of the new governor and his shadowy adviser, a superstitious centurion's struggle to save his faith in the faded ideals of the Republic, and two mismatched brothers' attempts to change the course of history. All are pitted against the gods, the emperor, and the decline and fall of damn near everything.

From Publishers Weekly:

"The Roman Empire is at a crossroads, and Emperor Hadrian, realizing that continued expansion will make the empire's borders indefensible, decrees consolidation to a size the legions can better guard. That story is told here in a confusion of the historical, the comical, the metaphorical, and the adventurous that mostly (and surprisingly) holds together fairly well. In the province of Hispania, the governor, Festus Rufius, has just taken over for his murdered predecessor, veteran centurion Marcus Valerius.

Surviving on graft, plots, kickbacks and bribery, the Empire lurches on while Hispania is beset by slave revolts, food riots, uncollected taxes, and bad wine. And so the province's leadership must resort to a series of desperate illusions to disguise its failings.

All this is recounted swiftly, with verve, panache, and a light tread that makes for a delightful, well-told tale."

Aqueduct To Nowhere

One
I

Tarraco, the capital of Hispania, swelled to twice its daytime population and quivered like a nervous bride. Costumed Spaniards emerged from every neighborhood and flooded toward the central forum.

On this, the first night of Saturnalia, the world officially turned upside down. Slaves became masters, and masters, slaves. For Hispania's farmers, the winter solstice approached with a sober reminder to plow, plant, and pray. For the province's city dwellers, tomorrow would be soon enough to worry about the future.

The cold sea breeze pulsed with anticipation

"Io Saturnalia!" shouted the two town criers. For once they agreed on something.

Gaius Severus pushed through the crowded streets, his heart pounding with anticipation for his first love and first Saturnalia. The Fates incarnate could not have prevented him from celebrating the longest and most festive night of the year. He was so flush with freedom that he did not feel the winter chill.

With his father and brother now halfway to Judea, Gaius was free to do as he wished. The world was tilting in his favor and nobody would tell him otherwise. His father hated Roman festivals and pageantry. His older brother, Marius, always warned against the dangers of "going Roman." In years past, the family would draw their tattered window shade and ignore the festivities. Marius and Father would have argued over a fragment of Pentateuch while Gaius struggled to forget the revelry below.

Gaius understood that Jewish law opposed Rome's profane gods and unclean rituals—but so far as he knew, there was no commandment against having a little fun. What kind of dreary, jealous God would object to shaking off the darkness of winter with a bit of music, drink, and dance?

Surely God had better things to worry about.

1

Gaius was skinny enough to weave through the colorful crowd. He advanced slowly, keeping his eyes peeled for the stocky Corsican who had raided their tenement a month earlier. In response to the suspicious death of Governor Biberious, the usual suspects—Jews, liberals, foreigners—had been rounded up and harassed. Having lived barely one generation in Hispania, the Severus family qualified as all three.

Gaius had escaped after a tense chase. He fled town and found accidental refuge with a legion cohort. His father and brother managed to escape from both prison and the province. By now the Corsican thug who had sent them reeling had probably returned to his island to wallow in sour wine.

If Gaius could ask God for one thing, it would be seeing that Marius and Father reached Jerusalem safely. If God had time for one more wish, Gaius would ask for the Corsican to drown in fish brine while choking on pig fat.

Severus was jostled from the memory by a small jackal pursuing a girl dressed as a faun. A golden butterfly with crooked antennae and silk wings flitted through the crowd and reminded Severus of all that he had missed growing up. Taller than most Spaniards, he scanned the costumed crowd for Lena. She once claimed to be a mountain cat's daughter, and Gaius had little reason to doubt her. Instead of a tawny lioness, an iridescent crow now angled toward him. The bird was Lena's height, but a crow was out of character for a girl who placed high stock in omens. The bird pecked Severus on the cheek and then cawed loudly in his ear.

Aside from childhood kisses with a neighbor girl, his life experience with romance was nil. His notions of love were based on faith. Springtime flirtations in the marketplace had never ventured past blushing. He now saw the many missed Saturnalias as lost opportunities. Costumes rendered first encounters less awkward, kisses less scarce. Improbable pairs of insects and animals peeled off into dark alleys. Disguised strangers were quick to embrace and slow to release. It was no wonder so many children were born nine months after the festival.

The curtain of night drew across the fire-lit capital. Smoke hung, trapped in patches. The smell of burning sage drifted through the alley. Chanting echoed and drums rumbled through the tenement canyons.

Spaniards spilled out from buildings and neighborhoods, crowding into the streets. Rhythms mixed and churned like rushing water. Colorful masks, capes, and costumes adorned even the poorest of the plebes who had scrimped and saved to conjure materials for a costume. Entire neighborhoods took up collections to buy banners and drums lest they be upstaged or outshouted by rival quarters.

"Io Saturnalia!" shouted a woman who had just drained a wineskin.

"Bonus solstice!" responded a man wearing nothing but feathers.

Severus stopped to savor the improbable moment. For the first time in his short life, he was in the thick of a true celebration. What had his father been so worried about? The festival was profane but harmless. Rather than feeling tainted with sin, Severus felt exhilarated to be on his own in a world full of possibilities.

Slaves had become the masters. By the rules of Saturnalia even Security Chief Ferro, his overbearing supervisor, would be subject to a subordinate's command. This probably explained why old Ferro was nowhere to be found.

The crowd quickened like a river through a narrow canyon. Severus' leaping heart propelled him forward. He scanned the crowd for Lena and tried to keep from bursting with anticipation. His first and only love had to be nearby. Tonight they would drink and dance and bathe in smoke and celebration. When the moment was right, he would ask for her hand. With no families to oppose them, they might even wed on the spot. Tonight they could join their lives together as the Fates so clearly intended.

Carried along by the surge, Severus bumped into a garish hooker trawling for business at the mouth of a dark alley.

"Security guard, eh?" She hooked a thumb in her low-cut tunic and revealed a deep valley in which a young man might easily lose his head. "You'll be busy tonight, my limp little lad."

"Off duty, ma'am." Severus smiled. All rules of public morality were suspended during the festival lest the prisons overflow like sewers in a downpour. With masters often behaving worse than their temporarily freed slaves, nothing short of murder was illegal. "Have a prosperous evening, *domina*."

"Prosperous?" She laughed and pointed to the silhouettes of two lovers rutting like pigeons on a stoop. "Saturnalia's bad for business."

Severus stepped back into the rushing crowd, hoping to find his lanky goddess. He had never imagined wanting someone so much that time spent apart would seem like torture. Knowing that his finger-wagging father and dogmatic brother would have disapproved rendered her all the more desirable. Lena was spun from a different thread of history than his loosely knit tribe. Tradition dictated that Marius should wed first, but something went wrong with every attempted alliance. There were only a few Jewish girls in town, and Marius had managed to insult them all.

With his kin so far away, perhaps never to return, Gaius Severus resolved not to waste his life as a tribe of one. Love made him feel invincible. He would defy the universe, sprout wings for Lena. Had he not overpowered a gladiator, stolen a horse and ridden with her until their bodies ached with freedom? Their combined audacity was far greater than anything he could have mustered alone.

Once safe in Tarraco, Lena had found work in the governor's kitchen. Severus parlayed his limited military experience into a job as a capitol security guard. Money was tight, but with a bit of luck and a lot of effort, they would scratch out a modest life, raise a family, and grow old together. The future glistened with possibilities.

Tonight, they had agreed to meet under the new statue of Hadrian, built in tribute to an imperial visit that had never occurred. Severus followed in the wake of a wide fellow who cleared a path forward.

Bonfires burned across the forum. Torches cast orange light upon the deified emperor whose great imperial nose had been broken off for the third time in as many weeks. People danced around the statue, placing flowers, fruits, and entrails around the granite base. Women smelled of juniper and rosewater.

Demons and cherubim gathered under the colonnades. A wave of painted faces drifted across the square. The crowd floated as if weightless on the wings of disguise. Girls climbed on the pedestals and flirted with the reaching boys below. Children waved banners. Women tossed colorful scarves into the air. A team of drummers wearing goatskins, horns, and spiked tails surged into the plaza. The pounding grew louder and more urgent until a thousand rhythms converged into one thunderous pulse.

Swept up in the celebration, Severus threw his arms in the air. His cheering was cut short when two men threw a canvas sack over his head and wrestled him to the ground.

Two
II

Gaius Severus had not intended to spend the evening with a sack over his head. He had just caught a glimpse of Lena's red cloak when two men accosted and dragged him from the celebration. Now, instead of dancing with the only girl he had ever loved, two thugs were bouncing him on the cobblestones.

Kidnappers would be angry that he had no kin to pay a ransom. Robbers would soon be disappointed. With no coins to pay Charon the Boatman, he was too poor to cross the River Styx.

Severus struggled and shouted, but the crowd ignored him. Tarraco, the capital of Hispania, was not a town where people meddled in the affairs of others. On an average night, the sight of a hooded man being dragged through the streets might be cause for curiosity. During Saturnalia it was easy to confuse a public kidnapping with street theater.

"Let me go!" Severus tried to shake off the hood, but it was secured tight around his neck. "I work for the governor."

He fought to break loose from the sturdy grip of two strong men, one of whom smelled like a wet goat. Severus was disoriented, but from the joyful noise around him he knew that he was still within shouting distance of the forum where, unfortunately, everyone was shouting louder than he.

"Help!" he yelled, in spite of being smacked by one of his captors.

Severus choked back his fear and tried to stay clearheaded. In comparison to all he had been through recently, tonight's incident was probably no more than a prank. Barely one month prior, his adopted cohort had earned swift, deadly punishment for laying siege to an innocent border town. A day later, he had fought a tavern brawl with a hairy thug who claimed Lena was a slave.

"Let me give him a kick!" said a voice Severus recognized. It was one of the villa's less trustworthy laundry slaves, a resentful little fellow who trafficked in stolen kitchenware.

"Stop!" Severus shouted. "I'm not whoever you think I am." He squirmed, but attempts to twist free were rewarded with more kicks.

6

A frustrated woman willfully mistook him for her husband and added insults to injuries. Others just needed to hit someone, anyone.

When the beatings stopped, Severus went limp as a jellyfish to inconvenience his captors, but his featherweight offered no gravitas. His captors spun him until he fell and then lifted him by the ankles to better bounce his head against the cobblestones.

Moments later, he was thrown down a stairway into a subterranean room. Dizzy and aching, Severus hardly realized that the beatings had stopped. He gathered his wits, verified that his bones were intact, then flipped over to get his face out of the dirt.

Someone untied his numb hands and wrestled the sack off his head.

"Don't worry," a familiar voice whispered.

"Pergo?" Severus recognized the bland voice of an old soldier who had been lucky enough to retire from the *Scipio IV Hispania* cohort alive. Pension poor, rumor rich, Pergo had joined the villa's security squad to specialize in avoiding work and spreading conspiracy theories. "Why are we here?"

"Tonight's our big initiation." The normally lackluster Pergo sounded excited.

The ceiling above them rattled as two planks slid apart. Weak yellow lamplight leaked through the lath work. Severus squinted up into the dim chamber hoping to glean some clue as to where and why they were being held.

"Vesuvius!" The cellar door creaked open just long enough for another captive to be tossed down the stairs. Reeking of wine and tavern sweat, the newcomer crashed into Pergo and knocked him to the ground.

"Dii immortales!" Pergo cursed. "Watch where you're going, Limbo."

Limbo—the nickname fit tight as an undersized tunic—had joined the security force after having been disowned for surpassing his family's hard-earned reputation for dishonesty. Needing a job and a roof over his head, the younger man followed the chosen path of many untalented and lawless teens and became a security guard.

"Listen." Severus tore the hood from Limbo's head. "As soon as we see an opening, we storm it and get out of here."

"Why?" Limbo wheezed and dusted himself off. "Maybe they're going to feed us."

7

Heavy scuffling was followed by a loose stream of bovine slop from above.

"Nero's nuts!" Severus could barely inhale. "They've got a cow up there."

"A bull." Pergo flicked shit from his shoulder. "Haven't you understood anything I've said?"

The hobbled bull shifted nervously. Three men wrestled the beast into the center of the room above. Severus heard the joists groaning and flattened himself against the wall.

Incense smoke hovered like an unheard prayer.

"From the East came Mithras," chanted a voice Severus recognized. It was Ferro, his supervisor, the domineering and opinionated security chief. In addition to leading the team of miscreants tasked with keeping order, it now appeared that Ferro was a priest in the not-so-secret cult of soldiers. "Lord Mithras, born of the cosmic egg, born of the immaculate Virgin Mother ..."

Ferro lit a pitch torch that illuminated two robed men on the far side of the bull. The three hummed a low, otherworldly incantation

"Mithras the Immortal," Ferro intoned as if entering a trance from which there was no exit. *"Deo Invicto.* Protector of truth and justice."

"What in Jove's name are they doing?" Severus whispered.

"Shut up and come into the center of the room," Pergo hissed. "We're the new acolytes."

Unconvinced, Severus crept up the stairs. The cellar doors were locked from the outside. He peered through a crack but saw no one in the dark alley outside.

"Mithras, our redeemer!" Ferro sang.

"Mithras!" Pergo raised his arms toward the bull. "Our savior."

"Destroyer of evil," Ferro waved the torch over the bull's arched spine. "We bring you three new ravens, unwashed souls to drink of the blood."

"Mithras resurrected," said a new voice with the power to stop Severus' heart. It belonged to of one of the four assassins who had attacked the legionary camp.

"Mithras immortal," chanted another voice Severus also recognized from the massacre.

Two of the ruthless praetorians who had punished the cohort had returned. Why were they officiating as priests? On a night less holy,

8

they had sent forty men to the afterlife. Roman justice flowed like blood in response to the troops' botched raid on a northern village. Had the killers returned to finish the job?

Severus sensed motion in the alley. "Open the door!" he shouted through a knothole.

The bull snorted. The floor joists sagged.

"Bathe in the bull's holy waters!" Pergo stepped into the bull's sudden shower. He moaned and swayed, possessed. "Drink!"

"Not thirsty," Severus almost choked on the acrid air. Convinced that someone was outside, he stuck his finger through the knothole and rattled the door.

"Come into the center," Pergo called to Severus.

"Mithras, Mithras." Chief Ferro sounded intoxicated with true belief. "Born this solstice night. Died as a man. Risen as a god."

"Mithras. Mithras," droned an assassin priest. "God of the great Alexander. Protector of soldiers. Accept our initiates on this solstice night."

"The solstice is tomorrow!" Limbo shouted, but it did not seem to matter.

Ferro drew a long knife from his sash. "From the flesh of the bull springs the fruit of the earth. From his blood flows life everlasting ..."

Ferro positioned a chalice to receive the bull's first blood and jabbed his blade into the bull's neck. Not fully committed to the initiation, the bull groaned loudly and sent Ferro sprawling.

"Mithras is displeased," Ferro shouted.

Oil from an upset lamp traced a trail of fire across the splintering floor.

The bull thrashed about with such force that Severus heard bones snap like dry twigs. A burning beam cracked beneath a half-ton of falling hoof, muscle, and horn.

Pergo would never collect his pension. The old soldier disappeared, crushed under the fallen bull.

Flames rained down from above as the building caught fire.

The terrified bull whipped its great head in a circle, struggling to right itself.

"He'll kill us," Limbo cried.

"Help!" Severus pounded on the cellar door.

"I'm working on it," a voice whispered through the knothole.

The beast rose and glared. Its eyes glowed red in the falling flames. The rope that once bound its hind legs had not held.

The bull lurched toward Severus as the warped door burst open. A strong hand reached in to pull him to safety.

"Marius?" Gaius was shocked to see his brother, who had supposedly left for Judea a month earlier.

"Move aside!" Marius shouted.

The bleeding bull struggled out onto the street and moved away from the smoke.

Limbo scrambled up the stairs. Covered in soot, he ran blind with terror toward the refuse pile at the dead end of the alley. "Mother of Mercury!" he shouted.

The bull turned toward Limbo.

"Over here!" Severus stamped his feet and whistled.

Distracted by the provocation, the sacred beast whirled around. It pawed at the pavement, lowered its head, and charged at the two brothers.

Three
III

Lost in the crowd and caught up in the rising excitement, Lena turned into yet another narrow passageway. By day, the town was a tangle of skewed lines and sagging canyons that she had yet to unravel. By night, it was a shadowy labyrinth.

"I'm your slave!" A short, furry fellow with a long tail dropped to his knees in front of her. "I live to do your bidding, young *domina.*"

Lena considered wrapping the tail around his neck, but knew it would accomplish nothing. Masters might be slaves; and slaves, masters, but men were still men.

Snaking through the darkness, she stumbled over a large man sleeping against the back door to a butcher shop. He gasped like a beached cod, grabbed the tail of her long red cloak and twisted it in his pudgy hand.

After a brief struggle Lena yanked herself free, only to find a raucous drum team now blocking her exit. The drummers were dressed as locusts with green and yellow bodies, stiff brown wings, and bobbing straw antennae. An elder member of the swarm noticed Lena, stuck out his tongue and wagged it lewdly.

Glancing back, she saw that the drunk who had grabbed her cloak was now sprawled across the cobblestone snoring. It gave her no comfort to remember that a more determined giant, might still be stalking her. She and Gaius had managed to escape him in a tavern brawl a few weeks prior, but the masquerade could provide the cover he needed to find and capture her. To remain free, she would have to remain vigilant.

A squad of pubescent, marriage-aged girls tossed weighted flags into the air. For lack of a dowry, the less fortunate girls might finish the evening engaged to lecherous old widowers. The others would be pregnant by next winter. Lena shuddered at the thought of being condemned to serve a husband. Had she not escaped, her fate would have been far worse than marriage.

Tum-ta-ta-tum-tum! Stomping feet and pulsing drums rattled and echoed off the walls. *Ratta-tam-tam-tam!*

11

Red-trimmed batons and yellow streamers spiraled into the sky. Spectators reached from sagging balconies and tried to catch the weighted pennants.

"Io, Saturnalia!" The girls spun circles and caught their falling flags.

Lena knew she was late. Her only hope was that the ever-punctual Gaius Severus had been distracted as well. Before coming to Tarraco, minutes had not really mattered, but city time seemed to be in constant shortage. It was as if everyone in town had a water clock dripping inside their heads.

The marchers stopped at a crowded intersection where a troupe of red-clad demons taunted spectators with pitch torches. The drummers halted, causing a few of the swirling flags to fall behind the rearguard girls. Lena caught a wayward pennant and waved it over her head. She swayed as if submerged in the pine smoke and perfume.

Tum-ta-ta-tum-tum! Ta-ta-tum-tum-tum!

Nothing in her seventeen years—not the first winter snow or last spring lupine—had ever seemed so pure and perfect. She singed the bottom of her cloak by leaping through the flames of a street-wide bonfire.

"Io, Saturnalia!" Lena threw her arms into the air and cheered.

Marching behind the red and yellow flag of Southwest Tarraco, Lena and the locusts spilled into the plaza. They drummed and chanted, loud enough to rouse the gods.

An old woman sitting on the stairs in front of the treasury basilica leaned forward to offer a candied mushroom. "Goddess be with you, my daughter," the old woman blessed Lena through missing teeth.

Lena popped the delicacy in her mouth. She had no coin to offer but reached down and held the woman's gnarled hand for a second. As the surge pushed forward the warmth of the moment lingered as if to remind Lena that the many years between them were but a season.

Drum squads thundered into positions at the four corners of the plaza. The demon troupe from Northwest Tarraco chanted loudly, trying to overwhelm a school of spotted fish from the docklands. Rival dancers dressed as horned and tusked beasts—goats, stags, and one very aggressive boar—gyrated as if springtime might never come again.

Flaming sticks spun into the air and hung like stars. Spiral shadows danced on the columns and statues. Rising smoke draped the full moon in a gray veil. Lena's heart pulsed like a star.

At each end of the forum, neighborhood teams erected human castles. Small children raced to the top of towers six and seven levels high. At the base of one castle men began to tremble and, within a second, the structure crumbled into a pile of legs and torsos.

Lena wove through cracks in the shifting crowd. She looked up at Hadrian's missing nose and recalled her promise to meet Gaius at the emperor's feet. She handed her flag to a child and joined in dancing around the statue. Rounding the emperor's backside, she noticed a pair of security guards removing a hooded captive. A compact, serious-looking fellow with a vague resemblance to Gaius followed the odd contingent with incongruous determination.

At once, all drums went mute. On cue, all torches were extinguished.

"*Io, Saturnalia!*" A resonant voice from the large stage in front of the temple broke the silence.

Yellow light bent through the creaking doors to the Temple of Saturn. Solemn, robed women emerged, followed by men dressed as hawks, goats, and demons.

Lena let her long hair fall below her shoulders. She felt the night's rhythm vibrating through the length of her body. Spellbound and lightheaded, she lost herself in the revelry and hugged a two-headed fish dancing beside her.

"*Bonus Saturnalia!*" she shouted. She felt one with the crowd, one with the night, one with the great mother whose boundlessness suckled the roots of every tree that had ever yearned for the sky.

A procession of elegantly dressed, torch-bearing slaves from the governor's mansion emerged from the temple. They fanned out across the stage and preened for the crowd. On no other night would slaves have been allowed inside the temple. On no other night would such transgression earn applause.

Don Rexus, the *Saturnalia Princeps,* rose from a hidden platform and was greeted by a fanfare of shrill horns and screaming women. His silver hair shimmered like a frozen waterfall. Men clapped politely, but to the swooning matrons it was as if a star had fallen from the constellation of Hercules. His bearing was regal, his dress

13

rich and colorful. Stage makeup deepened his eyes and raised his profile.

"Masters and slaves," he shouted, "subjects and citizens. Tonight the heavens are below us, the earth above. Tonight the world is upside down!"

The crowd cheered, stomped, drummed and trumpeted louder than they had all night.

"I declare masters, slaves; and slaves, masters," Rexus boomed. "The highest must attend to the lowest. The mighty must serve the weak."

"Serve me!" a middle-aged woman shouted to the agreement of others.

"In that spirit ..." Rexus reached over and laid a long arm on the narrow shoulders of the governor's tiny valet, "it is my great privilege to give you the cornerstone of the capitol! The spritely slave who keeps the vultures at bay and the pigs in clover! This little man has served and outlived every overpaid, overstuffed, and overbearing governor that you've had to endure. The one, the only ... Carbo the Kitchen Slave!"

A team of slaves lifted Carbo onto their shoulders and paraded him around the stage. Torchlight from below caused his shadow to swell against the temple columns.

Lena lifted her hands to join the sea of arms waving like a wheat field in the wind. Carbo had been the first person to befriend her at the villa. Jealous of her freedom, the other servants had been petty and spiteful. They hid her supplies and stole from her spice cabinet. Carbo alone had been kind and helpful. Now the governor's personal valet, he took more than a slave's interest in everything that happened in the villa. Older than water, he had the dirt on dirt itself.

Nearly lost in the governor's fur-lined cloak and crimson sash, Carbo took to the stage. Swaying as if drunk with freedom, he bathed in the crowd's adoration and waited for them to settle. When a tenuous quiet fell, he began the traditional verses that, one night a year, spoke truth to power.

> "Tarraco, Tarraco, our once-vibrant town,
> Like a sick old dog we need to put down.
> The wine tastes like piss, the bread dole's gone stale.
> No one's surprised another governor's failed."

14

Lena laughed at Carbo's cheekiness, but most of the crowd jeered at the timidity of his opening lines. A slave so close to the center of power could surely do a better job of skewering his famously inept and self-serving master, Governor Festus Rufius.

"Don't hold back," someone shouted.

"It's Saturnalia!" another yelled. "What are you afraid of?"

Carbo feigned embarrassment and disappeared into the many folds of Rufius' expensive cloak. When the crowd shouted for him to stop hiding, he spun until the fabric unfolded like an inverted flower. He turned faster and faster, stopping just short of boring a hole through the stage.

"The rich eat mutton; the poor chew bones,
Only hookers and thieves call Tarraco their home.
Taxes are missing, the province is broke.
The governor's naked and I have his cloak."

"Now you're talking!" a woman yelled.

"Talking pretty," shouted a tall man dressed as a birch tree. For a second, Lena thought he might be Gaius Severus, but the voice was lower and the trunk too wide. "Come on, Carbo! Let the bastard have it!"

Carbo now appeared to float over the spectators. He beckoned to where Vindex the ex-gladiator was lurking. The red-haired giant dragged a paunchy man wearing a commoner's tunic forward into the torchlight.

"Festus Rufius!" a delighted spectator shouted. "The worst governor ever!"

Rufius struggled in vain to break free. He twisted his ample girth and swung his arms. The lack of trust between the privileged governor and his sullen bodyguard was thick and obvious. It was clear from any distance that his resistance was not theatrical.

Word spread across the forum and the crowd cheered with a bloodlust normally reserved for the arena. The surge forced people in the front rows to seek refuge under the stage.

The hated governor had not been seen since the botched assassination attempt on Hadrian a few weeks earlier. On that gray day in November, Rufius had proved as inept at regicide as he was at

15

governance. Since then, the nectar of nepotism had turned to vinegar.

"Rufius, resign!" The taunts multiplied.

"Slit your wrists, party boy!"

The crowd jeered until Carbo flapped his sleeves like the wings of an imperial butterfly and signaled for quiet.

> "His brother's been murdered, his father's disowned him.
> Why must we suffer this fool of a Roman?
> Hadrian hates us thanks to old Rufius,
> A mystery why no one's arrested this doofus."

No further provocation was needed. Fists shot into the air.

"Arrest the governor!" The crowd teetered at the edge of riot. Some people climbed the pedestals. Others hoisted their children out of harm's way. Pickpockets worked quickly while wine vendors refilled drained bladders.

Carbo turned his palms upward as if seeking the gods' forgiveness and the mob's permission. The crowd pulsed with approval and eventually calmed long enough to hear Carbo address Rufius directly.

> "By popular vote, unknown since the Caesars,
> We condemn your short hairs to be plucked with old tweezers.
> Since master is slave and this slave is your master.
> I condemn you to prison. Go rot, you fat bastard!"

The air filled with roaring approval.

Still holding Rufius aloft, Vindex descended into the crowd and led a line of drummers and dancers snaking into the forum. The ex-gladiator draped Governor Rufius over one shoulder like a wet sack of wheat. A vengeful crowd danced behind them, drunk with condemnation. Vindex stopped at the center of the plaza and hoisted the protesting governor into the air. The former arena fighter stiffened his arms and danced a jig while his irate captive squirmed in panic. Fearing the hard fall of a well-fed noble, people gave them wide berth.

Meanwhile, flames from a burning building licked the sky. The shabby five-story tenement would be as quick to crumble as it had been to build. If Saturnalia had not already emptied it of people, escape from the upper floors would have required wings.

Far upwind from the fire, Carbo danced on the stage with fellow slaves. Inebriated with temporary liberty, some turned blasphemous.

"Carbo for governor!" a kitchen slave shouted. "*Ave* Carbo!"

"Carbo for emperor!"

"Hail the divine Carbo!"

Lena was delighted to see her friend being celebrated. Carbo's uncharacteristic mirth was infectious. Laughter swept over her, and she abandoned herself to the crowd's intoxicating power. Everywhere she turned there was motion. She tore off her red cloak and waved it overhead as if flagging a distant ship.

An old man grabbed her from behind with excessive familiarity. On a normal night, she would have sent him sprawling, but tonight she just twisted free. Her heart pulsed like a drum until a strange darkness crept over her. Joy gave way to a sense of danger rising beneath the frivolity. Sensing that something confused and powerful had awakened, she pushed through the crowd to find the source of the disturbance.

The feeling dissipated as Vindex's drum line passed by. The usually dour ex-gladiator bounced Festus Rufius on his broad shoulder and ignored the governor's orders to desist. Rufius had promised him freedom but never delivered. Vindex clearly savored the opportunity to return the disappointment.

Back on stage, Carbo strutted, waved and bowed. The tiny slave strained every sinew in his thin neck to shout over the roar of the crowd. "As your new governor, I hereby condemn the slave Festus Rufius to get what he deserves!"

"To the arena!" The audience cheered. The snaking parade of drummers, dancers, and festooned revelers wound into an ever-tightening spiral. "Send him to the mines!"

Carbo feigned a striptease. Accompanied by a horn player, he gyrated and teased the crowd by slowly removing the governor's lavish garment. He pranced along the edge of the stage, swooping and dipping, encouraging the audience to toss coins and rude suggestions. He finally peeled off the oversized cloak to reveal a tiny frame wrapped in a regal purple toga. The audience howled to see a kitchen slave draped in the color reserved for the emperor alone.

Bumping and grinding, he waved the cloak over his head and tossed it into the crowd. Surprised by his own audacity, he performed a perfect swan dive into the mob's outstretched arms.

"Io Saturnalia!" Vindex shouted. He shifted position to render the governor's ample posterior available for smacking.

"Put me down," Rufius insisted. "Saturnalia may pass, but death is forever."

"As you wish." The statuesque bodyguard dropped Rufius onto the pavement and the mob surged inward to salute with fists and heels.

"Pick me up before they tear me apart!" Rufius shouted.

"Make up your mind." Vindex cracked his knuckles one by one before scooping Rufius up and stomping off toward the arena. "Don't think of jail as being locked in. Think of it as the mob locked out."

Since Rufius had granted the traditional Saturnalia pardon hours earlier, jail would be safer than the streets. An empty cell under the arena would provide safe harbor from the present storm of projectiles and disrespect. No insults, slaps, or half-chewed fish balls would torment him behind the prison doors.

Four
IV

Unable to outrun the bull, the brothers Severus shook the threat off their tails by jumping into an elevated doorway. The steaming, two-horned hurricane blew past them and charged toward the celebration.

The beast cut a wide swath. A few celebrants scrambled onto pedestals and climbed up columns, but most escape routes were blocked like bad plumbing. A young daredevil lost a challenge when the beast outran him and threw him over its great steaming head. The fellow cleared the horns by just enough to inspire others to run faster.

"What are you doing back in Tarraco?" Gaius Severus could barely cough out the question. His chest felt tight as a drum skin. His eyes burned from the smoke but he could see his brother's tunic was frayed.

"I came back to find you." Marius' bushy hair was unkempt, his cheeks smudged with ash. The bulkier of the two, he struggled for balance on the narrow stoop. "Just in time, I see."

"Is Father here, too? Weren't you both on a pilgrimage to Judea?"

Marius stepped down from the doorway and turned to leave. "God had a different plan, though damned if I understand it."

"Wait." Gaius grabbed his brother's sleeve. "You show up from out of nowhere and now you're leaving? Tell me about Father."

"He betrayed the rebellion." Marius avoided his brother's eyes. He gestured toward the crowd, squinting at the dancing pagans. "This festival is an abomination, just like Father."

"Where is he?" Overcome by years of pent-up desire to knock sense into his brother's head, Gaius shoved Marius hard against a column. He tried to pin him there long enough to extract an answer, but Marius was heavier, stronger, and too scrappy to restrain. Within one beat of a nearby drum, Gaius was pinned against the fluted column.

"I just saved your life, idiot." Marius tightened his grip.

"That doesn't give you the right to ruin it." Gaius directed a weak knee into his brother's thigh, but it barely registered. "Where is Father?"

"He ran off with a woman. A pagan." Marius spat out the words as if they were coated with dirt. "He abandoned our cause. He defied the will of God."

"Fine." Gaius knew better than to debate politics or theology with his militant brother. "Just tell me where he is."

"Barcino." Marius shook his head in disbelief that their stalwart father had fallen so low. "Shacked up with a sinner."

"For that you sacrifice your family? According to you, we're all sinners." The terror and loss of the past few weeks flooded over Gaius Severus. His family had never been typical, but now they were scattered like seeds, drifting and rootless. "Why can't you just be happy that Father found someone to love again? He's an old man. Who cares if she's a pagan? Isn't this better than his crazy quest for a homeland he's never seen?"

"God gave us Judea! I'll teach you to blaspheme." Marius slammed Gaius against the column.

Seventeen years of living under his brother's thumb boiled like Vesuvius. Gaius swung a fist that Marius dodged with embarrassing ease. He threw another punch that somehow landed him in a stranglehold. Cain and Abel had probably been closer.

"Keep your crazy rebellion. Go, march off to Judea. Evict the Romans. Restore the temple. Bring back King Solomon for all I care." Gaius tried to wriggle free. His frustration echoed down the arcade. "Your stupid ideas have brought me nothing but trouble. You told me to join the legion, made me promise to kill the emperor—"

"And you messed up both assignments."

"I'm lucky to be alive."

"So is the emperor."

"I never got near the vexed emperor. I've lost more lives than a drenched cat, thanks to you. I'm through taking orders. I have a chance at a decent life here. I have a job and a girl and a future and you're not going to ruin it."

"A girl?" Marius let his brother drop. "Is she Jewish?"

Gaius stormed away. Given the choice between finding Lena and arguing with Marius, there was no contest. His brother was too full of anger to understand love. That's why he had abandoned their father. That's why he wanted to overthrow the empire rather than

20

improve it from within.

"Sellout! Traitor!" Marius yelled. "Don't bother to thank me for saving your worthless life. Don't cry for me when God laughs at you on Judgment Day."

Gaius disappeared into the crowd before his brother could ruin any more of the evening. He plowed forward, determined to locate Lena before the bull did. Not far from the treasury, he saw some of the town's leaders looking down from a balcony. Spectators on nearby roofs were pointing toward the temple.

Taxman Cassius Kleptus watched the bull circle like a hornet in a bathhouse. Beside him, Winus Minem, the tiny adviser whose business interests included half the province, studied the rising mayhem and offered commentary.

"As entertainment goes, this isn't bad." Minem had squeezed into what little of the balcony had not been consumed by the outsized taxman. "Turning a bull loose into a crowd is a lively idea, but the cleanup could be costly."

"What a show. Don Rexus is a genius." Kleptus scraped a long fingernail across his fleshy head and twirled his remaining hairs absentmindedly. "Such flair that man has! I think I'll ask him to organize my daughter's wedding."

"So tragic to lose her husband on their wedding night. I'm glad she recovered so quickly." Minem could barely mask his interest in the largest dowry the province had to offer. "Who will she marry next?"

"I haven't decided yet." Kleptus rotated his great neck toward the burning tenement. Flames were now visible above the skyline. He laughed and shook with such delight that the balcony pulsed under his strained shins. "That big bonfire is a nice touch."

"Smoke and fire, purification and renewal." Minem noticed Lena down below, waving her cloak and shouting. "Watch her," he said, pointing. "That girl's got balls."

Kleptus squinted. "The governor's scullery wench?"

"Spice girl," Minem corrected. "Name's Lena. Works in the kitchen."

"Pretty girls can be so dumb," Kleptus said. His clever daughter was one of the ugliest in the province. "What in Jupiter's name is she

21

doing?"

Lena cut through the crowd like a knife through goat cheese. She waved her red cloak to encourage people to evacuate.

"Feisty," Kleptus said.

Perched safe above the forum, Minem and the taxman watched in wonder. Rather than evacuate, people crowded closer. Drawn by her cloak, the bull faced Lena from across the plaza and then charged with concentrated malice.

To everyone's amazement, Lena stood her ground. As the bull neared, she deflected its charge with her cloak. Confused, the beast skidded to a halt.

"I wonder how long she'd last in the arena," Minem said.

"Interesting idea," Kleptus said. "Maybe we could charge admission. Perhaps you could convince your red-haired friend to teach her a few tricks. I heard he fought in the Colosseum at Rome."

"Friend? Vindex?" Minem stiffened. The balcony shook as the bull charged again. "He killed the former governor."

"Vindex says that was your handiwork, Minem."

"Vindex tried to kill me, too." Minem rubbed the scab on top of his balding head, a souvenir from the day Vindex dropped him from the governor's balcony. "We'd both be safer if Vindex got back in the arena."

Distracted by a deft flick of her cloak, the bull hurtled past Lena and knocked down a torch post. Drummers infused the night with fury, infecting the crowd and enraging the bull.

"Io Saturnalia!" People on the perimeter threw their empty wineskins into the air, and merchants were quick with refills. Nobody could remember an opening night like this.

The bull mustered another charge. Lena twisted to avoid being trampled, but her footwork fell short. The beast lunged before she could retract her cloak and recover her balance. She dove out of the way but not before a horn tore a hole in the fabric.

The point of no return seemed to have come and gone.

The crashing bull obliterated a post supporting the stage. Two drummers fell into the splinters; others scrambled away from the crumbling edge. The bull freed itself from the wreckage and locked eyes with Lena. Undaunted, she draped the frayed red cloak over her shoulder and extended an open palm toward the bull.

"Looks like she's trying to calm the big demon," Kleptus said.

22

No one dared breathe. To the dumfounded spectators, it seemed that she had pacified the monster. They could almost hear Lena's heart pounding.

The bull lowered its bloody head and charged again.

"Her talent's wasted in the kitchen," Kleptus said. Sweat streamed down his forehead, but he did not take his watery eyes off the performance. "I'll bet you ten *denarii* she goes down."

Minem accepted the wager with a quick nod.

The bull gathered its menace, circled and charged. Exhausted, Lena lingered a second too long, and the bull sent her stumbling sideways.

Some spectators gasped in fear, others with delight. *"Bovis! Bovis!"* shouted those rooting for the bull.

Lena grabbed the ripped cloak and regained her footing. Someone tossed her a lit torch, which she used to force the bull backward. She advanced as if defying death's hoofed apprentice, jabbing the flaming pitch at its snout until a mischievous spectator snatched the torch away.

The bull thundered toward her, steaming with rage. Two dark heartbeats remained before she would be gored, trampled and crushed.

Charon the Boatman had to be waiting nearby.

At the last possible instant, Lena threw her cloak over the bull's head and jumped aside. The blinded bull charged headfirst into the base of Hadrian's statue with a crash heard for blocks. Pulverized stone and plaster mushroomed into the air.

The deified emperor fell to earth, and no beast emerged from the ruins.

"Looks like you owe me ten," Minem said.

"That was a bet worth losing." Kleptus shifted his bulk off the straining balcony and shuffled toward the top stair.

The crowd's cheers were muffled by what sounded like thunder as the burning tenement finally collapsed in the distance. Crooked columns of flame shot skyward.

"Where smoke rises, prices fall," Minem said. He followed the taxman down the groaning stairs to where a smart, stern-looking woman stood waiting.

"A word with you, Governor Kleptus?" Her coal-black *stola* was tastefully accented by a pale silk scarf. Her bearing was affluent and indifferent. A long braid coiled and rose like a cobra atop her head.

"Saturnalia brings out some strange birds." Kleptus tried to waddle around her, but she blocked his escape.

"The name's Plotina," she said. Her gray eyes bored into Kleptus as one accustomed to staring down death and lesser suitors. "I have something that will interest you and your enterprising little friend."

"Plotina?" Kleptus looked her up and down. She was handsome and intimidating though too young to be the former empress of the same name. The royal Plotina had maneuvered Hadrian onto the throne just as Trajan gave up the ghost. This one was probably just a fishwife gone overboard for Saturnalia. "Plotina, indeed. Of what family?"

"The only family that matters." She reached into her fur-lined cloak and handed him a scroll bearing the emperor's seal. "Sleep on this," she ordered. "We'll talk more tomorrow."

Plotina disappeared into the crowd like a raven in a rain cloud.

"Creepy lady," Kleptus said.

"Not unattractive if you like the smell of money."

"You think she's for real?" Kleptus stuffed the scroll into his sleeve and wiped his nose with the back of his hand. "Why did she call me governor?"

"I believe she's the emperor's niece," Minem said. "She must know something we don't."

The cadence of approaching drummers announced the return of those who had delivered Rufius to jail. They were greeted by a wave of refugees from the fallen tenement. Hungry revelers dragged the bull from the rubble while others salvaged timber for a spit on which to roast it.

Dust from the pulverized statue settled over the plaza.

"I'm not an expert," Minem said, "but if Vindex and Carbo really threw Rufius in jail ..."

"See that they keep him there." Kleptus cracked a yellow smile. In spite of his forty-odd years, most of his front teeth were still with him. "Help me secure the governorship, and I'll put you in charge of whatever you like."

Five
V

Gaius Severus tried to sleep off the night's bruises and disappointments in the guard shack, but day broke early with the sound of destitute petitioners pounding the gates in anger. The homeless mob insisted that by the rules of Saturnalia the governor should allow them to live in his villa for the rest of the week.

"I'm sure the governor will help you," Severus assured the victims, if only to quiet them down. He could barely think for the clouds of exhaustion lodged in his head, but remembered to add, "These things take time."

"I lost everything in the fire," a man shouted. "I've nowhere to go."

"I heard that the over-stuffed taxman owned our building," another yelled. "It's all his fault!"

"I'm sure this crisis will be the governor's top priority." Gaius wiped his eyes and tried to shake off the aching cold.

"Getting out of jail so he can rob us again is the governor's only priority. Common people need to organize and take action against the rich and powerful who burn our homes just to collect the insurance." Marius stepped forward from the rear of the crowd and was clearly surprised to see his brother. "What are you doing on that side of the fence?"

"I work here," Gaius said sheepishly. "It keeps me fed."

Limbo, the only other surviving security guard, arrived just in time to save Gaius from an embarrassing family reunion. He looked massively hungover. The dirt on his tunic suggested he just woke up under a bush. "The Titans want to see you," Limbo said, gesturing toward the great mansion.

"Who?"

"Our new leaders: The Titans of Tarraco." After checking the lock on the gate to ensure that the agitated taxpayers could not enter the grounds they had helped pay for, Limbo shuffled off to the guardhouse to nap until the taverns reopened.

"Behave," Gaius whispered to his brother. "I'll be right back."

25

He ran up the path, slipped through the villa's grand entrance and did not look back to see Marius' glaring disapproval. Celebrating a Roman holiday and having a pagan girlfriend were minor offenses compared with working for the government. What Gaius considered a simple job, Marius would see as working for the enemy.

Tarraco, Hispania's largest town, suddenly felt too small. Gaius hoped for a career in government; Marius dreamt of overthrowing the Roman Empire. One wanted to raise his standard of living, the other wanted to raise the dead.

Gaius wondered why he had been called inside the imposing mansion. Trouble seemed the only logical explanation. He walked in a free man, knowing that he might leave in fetters. The notion that a son of a rebel family could eke out a living as a civil servant seemed a bubble made to burst. Logic suggested flight, but the smell of warm bread ovens drew him forward.

The opulence and excess he had expected were conspicuous only by their absence. Gray light leaked from an opening in the ceiling and spread across the dirty interior. The water in the oblong *impluvium* was green and stagnant. Pieces of tile from an unfinished mosaic lay scattered across the floor. Statues were missing from pedestals. Cracked plaster on the walls suggested that the painters brandished hammers instead of brushes. The neglect had not been benign.

Severus tried to remain calm but he worried that the Titans of Tarraco might have linked him to Marius' rabble-rousing or his father's arrest and escape from jail. Maybe Jews were being blamed for the fire the way they had been blamed for the death of the previous governor. Perhaps the Titans were also priests of Mithras. Would these rich and powerful men blame the lowliest survivor for the escaped bull and fire that killed the security chief and two praetorians last night?

The shadows crawling down the coved walls reinforced that it would be better to leave the grounds and skip town. He could start fresh somewhere beyond the reach of his dodgy past. Find a quarry, begin another apprenticeship and carve out a new life. He could say goodbye to Lena, avoid Marius and go north to Barcino in search of Father. With any luck he could hop on one of the small fishing vessels that plied the winter waters and never return.

He decided to convince Lena to join him. By now, she would

understand that the town that had rejected his family was unlikely to embrace her. What had he been thinking when he brought her back to Tarraco? She had to have realized that this was not where their destiny lay.

He knew she would be working in the kitchen and decided to surprise her. After a few false turns in the villa's confusing corridors, he followed the smell of bread toward its source and found that the taxpayers had not skimped on the governor's kitchen. The food preparation area was like nothing he had ever seen. Knife-scarred wooden tables stood ready to receive legs of lamb, piles of poultry, and delicacies he could not even imagine. Two slaves were scraping a stew pot that was big enough to bathe in. A few crusty washbasins captured rain along the exterior perimeter. In full service, the indoor kitchen and outdoor ovens could feed a legion. The ingredients for one dinner party would be enough to sustain a common house for a month.

Severus heard Lena humming to herself in the spice closet. He had spent the previous night looking for her, but between his captivity and the loose bull they had never connected. It felt like years since he had seen her. Perhaps love made time fly when together and crawl when apart. He snuck into the closet, grabbed her around the waist and kissed the back of her neck. "I've missed you!"

Exotic spices from beyond the edge of the empire infused the air. Lena smelled of clove, sage, and herbs he could not name. She twisted toward him and they locked lips until Severus lost balance and stumbled into a shelf full of ceramic jars. He caught a falling container. "What's this?"

"Spanish saffron." Lena opened the jar and offered him a whiff. "They say it wakens desire in old men."

"What about young men?" Severus inhaled deeply.

Lena drew him inward, crushing the jar between them.

"Do you have anything that can turn me invisible? I think I'm in trouble. I may need to escape."

"There's no escaping me." She nudged him deeper into the closet and shut the door with her foot. *"Veni, vidi, vici!"*

"I surrender." Severus nuzzled the warm crease of her neck, losing himself in the softness of her hair. He filled his lungs with her magic.

"Take this thing off." She pressed into his embrace and struggled with his sash.

"In the spice room?"

"Nobody ever comes in here."

Tunics fell and the moment sprouted wings. The two intertwined in the darkness and found an unlikely position amid the sacks and *amphorae*. They wrestled to a crescendo that left them tangled and panting.

The closet soon smelled of sage, sex, and saffron. Lena unraveled and pressed against his chest. For a long moment, Severus was unsure of his whereabouts. Dazed and delighted, he slumped backward against a sack of dry mint. Before Lena came crashing into his life, he had never imagined anyone like her. Now he could not imagine a world without her. Before Lena, his few encounters with girls had been awkward at best. With Lena, everything just seemed right. She was strong and sensual, uninhibited and unconventional. The tighter he held her, the freer he felt.

Severus took her hands and pulled her close. Now was the perfect moment to propose that they marry their futures together. He wanted never to lose her. "Lena, I've been thinking—"

"Shh!" She broke off his embrace and shoved him into a corner. A jar of ground cumin smashed onto the tiled floor. The pungent dust caused Severus to sneeze. "Stay quiet." She jumped into her tunic just as the door swung open.

Light poured into the closet as Carbo poked his head inside. The tiny slave either did not see or did not care that Severus was hiding naked behind a dusty *amphora*.

"Carbo!" Lena leapt out of the closet and tried to close the door behind her. "You were so noble onstage last night. Is the governor still in jail?"

"Lena, Lena, Lena!" the booming voice of Don Rexus echoed from the other side of the door.

Severus struggled into his tunic and saw the silver-haired actor grab Lena by the shoulders. Once finished with the Roman hugs and Spanish kisses, the lecherous actor stepped back to look her over. He clearly liked what he saw.

Lena had mentioned that Rexus often summoned her to his chambers to interpret his dreams. As a servant, she was expected to obey a nobleman's desires, but what he sought she refused to give. The last time he groped her she threatened to serve him diced and fried to the ravens in the courtyard, but her insolence only heightened his interest.

Rexus struck a statue's pose and smiled like a southern sunrise. "Lena my love, how would you like to be a star?"

Severus pressed against the door to better hear the conversation, but at Carbo's suggestion, Rexus and Lena stepped out into the corridor.

Rexus seemed to know the corridors and proceeded quickly toward the library where a merciful fire had recently destroyed tax records, proscription lists, and invoices from angry vendors.

"Lena, Lena, Lena." Rexus settled into the only chair in the room. "It's not enough that you interpret dreams? Where did you learn to fight bulls?"

"After fighting a bull, I'm not afraid of pigs," she said.

"That's rich!" Rexus grew animated. "Lena the Lioness! No, that's not quite it … Lena the Bull-Bashing Beauty from Babylon …. No, too big a mouthful." Rexus ran his hands down his broad chest and rocked backward in the chair. "Lena, today is your lucky—"

"Careful!" Lena jumped forward and grabbed Rexus by the blue trim of his toga. She yanked him to his feet just as the chair's rear legs snapped.

"Truly fabulous!" Rexus teetered for a second until Lena stabilized him. "How did you know that the chair would break?" He tried to draw Lena closer, but she resisted. "You have such raw potential. A bullfighting beauty who predicts the future can make a fortune with a little help from your's truly."

"The future I predict," Lena said, pushing him away, "is that if you don't stop bothering me, your face will be slapped."

No sooner had Rexus grabbed Lena's left hand than her right palm slapped his face. The loud smack left him stunned and staring at the only woman to reject his advances since he played Oedipus in Athens.

"Such insolence!" Rexus slapped her so hard that she spun past Carbo and out into the dark corridor. "You don't deserve my help, you spoiled brat!"

Lena wandered the twisted corridors until Carbo appeared before

29

her as if he had been waiting all morning.

"Come," he said. "I've something to show you." Carbo, slight but sprightly, led her on a zigzag course through the villa's internal labyrinth. "If you pay attention, you can smell odors and sense little breezes." He trod lightly until he reached a corridor where the air hung still. He felt along a damp wall until he located a panel that would have appeared no different from the others. He tapped and listened until he found the spot he sought and applied pressure with the palm of his hand.

The panel opened into a small chamber with a dirty skylight. Carbo entered and beckoned Lena to follow. "Rufius was collecting relics," he said.

The shelves were filled with household gods, charms, and talisman—some purchased, others confiscated in raids and evictions. A small, pregnant statuette appeared to glow as if lit from inside.

"Holy objects." Lena picked up a circular casting and traced her fingers over the Greek letters Xi and Rho that appeared as spokes in the *annulus*. She turned the pendant-sized circle in her hand as if deriving warmth from the dull bronze. "Some more powerful than others."

"That one's Christian." A quick hint of sadness passed over Carbo's wan face. "The letters signify Christos, the new son of an old god."

"Do you believe in him?"

"He's popular among slaves." Carbo took a small silver candelabrum from the shelf and exchanged it for the object in Lena's hand. "This one is Jewish, an old menorah."

"I might know the owner."

"Your friend Severus?"

"Why do you say that?" Lena was unsure how much to reveal.

"Aside from a few slaves, you don't know many people in town, and Tarraco isn't exactly overflowing with Hebrews."

"There's something here for everyone." Lena put the menorah aside and picked up a small pregnant figurine. "This is a fertility goddess. Why is Rufius collecting these?"

"We should leave," Carbo said. Though the air was still and the dim light steady, something had changed and he now appeared worried. "Please don't mention this to anyone."

"Our secret." Lena put the engorged goddess back on the shelf and took a last glance. A few objects had a radiance that suggested meaning beyond ceramic and metal. She whispered an incantation before Carbo sealed the door.

Lena followed in silence. She stood nearly twice the little slave's height and had to subtract one step in three to avoid overtaking him. She was happy that Carbo trusted her, but not sure why he had taken her into his confidence. He had to realize that the little gods could command a holy sum.

When Carbo stopped at a dark intersection, Lena noticed that the two corridors smelled different. A faint breeze to the right suggested the nearby kitchen; the other was harder to identify. It seemed that Carbo had not led her back the way they had come.

"Winus Minem's a murderer," Carbo whispered. "He killed Governor Biberious with dogroot, a poison that turns the lips green."

"I've never heard of dogroot."

"At Minem's insistence, we used it for cleaning. Works well against mold, but it turns out to have other benefits if you're trying to kill someone."

Lena waited to see what else the darkness would reveal. "Why are you telling me this?"

"A slave's testimony isn't worth a broken eggshell," Carbo said. Carbo paused as if deciding how much to reveal. "Minem tried to frame Vindex for the murder … came close to having him condemned."

Lena considered the story for a moment. She felt kinship for both Carbo and the morose ex-gladiator. There was no reason to doubt them. Her familiarity with Minem was limited, but his type— confident, fast talking—did not inspire trust. "What if you and Vindex were free?"

"What if cats turned into dogs?"

"No, really, what if we were able to buy your freedom? Would your words be heard?"

"Loud enough to get me killed."

"How much would it cost to buy your freedom?"

"Whatever the governor says I'm worth," Carbo said. "I've saved a bit of money from my, er, side ventures—"

"Selling food scraps and kitchen knives?"

"Something like that." Carbo smiled as if happy to share his small conspiracy. "Maybe you could help me."

"I was almost enslaved once. No one should be owned by another. With the gods as my witness, I'm going to help you." Lena crossed her arms. Her voice was firm. "We're going to buy your freedom and see that justice is served."

Six
VI

Gaius Severus tried to retrace his steps back to the spice closet but instead found himself lost in the villa's maze of dim corridors. He was about to shout for help when someone or something tugged at the back of his tunic. Surprised, he turned and saw Carbo flickering like a candle. The tiny slave stepped forward as if emerging from a dream and said, "Come with me."

"Is Lena in trouble?" he asked. "Am I in trouble?"

"Probably." Carbo gestured for him to follow. "Why else would my masters request your presence?"

"I'd rather face a Minotaur," Severus said, but he was too lost to do anything but follow.

After a few minutes of following the tiny slave toward whatever awaited, Severus abandoned any hope of memorizing the sequence of steps and turns. It seemed as if Carbo was intentionally trying to confuse him. After walking for what seemed like miles, they emerged into a small dining room where the ex-gladiator Vindex was leaning against a wall, feigning alertness.

Three men were eating and arguing. Severus recognized Rexus only too well. The other two looked familiar. Governor Rufius was conspicuously absent for a gathering of titans.

Carbo indicated for Severus to wait in a dark corner until the men were ready for him. After a few minutes, Severus felt like his stomach had sprouted eyes that could not help but stare at a nearby pile of grapes and peeled oranges. He was doing his best to live on one meal a day, hoping to adapt to austerity before it killed him. He tightened his sash to silence his growling stomach and wondered what his fate might be.

Cassius Kleptus, the big man who held the tax concession tighter than he now held a roasted goose neck, lay draped across a sofa normally reserved for three. In between red-faced rants and boiling reproaches, Kleptus shoved bite-sized cheese balls into the wide opening that crowned his many chins. The tables overflowed with nuts, sausages, and imported fruit.

Severus had no experience with Kleptus, but he knew that Rexus was a lecher. The silver-haired actor was famous for slipping his manicured hands into the purses of widows and the tunics of teens. Of the three so-called Titans, Winus Minem was the only one who seemed trustworthy.

Severus felt an immediate kinship for the small adviser. Wordy, wiry, and not much larger than Carbo, Minem was as alert as Kleptus was belligerent. Rumored to be nimble as a mouse on a cheese wheel, Minem currently seemed a bit off-balance.

Minem was an outsider who had achieved influence in an indifferent world. He appeared unbound to tradition, and Severus found this inspiring. Minem was worth observing, someone to learn from.

The porcine taxman stabbed at meatballs and drowned his prey with loud gulps of wine. Severus could not imagine how someone so obsessed with food could ever find time to collect taxes. To maintain such bulk, Kleptus would need to delegate everything except sleeping.

In the absence of Governor Rufius, the bulky Kleptus held sway. He appeared to have stumbled through the gates of power only to find them swinging on broken hinges. To hear him complain, the province had barely survived the long, lawless night between Rufius' arrival and his arrest. State treasures had been looted. Taxation and proscription lists had been torched. Bushels had disappeared from the grain stores, and the villa's wine cellar was reduced to a few *amphorae* of bitter plonk.

"Negligence!" Kleptus shouted. "Incompetence! Where were the security guards last night?"

"Ask Vindex," Minem said with unmasked enmity. "He probably killed them."

"Most of them died in the fire," Vindex said.

Severus now realized why he had been summoned. He was to be blamed for the fire and, as punishment, torn limb from limb by the gladiator. He knew better than to plead for his life; Romans hated cowardice.

"I wonder who arranged that fire," Don Rexus mused. He struck a grave pose. "Ever notice how convenient some tragedies are, Minem?"

The small Macedonian tensed and pivoted. His future as an adviser depended on whoever might seize the governorship. "Actors love tragedy. Real people prefer less drama." Minem's voice ran an octave higher than those of the larger men.

"Weren't you looking for a vacant property close to the forum?" Rexus asked. "Quite dramatic that one is suddenly available."

"Enough!" Kleptus ordered. "Our security squad was squashed. *Vigiles* and mercenaries can't be trusted, and the legion has marched north to build Hadrian's Wall. We owe the emperor a king's ransom, and the treasury is empty. We need to raise money or we'll lose control of this province."

"If the security guards are all dead, we could use actors to collect taxes," Minem said with an eye toward Rexus. "Actors aren't good for anything else, are they?"

"Not all the guards are dead." Gaius Severus stepped into the light. He was aware of his station as a plebe among nobles but saw no harm in pointing out the small detail of his existence. "I survived."

"But your shadow's gone missing." Kleptus glanced at the thin lad and laughed. "Interesting how your entire chain of command got killed, yet somehow you survived."

"Limbo Drekus made it out alive, as well."

"Drekus," Kleptus said. "I know the family. Equestrians. Above suspicion ... but you. What's your name? Who are you, anyway?"

"Severus, sir. Gaius Severus. A former stonemason seeking to better himself through public service."

"Admirable," Minem said. "I remember my first—"

"Common name, common profession, common alibi," Rexus interrupted.

Severus regretted having spoken. If these vindictive men were looking for a scapegoat, he had just handed them one. Had the proscription lists not been reduced to cinders, they would have had more reasons to doubt his good name.

"He looks like a common criminal, if you ask me." Rexus popped a handful of olives into his mouth and spat the pits onto the floor. "Probably an arsonist."

Severus knew better than to contradict his betters, but if these noblemen had already reached a verdict, he had nothing to lose by contesting it. "Why would I set fire to a building while I'm in it?"

"Perhaps you're also a fool," Rexus said.

"With all respect, I assure you—"

"No need to harass the lad," Minem interrupted. "He seems upstanding enough."

"For a plebe," Rexus snorted. "He's less trustworthy than you are, Minem."

"That's a high complement coming from an actor with no character." Minem smiled at Severus as if they had met before. "Not all plebes are common. I invited this boy here for a reason. Tell us what you know, son."

"Thank you, sir." Severus said. He sensed a brief opening in which to make his case without the appearance of pleading. "I believe the fire was accidental, the result of a religious rite gone wrong. As for myself, I may be a plebe, but I'm honest, law-abiding, and literate."

"Impressive," Minem said. He looked Severus over and then turned to Kleptus. "Given those qualifications, might I suggest that we put young Severus in charge of the front gates. I would be happy to advise him on dealing with the petitioners, vendors, and other riffraff."

A gray, well-fed cat poked a whisker into the room and decided not to enter. The sight of the cat made Severus want to sneeze, but he held his breath to avoid any hint of ingratitude. Being in charge of the gates was a step above his previous job and far better than the punishment he had expected.

"In charge of the gates?" Kleptus stuffed another morsel of grilled lamb into his mouth. As he cleared one plate, a kitchen slave brought in another.

"Why him?" Rexus asked. "Should we not consider someone with better standing and more experience?" His syllables stretched into a yawn that indicated just how unimportant he considered the matter. A red mark still graced the spot where Lena had slapped him.

"I think gumption counts for something." Minem seemed unwilling to let Rexus land an uncontested dig. "This lad was clever enough to survive an obvious attempt to assassinate the entire squadron."

"Perhaps you should consult with the governor," Severus said, regretting it instantly.

"I'm the governor now!" Kleptus shouted with such force that it sent linen wavelets through the pleats of his toga. He reached into his sleeve and produced the document Plotina had given him. "Read this."

The three men forgot about Severus who, for his part, was uncertain if he had been promoted or dismissed. Intrigued by the opportunity to eavesdrop, he tried to blend into the fresco on the wall.

"It's a writ of extradition." Kleptus was too impatient to let the others read the scroll. "Rome has relieved Festus Rufius of all duties. He is to be arrested, transported to Rome and tried for a number of very long accusations."

"My good friend Kleptus," Rexus beamed. "That makes it official. Congratulations, dear fellow!"

"Given what happened to the last two governors—one dead, one arrested—I'm not so sure I want this honor." Kleptus redistributed his bulk across the groaning sofa.

"Consider it an opportunity to do good," Severus suggested, before remembering that the goal of a fly on the wall is to avoid being swatted. He was relieved to have been ignored.

"I worked for Rufius. Rufius is gone. Therefore I'm free to go," Vindex declared in a tone that discouraged argument.

"Not so fast, Socrates," Minem said. "Poor, ignorant Vindex seems uncertain about his—"

"I'm certain that you're about to stuff a fish up my—"

Rexus seized the opportunity to irritate Minem by keeping Vindex in proximity. "We could certainly use him in the security forces," he said. "Given our recent losses, we need to rebuild quickly. That is, unless you want Vindex to serve as your bodyguard, governor."

"Bodyguard?" An involuntary snort from Kleptus rolled off the coved ceilings. He tried but failed to lift his bulk off the sofa. "Does my body look like it needs guarding?"

"Rufius hasn't paid me yet," Vindex protested. "I'm a free man, and I'm owed for my services."

"Excellent news! Heartiest congratulations." Minem smiled like a spider. "Can we see your proof of manumission? You have the document, don't you?"

Vindex reached for the adviser, but Minem jumped away like a grasshopper. On the fresco behind Severus a gaggle of wood nymphs waited for someone in the room to eat, speak, or throw a fist.

"I'm afraid your little friend is right," Rexus said. "Unless Rufius filed your manumission documents, you're still a slave."

"He promised," Vindex insisted. "He gave me his word."

"Which isn't worth much at the moment," Kleptus said.

"A document?" Vindex blocked the open door. The room seemed too small to contain his frustration. "A piece of papyrus?"

"Stay calm, Vindex. There's a simple solution to your little problem." Minem flashed the smile he used when asserting that an abject disaster was just a misinterpreted opportunity. "You can join the security force, right Severus?"

"Er—"

Minem did not give Severus time to respond. "Between your nominal base pay and whatever you can shake loose from the public, you'll raise enough cash to buy your freedom in no time at all. I'm sure your new supervisor is delighted to have you."

Severus had no time to think through the implications of working with an angry ex-gladiator. Minem appeared to be in charge, so Severus stepped into the game and played it for all he could. "Vindex would be most welcome on the force."

Vindex squinted at his scrawny new boss. "I'm not your slave."

"Of course not." Severus shook his head rapidly, almost straining his neck. He looked around the room, still amazed that he was holding his own with the men Limbo had called the Titans of Tarraco. *Limbo!* At this very moment, the lazy brat was supposed to be guarding the gates. If he was not sleeping off a hangover, he would be working on his next one. "If you'd be good enough to attend to the front gates, Vindex, I'll join you shortly."

Vindex scowled at Severus. "I'm the governor's bodyguard, not some scrawny mutt's sidekick."

"Vindex, poor misguided Vindex." If Minem's tone had been any more honey-coated, his words would have stuck to his tonsils. "Once again, the gods have blessed you undeservedly. Can you not see how trustworthy and likeable this young man is?"

"I trust no one." Vindex scowled and stomped away.

Suddenly the room seemed bigger.

Severus was unsure of what he had stepped into, but the possibility of having a patron like Winus Minem seemed worth risking an enemy like Vindex. Curious and apparently invisible

38

again, Severus stood at attention, unsure of what else to do.

While Rexus stared at some painted wood nymphs, Kleptus turned his attention to more urgent matters. "We'll need to neutralize that rich lioness from Rome."

"Plotina." Rexus perked up. "That slick *domina* we met last night? I'd like to neutralize her!"

"Hadrian's niece. If half of her story is true, we'll need to get down to the courthouse and straighten out the other half," Minem said.

Kleptus stuffed a hard-boiled egg into his mouth and spoke through the yolk. "Crawl across town to ask that half-dead magistrate for permission?" He swallowed hard and tugged at one of his remaining hairs. Satisfied that it was still well-rooted, he affixed it to a bead of sweat atop his skull. "Power is taken, not ..."

"Purchased," Minem said. "Plotina has a price, and she's in no position to bargain. Pay her off and put her on a leaky boat home. Let's have our new security guard go fetch her."

"Bring Plotina here, Severus." Kleptus eyed a fresh platter of grilled peafowl tongues. "She won't be hard to find. Look for a fancy dame who would seem out of place in her own bed."

Unsure of the protocol but thrilled to have been promoted so quickly, Gaius Severus saluted and bowed in one combined gesture. He had barely slept two hours in the past twenty, but the events of the past five minutes sent his thoughts and heart racing into what promised to be a new era. He had gained a foothold on the Roman ladder, and the next rung was in sight. He could not wait to tell Lena.

"Run along, young Severus." Winus Minem smiled. "Go make Tarraco safe for security guards."

Seven
VII

Gaius Severus stepped into the gray daylight just as a projectile sailed through the villa's great front door. The cobblestones would not remain mortared for long as homeless protesters shouted with more anger and determination than before.

"Your orders, Excellency?" Vindex's long ginger hair fell onto his broad shoulders. He had been waiting at the gates as ordered. No one dared hurl a rock in his direction. "Shall I tear a few of them limb from limb?"

"I'm not excellent and let's keep that technique in reserve." Severus looked for his misguided brother among the crowd. "Where's Limbo?"

"I think he's dead." Vindex nodded toward the guard shack.

Severus sidestepped the giant's cynicism and focused on dodging incoming stones. Once safe behind the guard shack, he roused Limbo with a swift kick. "Look alive! A major part of your job requires being awake."

"I'm tired," Limbo complained. He wiped his bloodshot eyes and felt around for the empty wineskin that he had used for a pillow. "When do I get a day off?"

"After you've done a day's work," Vindex said, quickly establishing himself in the pecking order.

"Give us a home or go back to Rome!" Stomping feet punctuated the shouting.

"Calm down! Be still," Severus shouted. "You need to form a committee, chose a representative, and present a prioritized list of grievances."

"Yes, that always works." Vindex scrambled over the locked gates and leapt down into the mob. He grabbed two protesters, hoisted them aloft and banged them together like cymbals. Panicked, the rest of the crowd fled down the narrow path. "They won't be back for a while."

"I might have played it differently," Gaius Severus said, "but your clear and direct approach seems to have worked."

"You've got a lot to learn, kid."

Gaius Severus needed to find Plotina. He had no firm description of her, but foreigners were scarce and she sounded fairly conspicuous. A strange face in a small town would not be hard to find.

Limbo unlocked the gates long enough for Severus to pass through.

Severus sped up to match Vindex's long strides. "What do you know about Plotina?"

"Her boat's in the harbor." Vindex seemed so eager to assist that small temblors spread from his every footstep. "I met some of her crew last night. Nice bunch of girls."

Most residents were still recovering from the night's festivities. The empty streets around the forum usually teemed with commerce. Open-air markets and unlicensed carts normally competed with the dingy shop fronts where women could find oil and grain, wool and thread. But Saturnalia marked the midpoint of fallow season. Southern oranges, priced just north of robbery, would be the only fresh fruit available until spring.

A damp blanket of ash had covered the town. It would take a good rain to wash all the soot down the gently sloping streets and into the pewter-colored Mediterranean.

"It is now the ninth hour." The forum crier shouted without conviction. Hungover and cold, his rumormongering was less creative than usual. "Governor Rufius has been sent to the lead mines."

"We need to hurry." Vindex left Severus panting to keep pace.

The path from the governor's villa to the cat-infested harbor crossed every stratum Tarraco had to offer and some that she would prefer to lose. The town's deep harbor brewed an unsavory stew of unmoored mariners. The unearned monopoly of maritime commerce enforced Tarraco's claim to capital status. Imported grain from Egypt and fine cloth from Italia were exchanged for Spanish olive oil and low-grade fish brine. Bustling during much of the year, winter found most larger boats gone for the season.

Vindex pointed to a wharf where a midsized ship bobbed like a sea sprite. The blue, green, and gray boat seemed to appear and vanish as clouds passed overhead. "It's painted to blend in with the waters," Vindex explained.

"I appreciate your insights, Vindex."

"You appreciate that I haven't wrung your neck."

"Yes, thanks. That, too."

Vindex led the way toward the sleeping ship until he was blocked by a crew of brawny longshoremen unloading some rare winter cargo. Foul-mouthed men with rickety barrows heaped with large *amphorae* restricted access to the wharf. The unhurried roustabouts appeared indifferent to Vindex's insistence followed by Severus' polite request to give way in the name of provincial security.

The two eventually slipped past the slow-turning cogs of commerce and proceeded down the long dock to Plotina's ship. The boat, simply named *Plotina* was a converted merchant vessel sporting an unusually muscular figurehead of the goddess Fortuna.

"*Salve!*" Severus' waved his skinny arms and tried to get the attention of a woman coiling a rope on deck. To his amazement, the crew appeared to be entirely female. "We request permission to come on board."

"Denied!" The woman did not look up from her work.

"That's Zinzin, the first mate." Vindex sounded almost happy. "I met her last night. She's from the Danube, not far from where I come from."

"How wonderful to meet someone from home," Severus said.

"I have no home." Vindex waved to the brawny woman now looking down at them. "I can get you up there if you promise never, ever to tell her I'm a slave."

"Deal," Severus said. "I don't believe in slavery anyway."

Zinzin's stern face softened when Vindex shouted something in a language Severus had never heard. She leaned over the gunwale and smiled down broadly at Vindex. Her short black hair stood erect against the breeze and her two-handed gesture would have made a tomcat blush. "Hey pork chops!"

Vindex blushed. "Isn't she something?"

"She's perfect," Severus agreed. "You two should marry and raise a wolf pack."

After a moment of flirtatious foreign banter in a tongue composed only of consonants, Zinzin lowered a rope that Vindex scaled with ease. Minutes later, Severus struggled over the top and fell flat on the deck.

"I need to see the captain." Severus rolled over and looked up at Vindex and Zinzin hovering above him. It wasn't clear to him which of the two was larger, or whether the ship could safely float both of them. They seemed made for each other, carved from the same tree trunk.

"The captain can't be disturbed." Zinzin shot a lascivious wink at Vindex followed by an elbow jab to his gut. "She's celebrating her wedding night."

"I have jurisdiction here," Gaius Severus asserted with low expectation of establishing any authority over the vessel.

"We have maritime immunity." Zinzin punched Vindex in a rock-hard bicep and feigned a hand injury.

"You're anchored in Tarraco," Severus insisted, though unsure where his authority ended and the sea began. "These are provincial waters."

"Same water everywhere." Zinzin landed one more jab at Vindex's solid abdomen before pretending to inspect a fitting. "You'll have to wait until the honeymoon is over."

"We need to speak with Plotina." Severus maintained a stern tone and a safe distance. "Governor's orders."

"Governor? He's on board, lambkins."

Vindex intercepted her next jab, spun her around, and disabled her with a bear hug from behind. Zinzin struggled with delight, refusing to surrender. After a moment of frolic, she slipped from his grip, opened a hatch and disappeared below deck. Vindex descended without touching a rung.

Severus inched down the ladder a moment later and found that the closed door to Plotina's quarters did little to mute a loud argument.

"Help!" a man shouted.

"That's Rufius," Vindex whispered.

"Sounds like the honeymoon is over." Zinzin landed a smack on the back of Vindex's head.

"I'll have you for supper," Vindex warned.

The two wrestled like bear cubs in a bathtub.

"Quiet!" Severus said, but the flirtation was thicker than the musty air below deck. He could barely hear what Festus Rufius was shouting at Plotina. By squinting through a tiny knothole he could see Plotina pacing. Rufius was tied to a chair.

"You've gone too far this time." Rufius struggled to break free but the cords held tight.

"Stop blubbering." Plotina's sleeveless garment was made of tiny leather diamonds stitched together to form a long jerkin that resembled lizard skin. The cobra braid coiled on her head looked ready to strike. She smacked Rufius in the face with a scroll to get his attention. "You have a very clear choice: You can sign the writ in my right hand, or you can suffer from the decree in my left."

"You've got no right to kidnap me," Rufius insisted. "As your husband, I order you to release me."

Severus peeled his ear from the knothole and looked up at Vindex. "Plotina and Rufius are married?"

"Love is strange." Vindex winked at Zinzin.

Plotina threw open the door so suddenly that Severus stumbled forward. Zinzin stiffened to attention.

"Raise anchor and throw all men overboard!"

Zinzin raced up the ladder. Within seconds orders were bouncing around the ship as women scrambled to make ready their departure. The pounding of feet made it hard for Severus to hear what Plotina and Rufius were arguing about.

"You must obey me," Rufius insisted. "Be a good Roman wife and stop this nonsense."

"I'm wearing the toga in this marriage." Plotina gave no indication that she had ever embraced the role of a politician's dutiful wife. "One final review of your options: In my right hand, I've got the divorce documents freeing me from your stupidity, indemnifying my family from your insolvency, and admitting that our arranged marriage was never consummated."

"It wasn't?" Rufius said, confused. "I'm pretty sure we ... don't you have a mole on your left—"

"Rodent! The only mole in this room is you. In my other hand is an extradition order signed by the emperor, may he show you no mercy, demanding that you stand trial on the floor of the Senate for more offenses against the gods than a decent woman could mention."

"When you find a decent woman, I'll—"

"Rig the sails!" Plotina stormed out of her cabin and shoved Severus aside. "Somebody get these boys off my ship!"

44

"Help!" Rufius yelled. He strained and twisted against the ropes, rocked his chair backward, and hit the floor with a thud.

Vindex entered the chamber but did nothing to set Rufius upright.

"Who wants to sleep with such a viper anyway?" Rufius hissed. "I'll bet she can't even cook! Untie me, Vindex. Get me off this ship!"

Vindex towered over his former master. "A little question of my freedom needs your attention."

"Take me to the magistrate, and I'll release you today." Rufius rocked from side to side like an overturned turtle. "Get me away from these harpies and you'll have your freedom."

"I've heard that before," Vindex said. "Why should I believe you this time?"

"You should never believe him." Plotina stood in the doorway. The light caught each scale on her jerkin differently and rendered it more colorful than a rainbow.

When Plotina returned to the cabin Severus saw that even Vindex was intimidated by her. There was little doubt that she could send them both to the afterlife with a twist of her thumb.

Plotina spoke with authority. "I am authorized to transport the former governor—"

"Your devoted husband!" Rufius interjected.

"—the scoundrel, Rufius, to stand trial in Rome."

Her quarters went silent. Each looked to the other to make a move until the ship jolted when the raised anchor dropped on the deck above them.

"You two trespassers have until the count of ten to get off my ship without swimming," Plotina warned.

"I'll sign," Rufius said, exasperated. "I'll sign your divorce documents, but mark my words, the gods will be angry."

"The gods are always angry." Plotina turned to Vindex. "Untie one of his hands. Let's see if he knows how to write his name."

"Don't let her take me back to Rome." Rufius scratched his name with a stylus.

Plotina opened the second scroll and smiled at the fine print. "Unfortunately, Rome does not absolve you from any local crimes you most certainly have committed," she said. "You still have to stand trial in Tarraco."

Plotina ordered the crew to reverse their preparations. Sails were lowered, oars were stowed, and ropes were coiled. A few moments later, she appeared on deck with her deflated ex-husband at her side. Zinzin produced a rope ladder and showed Rufius how to use it.

"I hate boats," Rufius said, returning to the *terra firma* of the pulsing dock.

"I'm sorry, sir, but my orders are to keep you in custody," Severus said. He turned to Plotina. "And the new governor wants to see you, *domina*."

"New governor? I'm the new governor!" Rufius protested.

Plotina looked at Gaius Severus as if considering how much weight to assign such a skinny lad. "I will accompany you if you leave your big sidekick behind as a hostage. You and I will escort Rufius to the magistrate, and my safe passage back to this ship will be exchanged for the return of your flame-headed friend."

Severus agreed. Zinzin and Vindex exchanged a furtive nod.

Plotina tightened her iridescent jerkin and climbed down the rope ladder with the ease of an acrobat. Severus ushered Festus Rufius toward the litter waiting on the wharf.

Four of Plotina's toughest-looking sailors stood ready by the enclosed chair. It was common for wealthy citizens to be carried around by slaves, but Severus had never seen or heard of women hoisting a litter. For that matter, he had never imagined a ship run by a female crew.

Saturnalia was full of surprises.

"You'll lead us to the magistrate by the most conspicuous route possible," Plotina ordered without looking at Severus.

The cold breeze broke her words into distinct syllables that took Severus a moment to assemble. Though he could not guess at Plotina's plan, Severus was sure that she had one. Rufius seemed to be Plotina's private jurisdiction. He would come to no harm unless she willed it. If the litter failed to protect Rufius from gawkers, the burly porters would fend off anyone bent on doing him harm.

Grumbling, Rufius climbed into the litter.

Severus tried not to be intimidated by the cobra and the tough woman beneath it, but there was no denying her bearing. If she claimed no lineage from Zeus, it was only because the Father of the Gods had disowned her.

"Technically speaking, *domina*, as the governor's representative,

46

that is, if you don't mind, I should be in charge of this operation."
Severus risked direct eye contact and instantly regretted it. In truth,
he was more accustomed to receiving orders than giving them.

"Of course." Plotina nodded curtly, with a look just south of
disdain. She stepped into the litter and her braided cobra arched as if
ready to spit venom. "And your orders are?"

Severus shut the door to the litter and addressed the nearest
porter. "To the courthouse."

Eight
VIII

Gaius Severus led the odd procession through the docklands. They crossed the maritime slums and marched up the gradual slope to where the courthouse basilica presided over the administrative corner of the forum. He prayed that his brother was not among the gawkers who followed and heckled the brawny women toting the litter.

"Such pretty pirates!" one man shouted.

Others were not as inaccurate with their insults.

"You freaks belong in the arena!"

Plotina's crew, a sisterhood of sea hawks, was as coarse as their captain was elegant. She rode as royalty, carried in the litter above their rough shoulders and sharp elbows. She was poise, they were power. The crew's stories could be read from their scars and tattoos. Each was a misfit from a different corner of the empire. They were strong as Spartans, stoic as statues. The ship was only place where they could be appreciated for the bone-crunching bruisers they were. From the wilds of Caledonia to the depths of the Danube, there were no tougher women.

"Go back to Germania, you monsters!"

Men were the most vocal, but many women joined in the heckling. Tarraco had not seen such a parade since a traveling gladiator show passed through town a few years prior.

Listening to Rufius' protests from inside the litter, Severus managed to place a few more tiles in the man's mosaic. Rufius' father was a powerful senator. His older brother, once in line for the throne, had been murdered in Londinium, probably by agents of a rival family. According to Rufius, he had been set up and knocked down in an imperial power play aimed at purging his bloodline. According to Plotina, Festus Rufius was a fanciful 'ne'er-do-well who clung like a nettle to his father's toga. He was mediocrity personified, a man whose name posterity would mispronounce.

Adding injury to insult, Rufius had attempted to kill the emperor.

Worse, he had failed. The family's reputation would never recover from being blamed for the mêlée that he had launched when Hadrian's ships tried to dock at Tarraco. Rufius denied having plotted the demigod's downfall, but his alibi rang hollow with the emperor's angry niece whose cold glare could freeze fire.

Severus marched alongside the litter, unsure of what his new job required. He surveyed the crowd, looking for trouble and danger, hoping not to see his brother who was both.

The procession entered the forum near the statue of Vespasian, the emperor who had commissioned Tarraco's administrative quarter. In the confusion after Nero's death, Vespasian had turned his sights on Rome leaving his son, Titus, to sack Jerusalem and lay waste to the province. Gaius Severus' grandfather, taken in shackles to Rome, had been among the few survivors. Someone, probably Marius, had painted "Free Judea" across the pedestal.

It occurred to Severus that more history was written in blood than ink.

Dust from Hadrian's statue had settled in swirling patterns, punctuated by footprints and pockmarked by raindrops. Charred bones and blackened cobblestones bore witness to the feast that had followed the beast's demise. A few overindulgent revelers still snored under the colonnades.

Unlike the ornate treasury building, adorned as befits a center for taxation and tribute, the stoic courthouse was drab and imposing. Plotina dragged Rufius into the antechamber while her women kept the crowd at bay.

"Festus Rufius arrested and dragged before justice!" shouted the docklands crier who had picked up the news. He ran north to spread the story faster than the other crier could run south to contradict him.

Fortunate to have avoided official contact with the courthouse, Severus expected to find a palace of justice stocked with well-read scrolls and crowded with scholars debating the law's finer points. Instead, he was surprised to find a sparse room crammed with hapless suspects and hopeless supplicants. Among them, Severus recognized Winus Minem, Rufius' former adviser, whose prowess with contracts and litigation often brought him before the court.

"Excellency!" Minem swallowed his astonishment at seeing his former patron and bowed before Rufius. He nodded to Plotina who, in return, ignored him.

"The man who sold the empire. The huckster who hocked Hispania," Rufius muttered. He shoved a chubby finger at Minem's round nose. "If I go down, you're coming with me."

"I'm devastated that you've fallen on hard times," Minem said. "But don't despair. Hard times can build character."

"That will never happen." Plotina opened her leather jerkin to reveal a dress woven from a posh fabric that radiated wealth and taste. The fine embroidery shimmered silver, gold, and azure like a radiant fish. When she moved, geometric patterns emerged from the ripples and disappeared in the folds. A thousand seamstresses had likely gone blind weaving such a garment. "If you're hoping to legitimize everything you stole from Rufius, you'll have to get in line behind me."

"On the contrary, *domina*," Minem said. "My claims are not in question. I'm only here to purchase a bit of land from the owner of the tenement that burned down last night."

"He works for Imperial Associates." Rufius pointed at his former adviser, jabbing the air with his index finger. "You can't believe a thing he says."

"That didn't stop you." Plotina shooed Minem from his seat, swept his documents to the ground and did not offer a space on the bench to anyone else. "You bought his stories and sold this province for a song without a dance."

"Speaking of songs and dances," Minem said, "If Governor Rufius is put on trial, we'll want to sell tickets. An event like that could bring in some much-needed coin to the treasury and provide some much-needed diversion to the long-suffering people of—"

"This isn't a theater." Plotina crossed her wide sleeves over her chest. "And I'm not a thespian."

A drunkard crawled over to inspect Rufius from head to toe and once over again. "I know you," he said, but Rufius refused to acknowledge the man's existence.

The drunk shuffled off in search of a warm spot among the homeless petitioners, citizens charged with infractions and slaves hoping to buy their freedom. The jostling continued until the town's bailiff, stout as he was wide, announced the day's docket at the doorway to the judge's chambers.

"How many fools must I suffer today?" Praetor Soranus, the impatient old judge, cut the bailiff short. Soranus was a psoriatic pile of wrinkles with lips as dry as stale bread.

Just looking at him made Severus itch.

The judge glanced up to verify that everyone in the antechamber could sense his frustration. He was as lacking in mercy as consistency was in his courtroom. In Tarraco, justice was valued at whatever Praetor Soranus said it would cost. He neither read the law's letter nor abided by its sprit. "How many dimwits on the docket?"

"Twenty-five, maybe thirty including the kids." The bailiff ran down the details in between bites of a honey roll. "Not bad for Saturnalia."

"Condemn them all!" Soranus snorted loud enough to shame even the most innocent. "Where's my drink? How can I condemn these clods when my throat is parched? Water down some *vino* and shuffle it over here."

The bailiff, who spread his profits evenly across sweetshops and taverns, waddled into the antechamber and flashed a beaming smile at Festus Rufius. "G'mornin', Governor," he said. "Sorry to keep you waiting."

"Vino!" the judge shouted.

Plotina passed a sealed scroll and a handful of coins to the bailiff when he returned. He was careful to leave the door to the antechamber ajar so the presumed guilty could overhear the sliding scales of justice being negotiated.

Winus Minem nudged Rufius and whispered in his ear. "As Imperial Associate's principal representative in Hispania," he said, "I'm obliged to bring a couple of contractual matters between my organization and yours before the court today. We would much rather settle this quietly. Going public with our arrangements could turn ugly."

"Ugly for you, you viper!" Rufius muttered. "Gods have mercy, I'm trapped between an angry wife and a thieving adviser. The only way it could get worse would be for you two to join forces."

"That's a good idea." Plotina stood up and yanked the scruff of Rufius' toga, jerking him back before he could swat the small adviser. "Now what's the matter?"

"What matters is not listening to every poser, peasant, and pissant you meet in these dirty streets!" Rufius' round cheeks vibrated with vexation. "Hispania is full of liars, losers, and loafers—bottom-fishing belchers trawling for—"

"It's a simple matter of a few unpaid contracts." Minem handed an example to Plotina, being careful to avoid her long, sculpted fingernails. "You're welcome to review these, *domina*, but the text is tight and the payment schedule is quite clear. I'm afraid the governor is underwater and overdue."

"He was over-duped," Plotina tore the document in half. "And you are overruled."

"You can't do that!"

"I'm the emperor's direct representative." Before Minem could argue, Plotina seized his yellow toga folds and lifted him into the air without breaking a nail. She brought her face close enough to bite off his nose. "Do you know what that means, little man?"

"Put me down," Minem said. "I'm heavier than I look."

"The emperor is a god. I work for the emperor. Therefore, I work for God." She dropped Minem onto the tile floor. "Any questions, Socrates?"

"None, *domina*." Minem scrambled upright before she could kick him. He arranged the folds of his toga and forced a smile. "Actually, I was thinking that you and I could come to a mutually beneficial understanding."

"*Vesuvius!*" Rufius blanched at the prospect of Plotina and Minem joining forces to suck the marrow from his bones. Lips trembling, he tried to sweet-talk the cobra down from his wife's head while pulling the document from her hand. "Actually, darling, this has all been due to a little misunderstanding ..."

"I'm not buying it, Festus." Plotina held tight to the contract. "You're in deeper than even you've ever dug."

"Minem's the one you want!" Rufius shoved Minem so hard the little man toppled back to the floor.

Gaius Severus rushed over to help Minem to his feet.

"This Macedonian midget!" Rufius was red-faced and sputtering. "This backstabbing ball-breaker hypnotized me. He forged my signatures on confusing contracts. He bamboozled me with self-serving schemes to turn this dogged province into an economic miracle. A miracle for him, maybe. He's the one you should drag before a judge."

"As a witness," Plotina said. "Now sit down and seal your lips before the magistrate seals your fate."

The man who had recognized Rufius earlier emerged from the courtroom bereft of his tunic. The disrobed drunk stood shivering in nothing but sandals and a loincloth and pointed at the ex-governor. "I know you," he insisted. "You're Julius Caesar!"

The bailiff poked his head into the antechamber and shrugged as if undressed drunks and disgraced noblemen were a routine occurrence in Praetor Soranus' courthouse. He pushed open the door to the cold courtroom, and the accused fell silent. The hour of judgment had arrived. Four trembling ten-year-old boys, their wrists joined by a rope, were dragged in front of the angry judge.

Like the wine, Soranus' mood was not improving with age.

"You rancid little lice buckets!" The judge took another drink and wagged a crooked finger. "Good thing we caught you brats early in life! I ought to condemn you today for all your future crimes." He ruffled a pile of bone-dry legal scrolls, some of which crumbled from disuse. "For your petty crimes, brazen thefts and public displays of immorality, I sentence—"

"Excuse me, sir," the bailiff interrupted, speaking through a mouthful of something sticky, "but, technically speaking, public displays of immorality are perfectly legal during holiday week."

The judge made a great show of extending his robed arms like a crow's wings. "In that case you toads have three blinks to get out of my sight."

The bound boys scrambled away like a clumsy spider.

"Don't come back unless you like hanging by your toes!" the bailiff yelled. He followed them out the door and delivered a few choice kicks to reinforce their good fortune.

Gaius Severus tried to eavesdrop as Plotina negotiated with Winus Minem, but it was difficult to glean much detail because the judge was berating a young woman for having been out alone and unmarried after dark. Severus managed to learn that Minem had a sizeable stockpile of signed contracts, verbal agreements, and general evidence of Rufius' profligacy. Dereliction of duty would be an easy accusation to prove. In exchange for a position near the head of the creditor's queue, Minem agreed to provide Plotina with documents, witnesses, and useful hearsay when the case came to trial.

The bailiff grumbled about the number of cases to be processed and indictments to be rendered. "The magistrate is offering a post-

53

holiday special," he announced. "Anyone who can pay a thousand in cash gets off with a half sentence. Jail is cheaper, but you get what you pay for."

Plotina took advantage of the ensuing clemency negotiations to step into the courtroom uninvited. A moment later, Rufius and Minem were summoned. Severus followed and, to his surprise, was not evicted.

"A bit of excitement today," the bailiff said as he refilled the judge's pitcher. "In addition to usual scum, we've got the ex-governor and some kind of Roman royalty. Judging from what I've heard so far, I recommend we execute Rufius immediately." He stepped back into the antechamber to continue collecting the price of penance.

"That's the thanks I get for trying to drag this province out of antiquity?" Rufius moaned. "I'm a Roman citizen. You can't execute me. *Civis Romanus sum!*"

"Put a scarf in it," Plotina whispered. "Stay quiet, and with any luck you'll just be tortured."

Rufius clenched his flabby mandibles.

The judge examined a few documents and handed them to the bailiff. "Divorce, bankruptcy, censure, and impeachment—we can't handle this kind of drama here. His father is a senator, for Pluto's sake. This case should be transferred to Rome."

"With respect, Your Honor, the prosecutor traveled all the way here from Rome." The bailiff appeared concerned that a profitable opportunity might be lost for the simple reason that their provincial court had no jurisdiction to pursue it. "She has the Senate's written permission for a fair trial to take place in Tarraco."

"Impossible!" shouted Rufius. "Nothing's fair in Tarraco."

"Honestly sir, this could be a golden opportunity," the bailiff whispered loudly. "Imagine how much Rufius will pay to save his skin. From the way he's twitching, I'd say the barrister babe's got some incriminating stuff on the old boy."

"A lady barrister?" The judge almost swallowed a molar. "A woman arguing law in my court?"

"The dishy *domina* … name's Plotina," the bailiff whispered. He nodded in her direction. "Claims to be Hadrian's niece, but so do half the girls in town. Judging from the steel in her eyes, I'd wager she's a tiger."

"Is nothing sacred in this god's forsaken dump?" The judge wiped his eyes, but they were too clouded with cataracts to see clearly.

The role of praetor was a common stepping-stone for young men working their way up the hierarchy. For Soranus, the stone had turned into island. After being ensnared in a scandal over the sale of fictitious land deeds, he paid a fortune in bribes and favors to avoid being hauled before the other side of the bench. Family connections saved him from being dispatched like a common thief. He was exiled to Hispania, which at the time was deemed better than Hades. He had rotted in Tarraco ever since while a generation of well-connected young prospects made their fortunes in the far north where justice was still lucrative.

"I'm going to die here," the old man sighed.

"There are worse fates." Plotina forced a shallow nod in deference to his gray hairs and lack of eminence. "May I approach the bench, Your Honor?"

"Why not? Everyone else does." The judge squinted and appraised her with more than professional interest. The value of her bright necklace was not lost on the nearsighted Soranus. He stood slowly, bones creaking as if they needed lubrication, and waved her toward the door behind his desk. "Given the nature of the case, perhaps we should retire to my private study."

"Three's a crowd," Minem said after Plotina disappeared with the judge. He gathered his documents and left.

Severus followed Minem and saw that the mob outside the courthouse had not dispersed. The mood was tense as a plucked string. Plotina's women looked like they ate gladiators for breakfast and were starting to get hungry.

"Don't let Plotina take Rufius," Minem whispered before disappearing into the twilight.

Severus understood that the ex-governor was a valuable commodity. Governor Kleptus wanted Rufius to reveal where any stolen tax money might have been stashed. Minem had unfinished business with him, and Rufius was of obvious importance to Plotina.

She had come to Tarraco to beat him with the scales of justice. Since feuds between patrician families could last for generations, she was honor bound to scorch his clan to cinders. Once she had collected Hadrian's missing tribute she would probably drag him back to Rome and parade him on a donkey through the Colosseum.

But Plotina was just one of many who might be after Rufius. Marius and his rebel friends had to be aware of Rufius' value as a hostage. Marius' failed scheme to kill the emperor and his constant talk of fomenting rebellion across the provinces might be bluster, but he was growing increasingly strident. For someone capable of plotting a regicide, kidnap would be child's play.

Marius was hotheaded and incautious. He had a knack for being in the wrong place at the right time, an uncanny aptitude for being within striking distance of Gaius' recent near-death experiences. Whether a hardened rebel or just a harmless lunatic, Marius could not be trusted.

Responding to Minem's instructions was a chance for Gaius Severus to show some initiative. Losing Rufius to Plotina or anyone else who might profit from a high-profile hostage would earn him a quick a trip to the sand on the arena floor.

Plotina would soon finish her business, so Severus clutched at the first plan that came to mind. Stashing Rufius in jail was an option, but his safety could not be assured under the arena—not with the way the old judge was condemning people today. The easily corrupted bailiff might sell Rufius' skin to the highest bidder or let an assassin share his cell. Severus was unfamiliar with its floor plan, but the jail's main purpose was to hold criminals and proscribed citizens condemned to the mines or the arena.

Gaius Severus approached the ex-governor and handed him the drunk's dirty tunic. "Wear this and I'll guide you to safety."

Rufius examined the soiled garment and tossed it onto the floor. "Not my style, kid."

"If you prefer leaving with Plotina, that's fine with me," Severus said. "But there's a mob outside, and they don't look friendly."

A snort of defiance gave way to a sigh of defeat. In Rome, a plebe like Severus would be whipped for addressing a senator's son with such candor. But Rome was a distant dream. Dejected, Rufius shuffled away to change in a dark corner. After donning the dirty tunic, he handed Severus his red-trimmed toga. "Don't lose this. It's imported."

Severus took the toga. The fine wool weighed more than the lamb it came from. "Wait in the antechamber."

"With the riffraff?"

"Try to blend in."

Severus stuffed the sleeping drunk into Rufius' regal toga and then sought two of Plotina's strong women. Gambling that they had not gotten a good look at Rufius earlier, he directed them to place the imposter in the litter.

When Plotina finally left the judge's private chambers, she looked impatient to leave. However justice had groped her would be paid back with interest.

"Rufius was so exhausted that he almost passed out," Severus told her. "We stuffed him in your litter. I suggest you take him back to the boat and keep him safe."

"Suggestion noted." Plotina swept through the courthouse with such a flurry of garments that the dust swirled in her wake.

"One more thing," Severus added. "I don't know how to put this delicately, but your husband got a bit sick. I did my best to tidy him up, but he doesn't smell like a rose. You might want to walk behind instead of subjecting yourself to the smell."

"Gods help those downwind." Plotina buckled her leather jerkin like armor against nightfall. Her stern glare cut a temporary canyon through the cold, homeless, and hungry people huddled along the colonnades.

Nine
IX

Lena stomped across town, enraged enough to send the rain boiling
back skyward. A low-flying crow confirmed that downhill was as
bad a direction as any. Heavy with scraps stolen from an altar, the
bird shed just enough ballast to clear the sagging rooftops.

Lena emerged near the arena where a group of young men were
loitering in front of the Gladiator's Goblet. They were playing a boys
game that involved bold dares and sharp jabs when Lena's
appearance attracted their attention.

"Hey, tiger eyes!" one shouted. Others joined in taunting her
with rapidly decreasing politeness.

She walked along the edge of the stadium, trying to ignore the
young fools, but their catcalls only grew louder.

"Why are you so skinny?"

"Why are you so tall?"

"I don't believe you're really a girl!"

She had endured far worse harassment, but tonight her anger
crackled like lit kindling. Young men, old men, rich and poor—why
did they all believe that a woman alone was their plaything?

"Resisting only makes you more attractive, my little lioness,"
Don Rexus had insisted, as if molesting servants was his birthright.
Early this evening he had torn her tunic in an attempt to paw her. "I
know you want me."

"Yes. I want you to stop." Lena struggled to break free without
inflicting visible damage on the man who was a superior in name
only. Self-defense was no justification for assaulting a noble.

Rexus grabbed her sash and pulled her toward him. "It's time
you learned your place, little servant girl."

Lena shook loose, grabbed his wrist and twisted it behind his
back.

"Hey!" Rexus tried to wriggle free without breaking his own
arm. "Show some respect!"

"If you ever touch me again, if you ever so much as get near me again, I'll break your arm in three places." She bent his wrist up into his shoulder blades until he howled for her to stop. Vowing never to return to the villa, Lena ran out through a delivery door with no plan other than ridding the world of the likes of Don Rexus and the rude boys now harassing her outside the tavern.

"If you're pretty, I'll buy the wine," a chubby fellow shouted.

"And if you're ugly, you buy the wine for us," another added. His laughing comrades, drunk with collective audacity, pushed him forward. "Come upstairs. I'll show you some moves you'll never forget."

"Moves?" Lena stepped into their midst. "Want to see some moves?"

Lena decked the first fellow who stepped into her orbit. She grabbed another and swung him in a wide arc by his heels. The remaining boys snapped like saplings in a windstorm.

"I'll be inside if you still want to buy me a drink," she said, nearly tearing the door off its hinges.

The tavern air was thick with stale perspiration. Oil lamps shone yellow light over the wrinkled faces of men who came nightly to drink, boast, and gamble.

"Not interested," she snarled at a red-nosed drunkard who bumbled toward her like a lost bee. She twisted his tunic folds and pulled him close enough to bite off an ear. "Go home to your sow and piglets."

She shoved through the crowd and sidled up to the counter. "*Vino,* no water," she demanded. She took a long swig of the sour plonk but found no solace in its fermented company. Each gulp made her blood boil hotter.

A young man bearing a familial resemblance to Gaius Severus entered the tavern carrying a small sack. He was shorter, rounder and lighter skinned than Gaius, but his nose and eyes were identical. Lena had heard Gaius mention a brother, but what would either sibling be doing here?

Marius looked directly at Lena but did not seem to see her. Neither did he notice a middle-aged woman approaching him with an unmistakable air of perfume and commerce until she was upon him.

"No thanks." Marius waved her away.

"Don't flatter yourself, puppy," the woman answered. She

pointed to a narrow stairway on the far side of the tavern. "He's waiting in the room upstairs. Make it quick, kid. The big boys are waiting to use the mattress."

Marius zigzagged through the tavern, sidestepping a weaving patron and avoiding the owner's lovesick dog. Lena maintained her distance, stooping a bit so as not to be seen towering over the steamy bald heads of Tarraco's most dedicated drinkers.

Lena squeezed up the stairs, inching past the patrons waiting to invest in the horizontal economy. The upper floor pulsed like a ship's deck. She tried not to worry about what kept the second level aloft as she spied on Marius.

There were three rooms off the short, dark hall that intersected the landing. Marius knocked on the door nearest the top of the stairs. A husky, breathless voice hissed at him to wait his turn. When Marius cracked open the next door a hairy arm shot out and yanked him into the dim room.

Lena peered through a knothole and saw that the bleak room housed a wash basin and an unpainted chair. Years of negotiable virtue had flattened the hay-stuffed mattress. A flickering candle cast wan light on a thin man in a brown tunic. Lena sensed power in the man's presence, a darkness that was not be trifled with.

"I've heard you're interested in holy objects." Marius reached into his sack and spread a few small ceramic figures across the bed.

The man arched his single wide eyebrow, examined the assortment and shook his head. "These are worth less than the gods they pretend to honor." The man's voice sounded rougher than a cart wheel in gravel.

"I'll be going then." Marius gathered his wares.

"Wait." The man leaned against the door, almost blocking Lena's view. "I've seen your Saturnalia antics around town. Do you really want to free Judea or are you just playing around?"

Marius wrapped a delicate statuette in protective cloth. "I'm serious."

"You've got the right spirit, but the wrong tactics. If you continue protesting after the festival is over, your brother will be forced to lock you up for good."

"Brother?"

"The security hack." The small man gestured for Marius to sit down and then did the same and continued speaking. "Do you want to do some real damage instead of fooling around?"

Marius perched on the edge of the rickety chair and fidgeted with a fertility goddess. "What do you want from me?"

"There's a stash of artifacts in the villa," the man said. "I'm prepared to pay a pretty coin for them."

Lena was more curious than Marius. The man knew about the stash of relics that she had planned to sell piecemeal to buy Carbo's freedom. It occurred to her that if she could arrange a larger transaction, the proceeds might free him and a dozen more.

"So you're a collector?"

"I work for the king of collectors." The man spoke softly but it did not soften his rough edges. "I understand that there may be an old silver candelabrum in the collection I mentioned."

Lena stiffened but Marius maintained his composure. If, as Carbo had suggested, the old lamp came from the Severus household, she wondered how the word had leaked to this strange fellow.

"Deliver the relic and I'll get you to Judea."

"Why would you do that?"

"I understand that your so-called god promised Judea to your so-called people. What if I told you that my god is more ancient and more demanding than yours?"

Lena pulled away from the knothole just as Marius stood up and turned toward the door. "Sorry, I'm not interested."

"Wait," the man said, raising his eyebrow. "They call me Monobrow."

"Call me Dayenu," Marius said, "because I've had enough."

Monobrow drew a small knife and rolled it across his fingers. His face, like his accent, was rough and eastern. His dark eyebrow looked like it had been applied with a trowel. His cavernous cheeks hung from weather-worn bones. "I wonder if your so-called promised land was empty when your sorry tribe found it. Don't you find it odd that a land of milk and honey would be vacant, free for the taking? If your god forbids stealing, why did he give you someone else's land?"

"You're holding me at knifepoint to talk philosophy?" Marius glanced at the loosely hung window. The cold air leaking through the rotting wood kept the room from smelling worse than normal.

Monobrow sent the small dagger spinning into the door frame.

From the whistle and impact, Lena could judge how deeply the knife had lodged in the pine. It would take strength to yank it out, and luck to avoid another.

Monobrow smiled at the sound of negotiated passion on the other side of the thin wall. "This tavern's full of hookers, but you're the real whore."

Marius jumped up and grabbed Monobrow by the tunic. He threw him to the floor so quickly that even Lena with her gift for premonition had not seen it coming.

"Good boy," Monobrow laughed. "Lots of spirit—there's hope for you yet." He stood up slowly, feigning injury and then leapt forward. He grabbed Marius' nose and twisted it until Marius dropped to his knees. "You think graffiti is going to free your homeland? You think slogans will rebuild your holy temple?"

Monobrow pulled his knife from the door frame and stuffed it back in his sash. "You can let a handful of old centurions turn Judea into a retirement colony or you can step up and make history. Your choice, Marius."

Marius did a poor job of hiding his surprise that the man knew his real name. "Why do you care?"

"I don't." Monobrow tossed a sack of coins onto the bed. "One third now, the rest on delivery. Free passage to the promised land. Just get me that menorah."

Ten
X

As soon as Plotina's entourage disappeared behind the temple, Gaius Severus sprang into action. "Let's go," he whispered to Festus Rufius. "We don't have much time."

"What's the rush?" Rufius seemed to be savoring his sudden freedom and anonymity. "Life is long."

"Not if we don't get you to safety." Severus reckoned it would take Plotina a few minutes to reach her ship. Even if she failed to detect the ruse before reaching the vessel, it would not take her crew long to fan out across town. There was barely enough time to reach the villa and stash Rufius in the *vomitorium*.

"As soon as Plotina discovers—"

"Relax, you'll feel better after a little drink. Isn't there a tavern over by the arena?"

"The Gladiator's Goblet? It's in the opposite direction. The villa is uphill."

"I know where the vexed villa is. I live there, you dull milkweed." Rufius adjusted the small tunic he had borrowed and took off like a homing pigeon.

Severus had no choice but to follow. "That tavern is a thieves' paradise. The scum there would make Nero blush!"

"Sounds perfect."

"There's no time!" Severus had not factored in a change of direction or stopping to drink at Tarraco's least auspicious watering hole. On the other hand, the Goblet was probably the last place anyone would expect to find a nobleman. As long as Rufius stayed quiet, the detour might not end in disaster.

"I'm sure the villa has better wine." Severus caught up to Rufius and pointed out a shortcut. "And a better class of people."

"Wrong on both counts. There's no *vino* left and, as for the people, well …" Rufius looked crosswise at Severus. "They have no respect for authority."'

"Visiting the tavern is a bad idea."

"Tarraco is the capital of bad ideas." Rufius loosened his sash and tugged on the shifting tunic. "I hope you have a few coins, boy. I need a drink almost as much as I need a bath."

"Sorry, sir. The baths close at sunset. It's the law."

"Laws are for commoners."

Seeing that Rufius was obstinate, Severus resigned himself to a difficult night. The difference in status, plebe to patrician, required deference. Perhaps Rufius would be more compliant after a cheap pitcher of local plonk.

The Gladiator's Goblet stood in plain view of the arena. Tarraco's poor impression of Rome's Colosseum could seat a thousand and stand a thousand more. The games and executions brought in patrons willing to exchange their last coins for blood, wine, and sausage. No games had been held since the budget for bread and circuses evaporated, but the downturn had not hurt the Goblet.

Outside the tavern, mariners who found the lawless docklands too tame cavorted with women of cut-rate affection. A handful of young men huddled for warmth around a small fire they had pitched in the middle of the street.

By the time Severus arrived at the door, Rufius was already inside the tavern. Severus stopped and considered the threshold from which there was no turning back. The Goblet was a place his father had warned him against. Gomorrah's debauchery would be tame in comparison with what Severus expected to find inside the tavern. He took a deep breath and inched forward into the dim light. Smoke stung his eyes. The thick stench of fish brine barely disguised the smell of charred gristle and unwashed fisherman.

Severus resolved to hold fast to as many of the Ten Commandments as he could remember. He vowed to honor his father, fear no evil, and try not to kill anyone. Father had warned that the true corrupting power of evil was that when surrounded by it, one could not help but succumb to its sway. Severus braced for the world's end only to find there was still time left. Once his eyes adjusted to the dim surroundings, Severus felt damp air escape from his over-inflated worries. He acclimated to the assault of smoke, shouts, and the thick smell of *garum*.

The walls were covered with weapons and tarnished armor. Weighted nets hung from the corners, and an array of daggers and three-pointed tridents were mounted for display. A blood-stained loin cloth hung from the tip of a sword.

A drummer in the corner tapped out a tepid rhythm while a trumpet player blew a minor scale through his dented horn. They were street performers, come in from the cold to play for drinks and a spot by the hearth. In response to the room's indifference, the horn player let loose a burst of dissonant notes that hung like frog spawn on a pond.

Severus had been in a tavern just once before, but the roadhouse where he and Lena had defeated the gladiator was tame in comparison with the Goblet. He thought back to the night he ran away from the Roman legion, the night he and Lena stole the horse. His nostalgia was interrupted by a boy in a grimy tunic.

"Cost's a copper to drink, three to gawk."

"I'm with him." Severus nodded toward the hearth-side table where Rufius was already tucking into a plate of grilled fowl and a pitcher of wine.

A dented shield and barbed mace graced the stone mantle above the fire.

"Got any money?" Rufius asked.

"Money … me?" Severus squeezed in next to him. "You're the senator's son! Don't you have money?"

"Not so loud, idiot!" Rufius stabbed a hunk of dark meat and washed it down with wine. "If I had money, would I be dining on red ink and road kill?"

"Probably." Severus reached for a chicken leg but Rufius slapped his hand away.

"Don't touch food you can't pay for."

Severus reached into his pouch, pulled out a *denarius*, and spun it onto the table. Rufius made a play for the coin but before it could fall the tavern boy scooped it away.

"See that guy over there?" Rufius jerked his head toward a squat fellow in a faded brown tunic. The man had just placed a sack on a table and was pulling out an assortment of strange objects. "I saw him once in Rome."

"He gets around."

"Most Greeks do. They've been a restless race ever since we brought culture to Athens." Rufius leaned over and spoke directly in Severus' ear. "When he gets started, put your money on the table and bet against the crowd. Do the opposite of whatever seems to make sense and you'll double your investment."

"Thanks, but I'd rather hold on to my last few coins."

"Lend them to me and I'll pay you back triple before the night is out."

"You already owe me for the bird." Severus grabbed a piece of chicken, shoved it in his mouth and washed it down with a gulp directly from the pitcher. "And for the *vino*."

"You should pay me to drink that swill. Come on, kid. I know this Greek's game. Within an hour, I'll have enough dough for both of us to go upstairs." Rufius shot a glance up toward the rooms where beds were creaking with one-sided intensity. An older woman with light hair and heavy breasts winked from the top of the stairs. Her cheeks looked to have been painted with a broad brush.

"We really need to go," Severus said. "Plotina—"

"Plotina wants money, and I know how to get it." Rufius put his palm out. "Give!"

Severus dug into his pouch and offered up his last three coins.

"How much do you get paid, anyway?" Rufius asked.

"Not sure," Severus said. "Minem said something about a base salary with room for sizeable commissions."

"Take it from me, kid. Don't believe anything that rat tells you." Rufius sauntered over to where the small, pinch-nosed Greek was attracting a crowd.

"I am afflicted with the curse of Pythagoras," the Greek shouted. His nasal voice cut through the din like a cawing crow. He produced a loop of twine that had knots tied at equal distance along the length. He held the loop above his bald head. "Observe this humble rope," he said.

"Use it to hang yourself!" a patron suggested.

"Hang I will if you can prove me wrong. Place one *sesterce* on the table, form this noose into any geometric figure you like and I will tell you the exact perimeter."

Before people could ask what a perimeter was, Rufius slapped one of Severus' coins on the table and laid out the twine in a rough ellipse.

"You may have me there, friend," the man said. He looked into the crowd, down at the rope, and up at a rafter. "I should have mentioned that the ancient secrets of Pythagoras only work with triangles. Your flattened circle could be the death of me."

Some patrons insisted that the shrill little man keep his promise; others claimed that Greeks never did.

"Since I appear to have made a fatal mistake," the Greek said, "I might as well wager some of my life's savings on the off-chance that I guess right. I'll offer two-to-one odds against my very self!"

People slapped their money down so fast that Gaius Severus lost count as the coins rolled across the table. He shot a curious glance toward Festus Rufius who smiled like a fox and tossed another coin onto the pile.

When the currency clattered to a halt, the Greek looked up in a panic. "My friends, it appears my story ends tonight. Unless I can guess the perimeter of that vexed ellipse, I'll die broke!"

Severus shoved closer to see the man close his eyes, run a finger over the loop and chant something about "foci" and "hypotenuse." His head bobbled. His chins vibrated. The corner of the room went so silent that other patrons came over to investigate the suspicious lack of commotion. The Greek appeared to be in some sort of trance until his eyes opened wide.

"Thirty-seven … no … thirty-eight lengths!"

"Let me check that," Rufius insisted. He counted the knots and nodded.

"I don't believe it!" shouted a local tile merchant. He grabbed the rope from Rufius' hand and reproduced the count.

Others did the same while the squat Greek swept the money off the table.

"Trickery!" A grumble welled up from around the table, but no one could explain the stunt or the money they had lost.

"I feel terrible to have denied you a good hanging." The Greek reached into his sack and pulled out an object that looked like a brass sea urchin. He offered the device up for inspection. "Have you ever seen one of these?"

"It's your left nut!" a drunkard shouted.

Gaius Severus examined the metal sphere. The spines extending from its equator were hollow; the bare ends slightly dented. He blew into a spine to see if the strange object might be an ocarina but no music sounded.

After the sphere made the rounds, the Greek placed it on a small stand. "This spiny orb can neither roll nor tumble, but using nothing more than two of the four basic elements, I can make it spin and whistle."

"Pish posh!" Rufius said, and the crowd agreed.

The Greek offered two-to-one odds that two basic elements would produce sound and motion. Before money could hit the table, Festus Rufius stepped forward and offered three-to-one toward the same proposition. The better odds attracted more wagers and forced the magician to increase his offer. Each time the increasingly flustered Greek tried to attract new wagers, Rufius offered more.

"Nothing more than two of the four elements," the Greek insisted, but after two more rounds of betting, the Greek was so confused he accidentally bet against himself. Sweat beaded on his head and soaked through his tunic. By the time the wagers ceased, the betting pool had flooded the table.

The odds were so high that Gaius Severus could barely exhale. A few minutes earlier, Rufius had borrowed money for cheap wine and a scrawny chicken, now he was running a casino with no funds in reserve. If his gambit failed, the patrons would pull the weapons off the walls and chop him into stew meat.

The Greek pulled at the neck of his tunic as if seeking relief from the overheated contest. "Shall it be earth? Fire? Air or water?"

"*Vino!*" shouted a spectator.

"Water!" The Greek opened a small hatch on top of the brass vessel and poured in a measure of water. He mounted it in the armature and gave it a playful spin. When it stopped, he asked for an oil lamp. "Fire!"

The gamblers crowded closer and watched the Greek pour a few thimbles full of olive oil into a tiny basin under the mysterious brass sea urchin. He lit the oil and waved his hands as if blessing the strange device. "Spirit of Archimedes ..."

Nothing happened.

"Ghost of Pythagoras ..."

The crowd purred with delight at the expected windfall, until a bit of vapor leaked from one of the hollow spines. The hissing grew louder until the spines began to whistle and the sphere began to spin. The magical orb rotated into a blur. As the water boiled away, the sphere coasted to a halt.

Rufius scooped his winnings from the table and bounded upstairs to celebrate.

The squat Greek tried to introduce his next trick, but the twice bitten men were uninterested in a third round.

The horn player blasted a shrill phrase to remind the crowd that he was still there. The drummer beat his taut skin as if administering justice to a child.

Considering Rufius to be safe for the moment, Severus elected to wait for him to return, spent and broke. An hour upstairs might even render him more compliant. He took a position near the base of the stairs and looked up to see a tall woman emerge from the darkness at the top of the stairs.

Severus wiped his eyes to be sure they weren't deceiving him.

It was Lena.

Only the gods knew how long she had been in the bordello, but there was no mystery about what took place up there. Their eyes met and her guileless smile nearly knocked Severus backward. She seemed happy to see him, though he could not imagine why. The thought of Lena working the sleazy rooms above the tavern was worse than drinking poison from a dirty cup. His stomach churned as if full of vinegar. Of all the unimaginable heartaches, there could be none deeper than this. He clutched the railing and blocked the bottom stair. "Have you no shame?"

Lena pushed through the throng of eager patrons. She looked tired and disheveled, apparently worn out by whatever had transpired in the rooms above the tavern.

Severus had to shout just to hear his own voice over his beating heart. "Are you completely without decency?"

"Decency? What are you on about?" Lena shoved past him as if he were a bill collector. "You're the one standing in line for a cheap round of thump-thump."

"Thump-thump? Me?" Severus followed her toward the door. "I don't have money for thump-thump."

"Here." Lena reached into her pouch and pulled out a handful of coins. "Go get some."

She shook off a couple of compliments, dodged an unwelcome embrace, and ignored the cat calls as she shoved toward the exit.

Severus followed and tried to shove the tainted coins back into her clenched hand. "How did you get so much money? You have a respectable job and a place to stay. You have me … had me … why in Jupiter's name are you working here?"

"Who are you, my father?" Lena's eyes tightened. She grabbed

Severus by the collar. "You don't own me."

"Own you? Until just now I didn't know you had a price!" Severus twisted away, angrier with each passing second. He knew she could be fierce when crossed, but holding the moral high ground emboldened him. "I saved you from a gladiator. I brought you to Tarraco and helped you get on your feet. I loved you and this is how you return the favor? I thought you were a goddess, but you're just a—"

"A what? I find you waiting in this line and *you're* the one who's angry?" Lena stormed out of the door and into the street.

"You think I'm joking?" Severus followed.

"Go jump off the mountain of your own stupidity." Lena slammed her fists against her hips, making it clear she was ready to use them. She cursed in a dialect that needed no translation.

A break in the clouds revealed a dark sky full of indifferent constellations.

"I don't understand why you did this," Severus said. "I thought we had something … something that would last."

"Nothing lasts. Don't you know that by now?"

"You're crazy." Severus stomped off toward the dark arena.

"Crazy? I pass my days among slaves in your governor's villa," Lena shouted, following him down the street. "*Slaves*—people owned by other people. You think *that's* normal? You dare judge me? I raise money to set people free and you call *me* crazy?"

Severus shook his head in disbelief. Her explanation was as wild as she was. Why had he ever imagined that Lena could be domesticated? She was like a lynx that could be caged but never kept. "Go," he said, waving over his shoulder without facing her. "Free the slaves. Free yourself from me."

Severus stomped away, wondering what purpose love served if pain was its only outcome. He stumbled blindly along the outer wall of the arena until he found the heavy door to the subterranean jail. He felt like admitting himself and volunteering to face a swift death. No cut delivered on the arena sand could be worse than what Lena had just dealt him.

Night dripped down the massive walls and trickled into the street. The arena loomed above him. Severus felt the crushing weight of a sadness well beyond his own. The bloodshed seen here was enough to make God weep. In the silence between his own heartbeats, Severus sensed the restless spirits of a thousand victims. They beckoned and moaned in undead tongues.

Lemures. Sprits trapped at life's gates whispered his name. Innocent victims who died with no coins for the boatman. There was no misinterpreting the sounds swirling around him. The restless spirits had come to claim him.

"You will join us."

"No!" Severus shouted at the arena and railed at the darkness. He refused to let the voices scare him. Nothing was written. The future was an open scroll. "I belong here in this world!"

Lena snuck up from behind and shook his shoulder as if rousing him from a nightmare. "Who are you shouting at?"

"You didn't hear them?" Relieved to find himself on the living side of the River Styx, Severus fought back a shiver. "Honestly now, what were you doing in the tavern?"

"I tell fortunes, you idiot. That's how I raise money to free slaves."

"A soothsayer?" Severus felt the dread dissipate. He reached out but she backed away. "Fortune telling? Seriously?"

"Why were *you* waiting in line?"

"I was standing guard." Severus shook off the phantoms and returned to the fray. "I'm escorting a high-profile prisoner to justice."

"*Seriously?*" Lena imitated his disbelief and threw in a measure of condescension. She was angry enough to defang a snake. "You throw dirt on me when you're covered with mud?"

"You're upstairs at the Goblet, and I'm covered with mud? I'm the most open-minded person I know. I can see three sides to every argument but if I bend any further backward I'll snap. I may be stupid, but I'm nobody's fool."

"You're everybody's fool. You think these Romans will ever accept you?" Lena stormed away. "As long as you live, you'll never be one of them."

Severus turned his back to the arena, its cheap phantoms and their empty cries. Perhaps Lena had chased away the boneyard spirits. In the brief clash between love and death, both had lost. He felt a shallow, short-lived rush of relief until he remembered that Festus Rufius, ostensibly his prisoner, had been left to his own devices.

Severus raced back toward the Goblet and found a handful of dazed patrons milling about in the street. Inside, the tavern looked as if a thunderstorm had erupted in the kitchen, spewing debris everywhere.

The tavern had been ransacked. Tables were overturned. Ceramic pitchers lay broken in puddles of wine. Most of the weapons were gone from the walls.

"Female gladiators," a traumatized hooker said. "Red tunics, cobras on their backs. They turned the place upside down and us with it."

Severus ran upstairs. One door had been wrenched from its hinges, another hung ajar. Straw from shredded mattresses drifted in the corridor. A few scattered coins were all that remained of the disrupted commerce.

Severus descended and found the tavern boy cowering under the counter.

"Giant women," the boy sobbed. "Warriors. Pirates."

"What were they looking for?"

"I don't know what they wanted." The boy clutched his forehead. "They just wrecked the place and left."

"Did they take any prisoners?"

The boy just twitched and withdrew into the darkness.

The ex-governor might have been lucky enough to sneak away before the raid, but with the streets now crawling with Plotina's pirates, additional luck would be in short supply. Gambling that Rufius would not have made for the port, Severus took to the streets and ran uphill.

Enjoying their shore leave, Plotina's crew was blowing through town with gale-force abandon. They kicked up trash, knocked over carts and left dirty whirlwinds spinning in their many wakes. The pirates scoured storefronts and alleys, looking high and mainly low for the ex-governor. They were brash and fearsome. Each represented the worst her province had to offer. Most had never seen Festus Rufius, but this did not dampen their enthusiasm. They were armed, determined, and not overly concerned with the basic rights of citizens. Any man within ten years of Rufius' age was subject to search and interrogation.

"Pirates of the Mediterranean!" shouted the forum crier before one of the invaders gagged him with her sash. The other crier, typically quick to contradict, had already been silenced.

Severus clung to the walls, trying to avoid the thin light glowing from illegal braziers on the sagging balconies above. He veered through slums and side streets, hoping to pass undetected by the formidable women patrolling the town. He tried to imagine Rufius' next move, but the ex-governor had proved unpredictable. Returning to the villa seemed too obvious. Depending on how much money he had spent in the bordello, he might have enough left to bribe a plebe into putting him up for the night. Rufius could hide in a tenement until morning and then make his next move.

Rufius seemed clever, but not particularly smart. A smart politician would never have been arrested, deposed, and manhandled by his ex-wife. Smart governors became richer senators. Ambitious senators became tribunes, counsels, and emperors. True, Julius Caesar had been a fugitive once, but Rufius was no Caesar.

The waterfront would not offer safe haven. Rufius was a noble, and the docklands were anything but. Even if he could avoid Plotina's crew, he would not last longer than a feather in a fire on the unsafe streets.

Gaius Severus feigned inebriation as two fierce women approached him. He sang an off-key song about a pig and a magistrate and stumbled along until the pirates turned the corner. Once sure no one was following, he yanked open the warped door to the plebian bathhouse, and slipped into the small vestibule. If going underground was impossible, Rufius might still go underwater.

Marius was working the night shift, sleeping on a chair leaning against the wall. He woke up with a start and raised one eyebrow that pulled his face into a half smile. "Look what the cat dragged in!" Marius rocked the front legs of his chair down onto the tile floor. "Where's your pagan girl?"

"Ancient history."

Marius stood up and cracked his back. "How's your police job going?"

"It's history, too."

"Hannibal's elephants?"

"More history." Gaius smiled, relieved that Marius seemed to be in a good mood. There was no telling how long it would last, but a few minutes free from reproach were always welcome.

"So what brings you here? Looking for a job? Need a place to spend the night?"

"Not just yet," Gaius said. He was unsure how much to confide in his unpredictable brother. "I'm looking for someone. Someone important. It's urgent."

"Nobody here but us plebes." Marius planted himself in front of the corridor leading to the baths. It appeared he did not want visitors. "I've been here all night. What's your friend look like?"

"Middle-aged toff—gray hair, Roman abdomen."

"Could be anyone," Marius said. "It's after hours. If you want to bathe, I won't stop you, but we already have enough spies in here without one more poking around."

"In that case, I'll need a towel."

The plebian baths were one of the better-maintained public institutions in Tarraco. There was always plenty of wood for the boilers. The towels were threadbare but clean, and a polite attendant could just about make a living from the *sesterces* in the tip bowl.

The baths took the edge off the cold and offered relief from large families and tight quarters. This was a place where a body could relax and steam. News was exchanged, advice was dispensed, gossip was vetted, and fresh rumors were started.

Marius stepped back from the closet and threw a towel at his brother. "It's quiet tonight," he said. "On earth as it is above."

"Not quiet where I've been." Gaius tossed the towel over his shoulder and motioned downward. "All may be well above, but I caught a glimpse of what lies below."

"The heating ducts?"

"Hades." As a child, he thought the hot air flowing through the brickwork rose directly from the underworld, but now he knew better. "I came across some kind of spirit tonight. Down by the arena … ghosts of victims, I think."

"Pish posh." Cold air whistled into the vestibule and Marius pulled the door shut. "Not even your fortune-telling girlfriend believes in ghosts."

Gaius shivered and positioned himself over the floor grill to catch a wisp of hot air rising from below. "You know about Lena?"

"Who doesn't?" Marius clearly enjoyed his brother's surprise. He reached into the tip jar and churned the coins. "Telling fortunes in the tavern is a better racket than working here."

"I'm such an idiot!"

74

"I've been trying to tell you that for years."

Gaius Severus confronted the possibility that Lena had been completely earnest. What had he called her? A *thump-thump girl*? Could he have been any more provincial? His narrow-mindedness had cost him the love of his life. Perhaps he and Marius were not so different after all. "Lena's telling fortunes. I'm seeing ghosts. I always thought you were the crazy one."

"Go take a bath before I remember that we're on opposite sides of the revolution. You should really—"

The swollen door burst open and two agitated women barged in wielding sticks.

"Sorry," Marius said. "Ladies bathe in the morning."

"No problem." One of Plotina's crew picked Marius up by the armpits and slammed him against the wall. "We're not ladies."

"Plotina would not want you rampaging through a bathhouse full of naked old men," Gaius insisted, trying to back out of harm's way.

"The captain will be sad to miss the fun." She lifted Gaius by the tunic and bumped his head against the ceiling.

"You know these charming girls?" Marius asked.

"Would you like me to introduce you?"

After dusting the walls with the brothers Severus, the women tossed them aside and stomped into the corridor.

"Vesuvius!" Marius cursed. "Are these the ghosts you were babbling about? What Greek tragedy did they come from?"

The brothers reached the *caldarium* just in time to find the muscular women pulling men from the soaking pool, inspecting them rudely and tossing them back in the water.

"They're worse than lava," Gaius muttered.

"Be glad we never had a sister."

The sailors stormed in and out of the drying rooms and exercise areas. Stiff bruises were freely distributed to all who resisted.

The women disappeared as quickly as they had arrived, though shouting echoed through the corridors long after the sanctity of the bathhouse had been breached. A few men claimed to have never been so offended, but most of the others seemed to have enjoyed surviving the excitement. The raid would give everyone something new to talk about. By morning the incident would spawn a dozen new rumors.

"Still need to search the place?" Marius scooped a towel off the floor and tossed it at Gaius. "Those she-wolves were pretty thorough."

Gaius noticed that the towel was cool. He touched the floor and felt no warmth, though he knew the furnace was nearby. He recalled the night he and Marius had escaped from the enraged Corsican mercenary by crawling through the heating plenums. He bent down and wrestled with a grill from which hot air should have been hissing.

A man was hiding in the ductwork.

Festus Rufius extricated himself from the plenum. A burst of hot air ruffled his torn tunic as he emerged half desiccated and covered with brick dust. His salt-and-pepper hair looked streaked with cinnamon.

"Nothing wrong with the furnace," Rufius said. He brushed off the dust and ran for the exit.

Eleven
XI

Gaius Severus awoke the next morning to the usual shouting. He peeled away the moth-eaten blanket, scraped his stiff body off the wooden chair and exited the guard shack. After rubbing daylight into his eyes he saw a larger than usual mob at the gates. Angry citizens left homeless by the Saturnalia fire had massed outside the villa to demand assistance.

"Housing now!" the crowd shouted, mostly in unison. "Housing now!"

"So begins the day shift," Severus muttered. He broke the thin layer of ice that had formed in a pitcher and rinsed his face. The bracing water jolted him awake but did not wash away the biting tang of failure. Distrust had cost him Lena. Distraction had cost him Rufius when a sudden commotion enabled the dust-covered governor to escape into the night again. Severus wondered if it might be better to tender his resignation immediately rather than waiting to be fired for such a lard-fingered blunder.

Vocal petitioners began shaking the governor's locked gates. Marius Severus was among them, dressed in a blue-trimmed tunic with a yellow Star of David painted across his chest. Marius thrust his fist skyward and shouted, "Rome go home!"

Most of the crowd had come to protest homelessness; others were angry about the pirate rampage. None had come to hasten the fall of Rome.

"Free Judea!" Marius appeared to be on a quest to win universal disapproval.

"No. Free housing," a man shouted back.

When the crowd parted to let Marius through, Gaius saw that some in the rear were gathering stones and readying projectiles. The cold, hungry, and homeless people of Tarraco were in no mood to bargain.

"We are all homeless!" Marius climbed on the gate, turned to the crowd and shouted, "Brothers in Babylon, join together to stop Roman oppression."

"Get down," a man tried to pull Marius down from the gate. "This isn't a Saturnalia prank. Stop turning our protest into a joke."

"You fools!" Marius managed to scramble higher. "You're doing exactly what Rome wants. Can't you see we're all on the same side?"

"No," shouted a woman from deep in the crowd. "You're Hebrew, we're just homeless!"

"We're all the same," Marius insisted.

"Homeless outranks Hebrew!" someone else shouted and threw a palm-sized cobblestone at Marius. "Jews go home!"

"Power to the plebes!" Marius climbed out of reach but not out of range. A stone sailed past his ear. "Follow me, citizens!"

Gaius Severus ran to the gates, waving his hands and wondering how to prevent his brother from being torn limb from limb. "What in Jupiter are you doing?"

"Rome, go home!" Marius yelled, ducking a projectile that whistled through the gate and just missed his brother.

Gaius Severus willed his brother to stop, but Marius was in one of his agitated states and there was no predicting when or how he might calm down. He had crossed the thin line between righteous and irrational. Was there no cure besides a hammer blow for these wild mood swings? "Back down or you'll get us both hurt."

"Remind me what you're doing that side of the gate," Marius said.

"I got a job as a groundskeeper," Gaius lied. His head was pounding and he was in no mood for the tirade that the truth might provoke. The best he could hope for was to inject a dollop of reason into Marius' thick skull and prevent a riot.

Another stone flew wide of its mark, and more followed.

"Halt!" Gaius shouted. "Stoning is not legal in Hispania!"

"Since when?" a man asked. "Besides, burning down our homes wasn't legal either."

"Right!" shouted a woman whose family had once lived in a windowless garret now reduced to cinders. "Since when is it legal to torch poor people out of their homes?"

"Since never," Severus said. "That's why we have laws."

"To Hades with laws," yelled a wrinkled old man. Though doubled over with age, he threw stones with surprising accuracy. "If we can't have justice, at least we can pelt the Jew!"

"Pelt the Jew!" people yelled in agreement as more rocks took flight.

Gaius scrambled up the wrought-iron gate until he was higher than his brother and tried to shout over the crowd. "Under Section 13:2 of Roman Civil Code, which is itself covered by numerous imperial decrees, I quote: 'Death by stoning is declared illegal in all provinces with the exception of Egypt and those cities in the East where this practice is consistent with previously recognized and registered cults and rituals.'"

"Huh?" someone said. "Aren't we in the East?"

"Don't think so," muttered a woman lucky enough to have a tattered shawl with which to wrap herself.

Gaius dropped back to the ground. He took advantage of the lull to address the crowd. "If you can elect a representative, prioritize your complaints and discuss your issues in a civil manner, the governor will hear your grievances."

"That will never work," Marius insisted. "The system is rigged."

"I saw Vindex coming up the path," Gaius said to the group. "If you'd rather throw rocks and climb the gates, I'm sure he will be happy to stop you."

The rearguard confirmed what Gaius had seen from his vantage point. The threat of gladiator justice had the desired effect. People put their stones down and disbursed quickly.

"You've just set us back a hundred years!" Marius hissed. He climbed down to ground level opposite his brother. "This could have been my moment to tip the balance!"

The balance. Gaius had heard this many times before. According to Marius, the overextended empire was like a giant pyramid of pebbles that would crumble when the unwashed masses finally awakened. It was just a matter of time before ragtag bands of rebels armed with faith, plowshares, and righteousness would defeat Rome's iron will and fearless legions.

"Collaborators like you will cost us Judea."

Gaius held his tongue. The idea that the Jews might win back their homeland was not one shared by the gallery of tyrants who had scattered them across the boneyards of history. In spite of all evidence to the contrary, Marius believed that the ancient and indifferent God of Justice would soon return to deliver His chosen people from tyranny. Had not the same God abandoned them in

Babylon?

"Rebellion in one province will spread to all!" Marius insisted.

"And then?" Against his better judgment, Gaius entered the debate. "Replace one master with another? For every tyrant you sweep away, there are two waiting in the wings."

"You talk like one of them." Marius gestured toward the governor's villa.

"Just trying to get by."

Where Marius saw collapse and decay, Gaius saw opportunity. Marius thrived on conflict; he relished being an outsider. His logic was simple: in a corrupt world it was noble to be an outcast. But was it not just as noble to fight corruption from the inside and make the world a better place, if ever so slightly?

Marius lowered his voice to a conspiratorial whisper. "Can you help us penetrate their defenses?"

"Vindex doesn't look happy." Gaius nodded toward the giant.

"Think twice about working for the occupation." Marius stomped away, taking care to avoid Vindex.

Gaius watched his brother leave and realized that the blood they shared was not enough to bind them. They had been raised under the same conditions—no mother, a dreamer for a father, few friends, and hardly any community, but they had emerged as different people.

"It's no use." Vindex approached the gate, apparently too depressed to climb over it with his usual aplomb. "I'll never be free."

"I need you to stand guard, Vindex," Gaius said. "We've had a bit of excitement already today. If the petitioners come back, please don't hurt anyone."

"She offered to pay my freedom."

"What are you talking about?"

"Rufius promised to free me, but he was lying. Lena raised money to buy my freedom, but Kleptus won't sell."

"Lena was raising money to free you?" Severus felt his stomach drop. He knew less about the ginger-haired gladiator than he did about Lena, which, in retrospect, turned out to be nothing at all. He unlocked the gate and bid the gloomy giant to enter. "If you'll stand guard, I'll find Lena and figure this out."

"She's not …" Vindex started, but Severus was out of range before Vindex could tell him that Lena had left to join the pirates.

Severus ran into the atrium and nearly crashed into Carbo. The former kitchen slave, now a valet, had a knack for showing up before he was needed and fading into the shadows before orders were given.

"Someone important wants to see you," Carbo said, beckoning. "Follow me."

"I need to see Lena."

"Follow me." Carbo padded away on bare feet.

Severus followed the sphinx-like slave through the atrium. Fresh, clear rainwater had replaced the brackish slime in the recently scrubbed *impluvium.* Missing tiles had been replaced, and mold had been cleaned from the corners. Carbo slipped between two painted columns and disappeared into a corridor.

"Where are we going?" Severus struggled to keep up. The confusing corridors led to an unfamiliar wing of the villa. "Who wants to see me?"

"In honor of Saturnalia, you're being promoted to emperor," Carbo said.

"Only because no one else wants the job." Severus resigned himself to whatever surprise Carbo had in store.

After more twists and turns, Carbo opened the door to a warm dressing room. "Welcome to the *caldarium.* Your life's desire is soaking in the bath beyond that door. Take off your clothes and immerse."

Carbo disappeared without further sound or substance.

Severus pressed his ear to the swollen door but heard nothing more than gurgling water. Whoever was waiting on the other side of the door had left no clue other than a pile of fresh towels.

Then it struck him that this was Lena's way of both apologizing and making up. No wonder Carbo had been so secretive. As much as Severus had talked himself out of loving her, the thought of her lithe body covered in nothing but bubbles hit him like the promise of spring. He tore off his tunic, pried open the door, and entered the steamy room in naked expectation of finding his Aphrodite waiting.

"My love," he declared.

"Darling!" said a voice that could never have been mistaken for Lena's. A burst of barrel-chested laughter suggested the thespian, Don Rexus.

It took a moment for Severus' eyes to adjust enough to see three familiar faces reddened by the heat. The Titans were having a soak.

"Ah, young Severus." Winus Minem's nasal voice cut through the fog. "Jump in if you can find the room."

Severus turned quickly sideways lest anyone notice his scar of the covenant. Circumcision was not something he felt like explaining to the Titans of Tarraco.

"In!" Kleptus insisted, but the outsized governor occupied most of the tub. Every time he shifted, wavelets sloshed over the rim and boiled to steam on the heated floor. "We're having an important discussion."

Severus submerged into a small space between Don Rexus and Winus Minem.

"We're thinking to promote you," Minem said. "How does chief of security sound?"

Chirps of agreement circled the tub like a lost bird.

"Seriously?" Severus sensed an inside joke. Were the men in the tub just having a go at him, a rags-to-riches ruse in the spirit of Saturnalia? If not, there was something decidedly off-kilter about the Titans of Tarraco naming him to the town's highest security post unless they needed a new scapegoat.

"It's a capital idea!" Minem's tiny face was visible above the waterline, eyes glowing like a kitchen mouse. "Much more profitable than your current position."

"I'm told that your intimate knowledge of Tarraco and her citizens will be a great help to us," Kleptus said.

Gaius Severus had lived in Tarraco all his life, but he never had reason to consider how or why things worked. Water had always flowed through the pipes, a governor had always lived in the villa, and garbage had always accumulated in the streets. As for knowledge of the citizens, all he could speak to was their superstitions and intolerance.

"... and you'll need to provide tight security around the jail," Kleptus was saying. "We wouldn't want any prisoners escaping."

Severus shuddered. Did they know about Rufius? Did they care? In either case, a promotion was not an opportunity a young man with nothing could rightly refuse. A few weeks prior he had been a fugitive; now he was on the threshold of the town's inner circle. Either the Fates had found someone else to laugh at or they were preparing their biggest prank ever.

"Cat's got his tongue," Rexus said.

"Too many vexed cats in this town. We need some dogs around here," Kleptus said. "So, what do you say, kid?"

Promoted! As the top security official in Tarraco, Severus would be able to make changes—perhaps even replace the town's current haphazard approach to law and order with something resembling justice. But instead of feeling excited, he sensed his brother's looming disapproval. Marius had always insisted that the empire whittled at one's soul faster than termites on timber. "I don't know what to say."

"Say yes," Minem said, beaming with approval. "I'll be happy to mentor you."

"Congratulations." Kleptus' red face floated on the water like a puffer fish. "Keep it up and maybe I'll introduce you to my daughter."

Rexus buried a laugh below the water line. He slapped Severus on the back, sending water gurgling into Minem's eyes. "The governor's daughter is a real prize."

"She's the most eligible, beautiful, and desirable girl in town," Kleptus insisted. A proud wave formed at his chest, traveled across the tub, and splashed over the rim. The big man turned to Minem and took up the next item of business. "About your idea for a big shop ..."

"The Mall of Rome," Rexus said as if sneezing out a nose full of lead dust.

"Super Emporium," Minem corrected. "It will be the greatest—"

"Where's Rufius?" The door opened and steam hissed past the familiar silhouette of an imposing woman in expensive clothes. Plotina swept into the bath chamber, indifferent to the heat and agitation provoked by her arrival. Her braided cobra rose with regal menace. She extended her arms like wings and used her billowing sleeves to part the vapor. "Where is he, you milk drinkers?"

Silence and steam hung thick and fusty. Severus held his breath. When Plotina saw the three Titans turn toward him, she added her glare to the gallery.

"He's safe," Severus stammered.

Plotina pulled the door shut. She planted her hands on her hips, exposing sharp elbows. "I need to see Rufius."

Severus wondered if Tarraco's Titans were afraid of Plotina. Her couture, her coiffure, and her steely-eyed superiority left little room for doubt that she came from the upper crust of the empire. But to Severus, there was something theatrical, almost comical about Hadrian's self-proclaimed niece hovering over a tub full of naked men. Plotina cut an intimidating figure, but she was far from Rome. She could lord over them all she wanted, but as long as she was unsure of Rufius' whereabouts, she had little to bargain with.

"Rufius. Here. Now."

"Rufius is being held in the prison." Severus had nothing to bargain with, but she did not appear to know this. All he needed was to buy a little time. Rufius could not remain hidden for long.

"Please join us," Rexus said. "The water's hot, and so am I." Rexus tried to stand up, but Plotina's sandal intercepted his shoulder and shoved him backward.

In spite of the heat, her face showed no hint of flushing. The yards of sleeves and pleated canyons of fabric seemed to have stiffened. Steam condensing on her feet suggested that the hotter the room, the cooler she became. "Rufius will see justice and I will receive compensation for the damage he's done to my house and good name."

"What good name was that?" Rexus asked.

"We expect to put him on trial by the end of the week," Kleptus said.

"This week?" The surprise escaped Severus' mouth before his teeth could bite his wagging tongue.

"He'll stand trial on the last day of Saturnalia," Rexus said. "In the covered theater. We'll sell tickets."

"The Trial of the Century!" Kleptus slapped the water and sent geysers spraying in all directions.

"You think I was born in Babylon? The only way I'll agree to that is if I serve as the prosecuting attorney," Plotina said.

"Can women do that?" Severus asked, regretting the question immediately. "I mean, argue a case before the court?"

"There's nothing women can't do," Plotina said slowly.

No one dared disagree.

"It's got dramatic potential." Rexus stood, thought the better of it, and sat down again. "The novelty of a female solicitor will help sell tickets. We've got the second half of a good story here. All this lacks is a strong leading man like me to play Rufius' attorney."

"You?" Minem could not hide his incredulity. "Doesn't law

require logic?"

"I taught rhetoric before becoming a thespian." Rexus did not acknowledge his detractor. "Trust me on this one, Governor. A famous actor and a mysterious Roman woman locked in mortal combat ... hints of romance, overtones of betrayal ... two eloquent gladiators battling over the fate of a senator's wayward son. Demand for tickets, snacks, and keepsakes will be sky high."

"It just might work," Kleptus said.

"So, now that we're all friends, why don't you soak with us a bit, *domina*?" Rexus insisted. "Nothing to worry about from this lot: Minem's queer, Severus' balls haven't dropped, and I'm famous for discretion."

"If I get in that water, it will be to wring your neck."

Rexus submerged and let a chain of rude bubbles rise in response.

Plotina eyed Kleptus with a look that could have shriveled a lesser man. "I'm here as the emperor's representative, charged with collecting back taxes and leaving this blighted province cleaner than I found it."

"I'm sure we'll come to a satisfactory arrangement," Kleptus said.

Watching the exchange, Severus saw that Kleptus wasn't quite the rock he appeared to be. He had thrived during the salad days and did not appear to be starving during the downturn, but Plotina was a factor he had not anticipated. She had the power to disrupt what had been a long, profitable run for him.

Severus realized that he would have to choose allies wisely. He scratched Kleptus and Rexus from the list. It would be unwise to cross them, but neither could he trust them. That left Winus Minem, the scrappy little adviser who found profit on both sides of a battle. Winus Minem.

Minem had an outsider's perspective. He was smart and full of modern ideas, but he wasted no loyalty on anyone. His knack for aligning with winners made him a safer bet than the other two. Minem might prove dangerous in the end, but for now he was the smallest of three evils.

Plotina gathered her sails and turned to leave.

"Wait. I have an idea."

All eyes turned toward Severus. Plotina crossed her arms and raised an eyebrow.

"Nothing earthshaking … but it's mutually beneficial."

Minem smiled. Rexus sulked. Kleptus wheezed.

"*Domina* Plotina," Severus began. "Your crew went on a rampage last night. As security chief, I can't allow our citizens to be terrorized by irregulars, male or female."

"Irregular," Rexus said. "That's the right word for those misfits."

"I understand that being cooped up on your ship is less than ideal for such a, shall we say, robust and energetic group of women." Severus shot a preemptive glance at Rexus. "Perhaps your crew could provide security services for the duration of their stay."

"Security! Exactly." Kleptus became animated. "I was just thinking about how to put a bit of muscle back in tax collection."

Knowing that a good idea has many fathers, Severus smiled and let the notion play out. If the idea turned out to be bad, the blame would roll downhill. But if it worked, he had just made a powerful friend. Minem agreed immediately, and Rexus' opinion on this topic clearly did not matter.

"Severus will escort you out," Kleptus said. "Next time you visit, please give me advance notice so we can welcome you more appropriately."

"We'll make sure there's room in the tub," Rexus said without looking up.

After a brief negotiation and a careful dance with a towel, Severus got dressed and led Plotina through the confusing corridors to the atrium.

After she exited through the great doors, Carbo emerged from a shadow and whispered to Severus, "Minem's a murderer. He poisoned Biberious with dogroot. That's why the corpse had green lips."

"What?" The new chief of security was caught off guard by the sudden accusation.

"One other thing," Carbo said. "Your brother's been arrested."

Twelve
XII

The jail cells under the arena served as a holding tank for those who could not afford better justice. Father and son had spent time there, and now Marius had returned. As family traditions went, incarceration was not one worth passing on to future generations.

Gaius managed to pry the door open after a brief struggle with the bent key. The stench that hit him triggered an immediate oath to have the cells mucked out. If he could not shut the jail outright, at least he would see that it served the cause of justice, not just the public's thirst for blood.

He took a last gasp of fresh air before entering the reeking chamber. Once his eyes adjusted to the gloom, he saw a group of bound adolescents trying to stand. They tugged in all directions before falling back into the mud, arms and legs waving like spines on a scared hedgehog.

"One at a time!" Marius shouted from somewhere near the bottom of the pile.

Two of the young prisoners finally untangled themselves and pulled the rest upright. In the dim light cast by the open door, Gaius could see that his brother was filthy. Had Marius learned anything from his brief incarceration? Perhaps a few days of gruel and bad hygiene would smooth out his self-destructive mood swings.

Perhaps ducks would shit gold.

Before deciding what to do about his brother, Gaius took a few moments to peer into the other dark cells. The odds were slim, but he hoped to find Festus Rufius languishing in relative safety. Gaius fondled his key ring and considered his obligations. As head of security, he was expected to keep Tarraco safe. In the past, this meant filling the jail with anyone who couldn't pay a bribe. Some would be sprung by family, a few might die in captivity, and the rest would feed the arena and the mines. Severus vowed to change this. Shutting down the arena was beyond his ability, but he could slow the supply of human fodder.

Most of the cells were empty. The Saturnalia pardon, Festus

Rufius' last and only decent act as governor, had reduced this week's inflow to a hapless trickle. Aside from the youths that Marius was chained to, few people had been incarcerated since the festival.

Flush with his recent promotion to security chief, Severus was about to lecture his captive audience when a loud snap crackled through the dank air.

"We're going to be tortured," cried one of the prisoners.

Severus hopped between dry spots to where a small, bony man stood cracking a riding crop against the door. On first glance, the fellow's gray tunic appeared to have an expensive sheen, but proximity and light revealed the opposite. The fabric was encrusted with dirt.

"Who's in charge here?" The fellow cracked the riding crop again. His hollow face clung to his bones like an old cadaver.

"Excuse me, sir," Severus said. "Your whip is scaring the prisoners."

"That's rich." The man's serrated grin radiated false warmth and cheap dentistry. "I love a jailer with a sense of humor."

Severus recognized the throaty accent of the empire's doctors and grammar instructors. "You're from Greece?"

"Indeed, I've come all the way from Athens just to visit your fine facility. May I come in?"

"Come in? Most people want out." Severus stepped outside to get a better look at the odd fellow who appeared not to have bathed since the fall of Sparta. His tunic read like the history of dirt. A rickety cart stood in clear violation of the town's ban on vehicles during daylight hours, but it looked ready to fall to pieces should anyone attempt to enforce the rules. His bow-backed donkey chewed on a soggy nettle.

"Philo's the name." The man pumped Severus' reluctant forearm. "And you are?"

"Late." Severus wriggled free. "So, if you'll excuse me."

"Wouldn't dream of it. We've got important business right here." Philo forced his way into the cavernous jail. "Mind if I tour your fair facility?"

"As a matter of fact—" Severus began, but Philo was already inside.

Indifferent to the odor, the road-worn Greek sloshed through the mud and peered into the cells. Prowling like an alley cat, he seemed to be in his element. From time to time he shook his head in condemnation. He made his progress known with disapproving clucks and woke a sleeping prisoner with a snap of the riding crop. "Just as I suspected: This facility is deficient, seriously lagging. Sorry to say it, chum, but you're not nearly up to imperial standards."

"Perhaps you could come back tomorrow?" Severus tried to herd Philo toward the door.

"Nonsense! Why, for a small fee, I can have your prisoners confessing by sundown."

"Not interested," Severus said. "I really must be going."

"*Vesuvius!*—it's quiet around here. Too bloody quiet. No shouts of pain, no one begging for mercy. No wonder you've got problems in this town!"

"Actually, this is a fairly law-abiding—"

"Law-abiding?" Philo stroked the stubble on his broad, flat chin. "No theft, adultery, public drunkenness … no sedition. The plebes pay their rent on time, structures never collapse, and wives don't smash pots over their husbands' heads ..."

"I didn't say that."

"Wait! Isn't this the town where the governor was murdered? Correct me if I'm mistaken, but isn't Tarraco the lawless backwater where rioters tried to kill our beloved emperor?"

Philo now blocked the door.

Severus suspected he might have to kill the man to escape the sales pitch. "What exactly are you peddling?"

"Civilization, son." Philo examined the crowded cell where Marius was still bound to a pack of frightened boys. "This is clever." Philo smiled widely. "With any luck they'll kill each other and save you the expense."

A new commotion by the entrance attracted Severus' attention. He started toward the noise, but Philo grabbed his arm.

"I can see you're in a hurry, so I'll make it brief. I offer an affordable, six-step program. Six practical measures and a reasonable payment plan that will get this prison humming. The first step is simple and cheap: hire a screamer."

"A screamer?" Severus was distracted by what sounded like Limbo on the threshold of murder. "Someone is screaming outside the door right now."

"Not an outside screamer! An inside screamer." Philo spoke fast and refused to let go of Severus' sleeve. "Trust me, there's nothing like the sound of bloodcurdling howls coming from the bowels of a prison to discourage crime. Of course, the best screams come from people being tortured, but for those rare times when nobody's getting flayed or beaten you'll want a big man with a booming voice. Screaming women are everywhere, nobody cares when a woman screams, but when a man howls, that sends a clear message to troublemakers. If you don't believe me, go outside and listen while I scream."

Severus pulled away, but Philo followed and spoke faster. "Suggestion number two is even cheaper than screaming. Know what it is?"

"Starvation?" Severus said, not turning around.

"You mean you're not already doing that? Starving prisoners is a given."

Philo was interrupted by a scuffle by the door where Limbo was shouting insults that would have offended a stray dog. Seeing Limbo about to slap a hooker, Severus grabbed his assistant's wrist and held it long enough for the woman to scurry back across the road to the Gladiator's Goblet.

"Arrest her!" Limbo protested. "I swear she's a criminal."

"Overcharging you is not a crime." Severus dragged Limbo into the jail where Philo was now terrorizing the prisoners.

Philo eyed Marius Severus with sudden delight. "Now there's a hardened criminal. Just the type I'm talking about … a hate-filled nutter, that one. You owe it to the emperor to let me squeeze out a good confession and publicly relieve him of his undeserved life. I've got a couple of half-priced horse whips that are almost too good for a scoundrel like him."

Gaius Severus resisted the urge to pound Philo into flatbread. He had heard that the official guideline on beatings was to avoid witnesses, but there had to be an exception for salesmen.

"That's the fool who arrested me!" Marius shouted, pointing at Limbo.

Gaius Severus ignored his brother. "My associate is the one you should be discussing business with." Severus pulled Limbo into the conversation by the folds of his tunic. "Limbo's in charge of upgrading our facility and would love to discuss it over a jug."

90

"The Gladiator's Goblet is just the place," Limbo said. He winked at Severus, nodded toward the tavern, and smiled in anticipation of his next drink. "That's the place we security blokes do business."

"Limbo, Limbo, Limbo," Philo said. "The moment I saw you I said to myself, now here comes a reasonable fellow. Let's head over to the tavern and discuss business."

The two walked away to discuss modernizing Tarraco's prison system over jugs of mulled wine that neither intended to pay for.

Gaius Severus waited until Limbo and the salesman were safely out of range before unlocking the chain that shackled his brother to the others. He released the young prisoners with an admonition to behave, and they disappeared faster than startled farm mice. "Have you learned your lesson, Marius?"

"I could ask you the same question, but I see you're working for the Romans."

"You don't know the half of it," Gaius said. "I could have been the one in chains."

"You swore an oath to kill Hadrian. Instead you let him live." Marius poked the security insignia on his brother's clean tunic. "You even joined his henchmen. You've betrayed our people for a handful of silver."

"Silver? I've yet to get paid a copper. Speaking of betrayal, suppose you tell me the truth about our father?"

Marius arched his sore back and squinted into the daylight. "I lost him in Southern Gaul."

"Lost him?" The last time Gaius had seen his kin was on the night his cohort was attacked. He had been on sentry duty when distracted by sounds coming from what turned out to be their camp. While Gaius was off investigating, many among his exhausted cohort, drunk on the spoils of war, were murdered in their sleep. Gaius had been lucky to survive and luckier not to be blamed for the role his negligence had played in allowing the disaster. "Tell me the truth. Is Father dead?"

"I already told you." Marius spat on the ground. "He shacked up with a pagan, a northern widow with legs like a spider." Marius rubbed his wrist where a rope had chafed him. "Like father, like son, I suppose."

"Safe and happy."

"But Mother's barely been dead ten years."

"Father's too old to go traipsing off to Judea. Besides, an old man can't be expected to mourn forever. If he found someone—"

Shouting interrupted the reunion.

"Innocent," the remaining prisoners chanted. "We're innocent!"

"Who are these prisoners?" Marius asked. "Why are they being held?"

"Feed us!" More shouts rang through the subterranean chamber. "We're hungry."

"I intend to free the innocent among them." Gaius took his brother's arm and pulled him gently to freedom. "I know what this looks like to you, but it's just a job. We're all just trying to get by in this world."

"Some more than others."

Gaius Severus could not get over the growing chasm between them. Their father had always provided balance, but now that he was gone, Marius was more strident than ever. "After years of living hand to mouth, you should be happy that someone in this family has a chance at stability. One steady income could keep our clan in clover. Why are you determined to destroy my good fortune?"

"Fortune? Is that what this is about? You can't embrace some of Rome without embracing all of it. Don't you see that the empire won't tolerate a partial commitment?"

"A bit extreme, no? Do you think I'm too dumb to hold a job and principles at the same time?"

"It's because you're smart that I'm worried. You'll find a way to rationalize this. You can't serve Rome on your own terms. In no time at all you'll be one of those snappy fellows in white starched tunics ordering police raids on citizens."

"Police raids? Have you forgotten that I was a victim of a police raid?"

"Without the threat of force, there is no empire. Everyone who serves Rome is guilty of murder."

"Nonsense." The futility of arguing with his brother was evident, but Gaius could not resist. "Trash collectors aren't guilty of murder. Towns have to function, ports need administration. There's nothing wrong with bridges, roads, and waterworks."

"Then why are we required to believe Hadrian's a god?"

"You can't bring down the empire with two pebbles and a stick, and you can't escape jail if you remain locked in your convictions. You need to adapt to the world as it is, not as you want it to be. I'm not the enemy, and Father hasn't betrayed anyone."

"Before Mother died I wasn't sure if Father knew how to finish a sentence." Marius stepped into the street. He scraped his soles against the cobblestone and wiped muck from his face. "She was pretty tough."

"I barely remember." Gaius was relieved that Marius' short attention span had moved on to a new subject.

"The way she used to talk about becoming a grandmother!" Marius laughed. "How did she ever expect us to marry? There were two Jewish girls in town, and neither was good enough."

Gaius laughed. It felt good to be with family. Too good. He knew not to trust the feeling, but gave in to it anyway. "I'm sure Mother had a soft spot for you."

"Nothing I did was ever right by her."

"She wasn't well."

"At least now she's out of pain," Marius sighed. "She's in heaven, complaining. Some days I can even sense her presence looking down from above and criticizing me."

Gaius watched Marius disappear and then left in the opposite direction. Seeing that the salesman's donkey cart had not moved, he knew that Limbo was still inside the Gladiator's Goblet talking shop and filching drinks.

A stray cat—one of many running rampant through town— nearly tripped him as it darted across the street. Its feral confidence and ability to disappear into thin air reminded him that Festus Rufius was still missing.

Thirteen
XIII

Lena awoke on the ship and listened to the murmur of lapping water. Soon the chatter of Plotina's crew would fill the air, but for the moment, the morning was still. She was relieved to be away from the unwanted affections of less than noblemen, happy to be accepted among Plotina's strong and sturdy women.

The crew had welcomed her as one of their own. Plotina had even invited her to join them on the open water. Lena understood many of the dialects spoken on board. Even the quietest voice hinted of far greater adventure than a life spent arranging spices or spinning flax. Hoping to see the sunrise, she tucked a blanket under her arm and slipped out of the crew's quarters.

She squinted until her eyes adjusted to the sliver of clear, December light scraping across the flat gray water. Standing alone at the bow she felt like a restless daughter of the sea.

The hopeful hues of dawn swept westward when the sun squeezed through an opening in the clouds. A lone bird patrolled the shoreline as if guarding the border between air and water. The gull's cry broke through the crew's rising chatter.

Lena unfurled her blanket and let it catch the breeze like a sail that might carry her beyond the horizon, far from Tarraco. A dock's length behind her, the town woke to another day. From a distance it was certainly no worse than other towns she had seen. The muffled din of delivery carts mingled with sounds of storefronts opening. The cry of a hungry child drifted down from a tenement window.

Lena inhaled a deep breath of freedom before descending into the galley. She ladled a bowl of barley mush and sat by a porthole to eat and watch the birds. A few women shuffled in to grab a meal before attending to their duties. Determined to earn her keep, Lena finished her Spartan breakfast and helped a crew member get the kitchen in order.

Lena completed her chores and walked into town. Soon the delivery carts would withdraw, and people would throng the shops to negotiate another day's provisions from tightfisted merchants. Early risers had already emerged, drawn by daylight and the smell of fresh bread. She cut a gradual path to the forum but did not recognize it upon arrival. An elaborate homeless camp had sprouted overnight. The victims of the Saturnalia fire had created a sprawling tent village across the plaza and under the colonnades.

Those rendered homeless by the torched tenement had let nothing go to waste. Charred timbers and wood fragments were piled at intervals where small fire pits dotted the plaza.

Smoke rose from the center of the square where a scrawny goat was roasting on an improvised spit. A large stew pot bubbled on a bed of coals. The smells were simple but savory—roasted meat, scrounged herbs and turnips, maybe an onion to augment a weak broth.

The remains of curtains and cloaks had been stitched together to serve as protection against the rain. Threadbare blankets had been hung to provide privacy. A few makeshift beds were shared by the tired and the weak.

The Saturnalia festival had been transformed by fire into a pageant of poverty. People had banded together to reduce the suffering. Girls looked after the young children. Boys returned from scavenging expeditions with loose bricks and arms full of wood. Young men patrolled the perimeter and old women shooed away the thieving cats.

"Got a coin?" A small girl tugged on Lena's tunic. The child's face was smudged with ash. Her clothes were torn, her sandal straps broken. Swollen eyes expressed weariness beyond her few years.

Lena pulled a coin from her pouch. She tried to stroke the girl's disheveled hair but the waif scampered away to where an old woman tended a steaming pot.

Lena wondered if these families were living better in the open air than they had under their landlord's sagging roofs. Sleeping outdoors did not have to be a punishment. She had spent many nights under the stars when traveling with her mum, though not tied to any one place. She wondered where Mum was now.

Lena had never known her father, but her mother more than filled the void he left behind. Mum once claimed to have fallen from Olympus after being abandoned by the gods. She was ambitious, iron willed and determined to prove wrong all who doubted her.

When Mum discovered Lena's knack for prediction, they left poverty behind. Lena's gift for augury matched Mum's gift for self-promotion. Depending on the town, the street corner, and the season, Lena performed as the "Daughter of Aphrodite" or "Minerva's Maiden." People threw coins. Bronze turned to silver, silver to gold. Mum bought a donkey and a covered cart. They traveled from village to village with no greater plan than staying ahead of hunger.

Lena read palms. Mum sold powders. They crossed the great river into Gaul and back, never nesting long enough for a chicken to hatch. Mum sweet-talked the tax collectors. Lena fended off the lechers. Both repelled the thieves. Somewhere along the rutted roads, Mum acquired an awkward teen whose precocious feats of strength defied his years. Mum's claim that he could bend iron bars brought howls of incredulity and ten-to-one odds that always paid in her favor. She dubbed him "Young Hercules" and treated him like a lost son. Hercules wrestled any opponent who could afford the fee and won more purses than he lost. Mum called the two her family, but Lena never accepted the boy who had muscled into her mother's orbit. He grew strong and brazen and eventually drove Lena away.

"Smart landlord," a woman was saying. "The insurance was probably worth more than the rent."

"I heard that someone had a bull in the basement."

Snippets of conversations brought Lena back to the present.

"There ought to be a law."

"Laws don't apply to bulls."

"Or landlords."

Or Mum. Mum was a law unto herself. She managed the money and kept a tight rein on her troupe. She strong-armed the legionaries, evicted the drunks, rolled over the equestrians, and outfoxed the dandies. As they worked the back roads and byways, she assembled an eccentric collection of performers, both human and animal. The wagons multiplied. A contortionist and a magician, acrobats and fire-eaters—the cast varied, performers came and went depending on the local price for talent. Mum demanded obedience and ran a tight show. Anyone she caught conducting unsavory side business paid double in fines.

Lena learned tricks and dialects from the shifting members of the troupe. During one particularly lucrative season, Mum hired a *Grammaticus* to teach the performers enough Latin to trade insults in a common tongue. Lena learned to read and figure. She learned that a crowd is fickle as the winter sun.

Her growing powers and rough beauty did not always attract the right sort of admiration. Fans had a way of turning fanatic. She learned how to deflect wealthy men seeking more than a simple palm reading and lonely boys looking for solace.

To ease the boredom between market days, Lena trained with the wrestlers and sparred with the pugilists. With the exception of Young Hercules, Lena soon reigned undefeated within the troupe. When it became clear that Mum favored the idea of a dynasty and Hercules fancied more than a training partner, Lena fled.

"Lena?"

Gaius Severus appeared before her. She brushed a tress of brown hair off her face and offered a shallow nod.

"I'm so sorry about last night," he said. "I was such an idiot."

"You were an idiot long before last night."

"Guilty as charged. I'm sorry for misjudging you."

"Being misjudged is the story of my life." She added a comment in a foreign dialect that was better left in the vernacular.

Fourteen
XIV

It was the first time Gaius Severus had seen the encampment in all its hopeless glory. Tarraco had its share of poor, there were even a few homeless, but this amount of misery was without precedent. "Look at this camp," he said. "People uprooted from one day to the next. It looks like the exodus from Egypt detoured through Tarraco."

"The money I've raised to free Carbo wouldn't pay for one meal out here," Lena said. "What can be done?"

"I'm going to speak with the governor. He needs to do something about this."

"Go ahead." Lena pointed. "He's over there."

Kleptus and his entourage had entered the forum at the opposite corner. Before Severus could compose an appeal to the governor's sense of civic responsibility, a small boy approached to ask for a coin. Lena mussed his hair and sent him off with a *sesterce* and a smile.

"He reminds me of the little boy from your village. Little sprite of maybe five years old. What was his name? Remo?" Severus did not mention that the boy was cute and toothless for now, but without a proper upbringing he would soon join the ranks of trouser-clad barbarians. "Do you miss Remo?"

Lena looked away.

"He was a cute little rascal. Who does he belong to?"

"Belong? He's not a slave."

"It's an expression. Like, 'you belong to me.'"

Severus watched her consider this for a moment. She seemed to be turning the notion of belonging—to a person, a place, or a moment—over in her mind. He wanted her to see that she could belong to this place, this moment, this person. Severus felt a sudden heat rise and rattle like lightning in his rib cage. His heart scorched his chest. This moment would not come again. He lifted the hair gently away from her ear and was about to propose marriage when she pulled away.

"Sorry." She turned to go. "It's just not meant to be."

Severus felt his heart chill, his inner flame sputter. A slap in the face would have been preferable to her preemptive rejection. At least a slap implied some underlying feeling.

After Lena walked away, perhaps for good, Severus swallowed his hurt and approached the governor. Better to assist those who could be helped than to feel sorry for one who could not.

Kleptus and his two advisers advanced across the plaza, their pace limited by Kleptus' slow waddle. Severus stepped carefully through the camp and joined them near the treasury basilica. "Citizens," he said. "Lovely day for a stroll."

"Not really." Kleptus parked his bulk against a column and looked out across Tarraco's once upscale forum. "I hate walking."

A group of destitute men warmed their hands over a pile of burning debris. Haggard women tended salvaged braziers. Half-dressed children played tag in the cold.

Gaius Severus assumed that the Titans would share his admiration for the resilience and ingenuity of the unlucky citizenry. No matter what the Fates threw their way, poor people recovered from calamity like ants from a flood. "Amazing, no?"

"Amazing mess!" When Kleptus was angry the folds of his neck tightened and created new folds. "Who turned my forum into a rubbish heap?"

"Looks like the fall of Carthage," Rexus said, looking over the scene as if it were a long mural.

Severus scanned the crowd to see if Festus Rufius might be hiding among the homeless. Instead of detecting a fugitive, he noticed his brother Marius deep in conversation with a handful of young men gathered around a sputtering fire. Gaius hoped Marius was applying his talents to help Tarraco's unfortunates rather than shouting slogans about faraway places. Maybe Marius had finally realized that improving the plight of real people was more useful than waving fists at impossible causes. All hope dissipated when Marius pointed an accusatory finger at the province's new governor,

"Give us homes, give us homes!" Marius raised his fist with indignation.

The cold, angry young men around him joined the chant. A few pulled burning sticks from the fire. The small mob marched toward the governor's retinue.

Gaius Severus was crestfallen. The peaceful commune had not lasted the morning. Any semblance of patience had been temporary. Did hope spring eternal only because it never lasts?

"This doesn't look like a Saturnalia party," Rexus said.

"Time to go," Minem suggested. "I'm not a big fan of riots."

"The reason you're so small is because you have no spine." Governor Kleptus said, determined to hold his ground. "If they have a grievance, I will hear it."

Gaius Severus rubbed his forehead and wondered if it were too late to have never been born.

"We want homes, not catacombs!" A vocal minority marched toward the Titans of Tarraco. Spurred by cold, frustration, and hunger, their gestures and demands grew more brazen as others took up the cry. "Roofs and walls or Rome will fall!" they shouted.

"No sense of decorum," Rexus muttered.

"They have nothing left to lose," Gaius said.

"Do these plebes know who torched their tenement to clear land for your store site?" Rexus asked Minem, loud enough to be heard. "Maybe you'd like to be introduced?"

"Severus said that religious fanatics set that fire." Minem pursed his lips so tight his words seemed to whistle. "These wretches are exactly the people I'm trying to help."

The mob swirled like a dust storm. Gray-blue smoke hissed from their smoldering sticks. Marius ran to the fore and tried to lead, but every time he appeared to be in command the mob would change direction. Once they had gathered enough anger and momentum to be reckoned with, they approached the new governor.

Gaius Severus stepped in front of the Titans, crossed his arms and glared at his brother. Marius seemed determined to ruin everything, and for what? Fists and sticks were no way to help the homeless. Did Marius even care about what he championed, or did he also oppose himself when no one else was present?

Gaius beckoned to Marius, hoping a parley might avoid mayhem. "This crowd is less predictable than a wildfire," he said when Marius stepped forward. "One minute they'll follow you, the next they'll howl for your crucifixion."

"If you're going to live for nothing, I might as well die for something."

Neither noticed that Winus Minem had stepped forward to listen. Marius was clearly not in a conciliatory mood.

"Remember when you told me to join the legion?" Gaius felt sadness settle in the canyon between them but doubted that Marius suffered any remorse. "You wanted me to learn to fight and understand the so-called enemy from the inside. You told me that the movement needed warriors or something like that."

"What of it?" Marius was barely paying attention.

"That's what I'm doing now." Gaius knew that any chance of dialogue—fraternal or political—was fading fast. He needed to appeal to Marius' rational side before the mob exploded or one of the Titans noticed the family resemblance. "Give me a few days to solve this."

"A few days?" Marius laughed. "I see what you're doing. You're waiting for Saturnalia to end so you and your thug friends can crush this rebellion the old-fashioned way."

Gaius looked up to see the stone likeness of an old emperor glaring down from across the plaza. "As an insider I'll be able to do more for these people than you will by shaking sticks."

"You'll never be an insider. You're a Jewish Icarus." Marius shook his head like a teacher giving up on a hopeless student. "I need to go. Being seen with you is hurting my reputation."

The ties that bind had broken. Common ground had turned to dust. Marius had chosen the road to ruin; Gaius, the road to Rome.

Marius returned to the fold of angry young men who, seeing no path to a better future, were willing to set fire to the present. He raised his fist and locked eyes with his brother. "Give us homes or down with Rome!" he shouted.

The mob was about to explode like lightning in a lamp.

"Friends and citizens!" Don Rexus stepped into the impending fray. "There's an audience at the heart of every mob," he whispered as he nudged Gaius Severus aside.

Rexus scrambled up to share the pedestal that boasted a poor likeness of Emperor Vespasian, the great visionary who once had taxed urine. Rexus bowed deeply and invoked his most resonant baritone. "Freedmen and citizens, slaves and subjects ..."

"It's the Prince of Saturnalia," a protester said. He stepped in front of Marius, dropping out of formation to get a better look. "He's famous!"

"A famous actor!" another protester chimed in, apparently relieved that someone noteworthy cared about their plight.

The crowd hushed.

Fatigued from shouting and seduced by celebrity, the star-struck

101

rabble abandoned Marius and gathered around the pedestal. A clutch of young women set aside their chores and children. They pushed to the front, fluffed their rain-flattened hair, and pinched their cheeks to appear more desirable than destitute.

Rexus leaned against Vespasian's marble leg like a small boy with a tall father. He smiled and waited until the crowd grew large enough to make the performance worth his effort.

"Cassius Kleptus, our gracious new governor, understands your pain." Rexus gestured toward Kleptus, whose thick neck and large square nose bore an odd resemblance to the statue's. The man and the marble both appeared too stern and too rich to enjoy life's simple pleasures. "If you stand down now, your governor's top priority will be to solve the housing crisis and punish whoever started that unfortunate fire."

"It was arson!" shouted a woman clutching a newborn. She pulled a threadbare blanket over the agitated child to protect it from the cold and pointed an accusing finger at Winus Minem. "He did it. I saw him!"

"We will find and punish the guilty party." Rexus looked at Minem and flashed a mouth full of perfect teeth. He ran a hand against the painted hem of Vespasian's stone toga and savored the concern on Minem's face. "Our security forces are investigating the fire."

"Down with Rome!" Marius fumed at seeing that the plebes were distractible as crows. Well-fed citizens never rebelled, and hungry people were easily co-opted with the promise of a meal.

Gaius Severus smiled. Other than a love-struck teen who probably mistook anger for passion, no one was paying Marius any attention. Looking at his brother but addressing the crowd, Gaius said, "We have laws against substandard firetraps."

"Easy, kid," Kleptus whispered. "I know the man who owned that building."

"That firetrap was my home," a woman yelled so loud it woke another woman's baby. Within a second all three were hysterical.

"In place of that dangerous structure we'll build you the biggest marketplace in the empire." Minem stepped forward. "From the ashes of misery will arise the greatest shopping experience in the known world—a city block full of exotic treasures and low-priced pleasures."

It was as if Winus Minem's sandals had sprouted wings. Even Rexus went silent as the Macedonian Mercury bewitched the mob with promises of unimaginable bargains. "No more haggling with thieving merchants! No more slogging through the dirty streets. The gods themselves will descend from Mount Olympus to sample the cornucopia at Super Emporium."

"Super-what?" Most people were simultaneously confused and seduced.

"In just one short month," Minem promised, "you'll find everything you can imagine in a shop so friendly we'll have people waiting at the entrance just to say hello."

"Pish posh!" Marius shouted. "People don't need better shopping, they need better housing." He turned his back on the governor's staff and searched the tired eyes of the mob he had hoped would launch a revolution. He urged them to remain steadfast in their demands, before another opportunity for change passed them by. "Don't be seduced with bribes and baubles. You may be poor and homeless, but you still have dignity."

"Guaranteed low prices?" the woman with the screaming child asked. "Sounds pretty good."

"Are you hiring?"

"Who do I bribe to get a job for my son?"

"We've already cleared the old home site of everything that burns," a middle-aged matron said. She gestured toward the wood piles scattered across the forum. "You can start building tomorrow."

Rexus descended from Vespasian's pedestal. The women who had swooned seconds earlier were now gathered around Minem, peppering him with questions. By the time Rexus reached his rival, it was clear that the crowd's interest had shifted. All Rexus could do was to pat Minem on the shoulder with enough insincerity to win an election.

"The salt of the earth just bought the store." Minem elbowed Rexus with undisguised spite.

"The salt of the earth can't taste the spice of life," Kleptus muttered. "At least they've calmed down."

Minem's promises of jobs, deals, and weekly specials grew larger than the city block it would be built on. When people's hope finally outweighed their despair, they returned to their chores, drunk with dreams of better days ahead.

Fifteen
XV

"Abandon camp! Every man for himself!" The town crier ran through the plaza flapping his arms in panic. "Pirates!"

A line of barefoot women appeared at the far end of the forum, stomping in unison, pulsing with determination and power. They wore sleeveless gray tunics that left little mystery as to their collective muscle.

Severus recognized Zinzin at the fore. The last time he saw her, she and Vindex were flirting like horses. Now she and her shipmates looked ready to deliver a torrential beating. Had Plotina misinterpreted Severus' request for added security? If so, she had wasted no time or subtlety in asserting herself.

"Gladiatrixes!" a young man shouted, his face half contorted with fear, half with intrigue. "Run or they'll tear us to pieces!"

"You are ordered to disperse," Zinzin shouted. She uprooted a tent and sent it flying.

Twice homeless in as many days, a terrified family abandoned what had been their campsite. Fear spread like puddles on pavement.

"This should be worth watching," Don Rexus said. The actor climbed onto the base of a column to get a better view.

"Too bad we can't charge admission." Winus Minem scrambled up to join Rexus.

"On whose authority is Zinzin acting?" Severus asked. The assault about to sweep across the plaza promised to be worse than the legion camp massacre. Anyone left standing by the pirates would be flattened by the impending stampede. "I thought I was in charge of security."

"Yes, but the governor's in charge of you." Minem nodded back to where Cassius Kleptus was securing the treasury door.

More tents fell as Zinzin's militia advanced. Fearful refugees pushed toward the far end of the forum. A squat-legged sailor hoisted an angry man over her shoulder and advanced as if unburdened with weight or conscience. Even the town criers would be hard-pressed to exaggerate the situation.

104

The clatter of bangles and beatings established a menacing rhythm as Plotina's pirates spread like a slow flood. Nobody's darlings, they had clearly been on the boat too long. Sparks rose when two barefoot pirates kicked a pile of burning timbers. Fire would have found purchase on the downwind rooftops were it not for the drizzle

"This is not what I had in mind when I requested help maintaining order," Severus said to the Titans. "Did one of you authorize this display of excessive force?"

"Fantastic, aren't they?" Kleptus was clearly enjoying the spectacle. He waddled toward the column where Rexus and Minem were perched. "By the gods, we need to get these girls into the arena."

"That's where they belong." Severus had hoped to rouse the governor's indignation but found there was none to awaken. Seeing that his employers might find entertainment in a massacre of innocents reminded him how far he was from becoming a true Roman. His only solace was not seeing Lena among the aggressors.

"I've never seen such talent," Rexus said with admiration usually reserved for himself. "This is far better than a chariot race. Frankly, I've never understood our fascination with horses."

"Such a pity," Kleptus said. "A performance like this is completely lost on the victims."

"Wait!" Severus said. "These people have lost their homes. They've hurt nobody and have nowhere to go. They need our help to get back on their feet again."

"They should go to Rome. As governor, I won't tolerate freeloaders in Hispania."

"See that?" Minem had climbed halfway up the column from where he could see an old woman slapping a pirate. "That lady is attacking our security forces."

"There's no excuse for violence." Kleptus shook his head with great gravity. "You need to make it clear that uncivil behavior won't be tolerated, Severus."

"Uncivil? Why does the definition of uncivil behavior apply only to civilians? These people didn't set fire to their own homes," Severus insisted. "Wouldn't we inspire more loyalty and civic pride by helping them?"

"This rabble threatens our very notion of civilization." Kleptus

105

patted Severus on the back as if comforting a confused child. "If we don't respond, the pillars of society will crumble."

It seemed to Severus that the very notion of society had already crumbled from above. Was it preordained that the innocent suffer when the mighty tangle? Somewhere between common decency and common sense the common man deserved better. How to convince his calloused employers without sounding like Marius? "Persecution only inspires rebellion. It's simple math, sir. If the common people ever understood their collective strength—"

"It will never happen," Kleptus snorted. "Stop talking nonsense and just enjoy the show."

Impervious to pain, one pirate woman—a Caledonian judging from her pale eyes and flaming red hair—overturned a boiling pot. Steam rose from the quenched fire. She arched her back, howled like a jackal that had swallowed hot coals, and proceeded to stomp on a nearby fire with her bare feet.

The statues of former emperors looked down with indifference. The stone gods afforded no protection to the empire's forgotten poor.

"There are plenty of able-bodied men in this crowd." Severus was unsure if anyone was listening, but he pursued his last line of logic just the same. "What if instead of beating and banishing them, we put them to work building the Super Emporium store?"

"Yes, let's arm them! Your radical little friends would love that," Rexus muttered. "Angry workers cracking our skulls with their hammers and trowels. Is that what you want, Severus?"

Minem jumped in once he saw that Rexus opposed the notion. "On the other hand, we could offer them a place to stay in exchange for digging a foundation."

Severus was glad for Minem's agreement. Convincing the governor was all that remained. "Super Emporium will help these people work their way out of poverty."

"Work? This lot doesn't want to work," Kleptus said. "They just want to destroy what they didn't create and whine about not being fed with silver spoons they didn't pay for. Mark my words, Severus; you'll soon outlive that youthful idealism."

"He's right," Rexus added. "Someday you'll regret having ever been young in the first place."

"Perhaps, but if we don't prevent a massacre, the taxpayers will be stuck with the cost of cleanup." Severus groped for an argument that would sway the governor. "Bloodstains on stone will be expensive to remove."

"Fine! If these bums are willing to work, so be it, but good luck getting Plotina's delicate *dominas* to stand down." The governor laughed at the prospect. "They're having way too much fun."

Agreement was one thing, execution another. How to stop the violence without getting crushed in the process? Severus tried not to dwell on the possibility that the entire incident might have been his fault. Was attacking the homeless how Plotina had interpreted his request for help with security? Perhaps she was just sending Kleptus a message: *If you don't restore order, I will.*

Severus wracked his brain for a solution. Short of throwing his corpse under the advancing chaos, he saw no way to prevent the wheels of injustice from flattening the homeless camp. His spirit sunk further when he noticed his brother at the edge of the fracas, organizing boys to gather cobblestones and encouraging young men to assemble barricades from scraps of wood. They looked intent on fighting the pirates regardless of the long odds against them.

Gaius made eye contact with Marius, silently imploring him to hold back and not to throw the first stone. A third of the tent village was gone and the rest would soon crumble, but so far, the pirates had not killed anyone. That would change if Marius started a fight he could never finish. Armed with sticks and stones, his minions advanced through the retreating wave of refugees.

The pirates pillaged onward.

Unimpeded by lack of a plan, Gaius leapt from the shelter of the colonnades and ran to the center of the forum. Mothers and children spilled past him like water from a breached dam. The air smelled of fire and fear. People were footsteps away from being trampled.

If the Roman gods had abandoned their people, perhaps the one God would still listen. Gaius Severus tried to invoke the spirit of Joshua at Jericho. He conjured David facing a line of female Goliaths. He stood before the flood and prayed that his raised arms would part the waters.

But nobody's god was listening.

"Stop!" Gaius knew that the first stone would trigger a terrible spiral. Once Marius got to within throwing range, a landslide of misery would break loose.

The marauding women approached. Gaius Severus looked into their angry eyes and remembered something his father once said about making the best of what limited time one has. For a second, he felt like an air bubble trapped in honey. The forum's straight lines seemed to curve around him. The din went silent except for the sound of his pulse. Unarmed, out of ideas, and out of time, Gaius Severus stepped forward to confront Zinzin. "I have something Plotina wants."

She smiled like a hawk about to strike a field mouse. "What have you got besides the clothes on your back?"

"I am Tarraco's security chief." Severus addressed the pirates but spoke loud enough for his brother's armed boys to hear as well. "Governor Kleptus and Captain Plotina both order you to stand down."

"I doubt that." Zinzin made an exaggerated point of looking Severus up and down and finding him lacking. "Get out of the way, goat breath."

Severus planted his feet before the tense wall of spite and muscle and held his shaky patch of bare ground. "You were asked to maintain order. Not destroy the town."

"The town was disorderly," Zinzin objected.

"What if I offer you something better?"

Zinzin raised a bushy eyebrow, but did not lower her guard.

Gaius remembered what Carbo said and embroidered it into a threadbare proposition. "The former governor was murdered. I know who did it. Tell Plotina that I will produce enough evidence to convict the perpetrator if she agrees to stop this violence."

Gaius turned to the crowd before Zinzin could reject the offer. He tried to forget that he had a solid line of rough women at his back. "We have jobs for you building Super Emporium." He gestured to Winus Minem, who waved in timid agreement. "Those of you who can't shack up with family around town can live at the construction site until you've earned enough to get back on your feet. Either way, you cannot continue to live in the forum."

"What's Super Emporium?" someone who had not heard Minem's earlier speech asked.

"The biggest and most wonderful shops this side of Rome's seven hills," Gaius said, though he was still unclear on the details. "We need people to build the structure and more people to work inside."

"We don't need another damned store!" someone shouted.

"I'm not here to negotiate and neither are the women behind me," Severus said.

Most of the angry young men dropped their stones. The chance for work and wages outweighed the certainty of being crushed by pirates. The thin ray of hope was better than the promise of darkness. People began to disperse.

"Do I have both sides' agreement?" Before turning back to Zinzin and her crew, Gaius scanned the crowd for Marius. His brother looked unconcerned with having led a group of innocent boys to within a stone's throw of being crushed. "Plotina's crew will return to quarters. The rest of you will clean up the forum and move your camp to the construction site."

"We'll need a hostage to assure our safe passage." Zinzin insisted, though her passage was never in doubt.

"Take Rexus!" Minem shouted from the sidelines.

Sixteen
XVI

Gaius Severus followed Zinzin's entourage at a safe distance to verify their return to quarters. He considered confronting Plotina to demand a promise of better behavior in the future but knew that without an army any such vow would be unenforceable.

Thanks to the town criers, exaggerated versions of his confrontation with Zinzin spread across Tarraco faster than any truth could ever travel. In one variation he had vanquished the pirates with his bare hands. In another, the fierce warrior women had torn him limb from limb and reassembled the pieces backward. He knew that the gossip would ebb and flow until washed away by fresh scuttlebutt. After growing up feeling invisible, the short-lived surge of winks and whispers was not unpleasant.

Severus had promised the impossible to prevent a rout. He had bluffed Zinzin with a thin ruse based on a slave's accusations. His promise to produce a murderer depended on solving a crime whose path had long been swept clean.

"Severus! Just the promising young fellow I was looking for."

He had not expected to see Winus Minem so soon, though it was not unusual to find him snooping around the port. Festus Rufius had allowed Minem to wrest control of the docks from the provincial administration. Minem now ran the operation for a profit on behalf of Imperial Associates. A few coins flowed as taxes to government coffers; more flowed directly into the governor's pockets.

Minem was the closest thing Severus had to an ally. He was a self-made man who had risen by moxie and will alone. Minem would be a good example to follow if he were not also a murder suspect.

"Good job at the forum just now," Minem said. "You'll make a great negotiator someday. In the meantime, I wonder if I might ask you a favor."

"A favor? From me?"

"It's about the Trial of the Century." Minem lowered his voice as if sharing a state secret in a bathhouse full of spies. "Can you come inside my office for a quick chat?"

Severus followed Minem down the wharf toward a bland administration building, the nerve center for extracting fees from ships using Tarraco's deep harbor. A manicured brunette sat behind an empty table. Her apparent job was to do nothing except look beautiful. Her cold demeanor ensured that the lobby would never overheat.

"Good day, *domina*," Severus said, but the woman was too intent on shaping her nails to acknowledge his presence.

"Good afternoon, Tertulia," Minem said, but she did not reply to him either.

Minem ushered Severus into a disorganized office where a pile of papyrus sagged on a bowlegged table.

"I've been impressed with you since you sang that song at the banquet," Minem said.

"Thank you, sir, but you've got me confused with someone else."

"That wasn't you who sang the ballad about the pig and the magistrate?" Minem sorted through a stack of scrolls. "We've been running behind ever since I fired our accountant for massaging Tertulia more than the taxes."

"I'm good at sums, sir. I'd be happy to assist."

"I'm sure of it." Minem found the document he wanted and looked up. "As you know, our former governor is accused of corruption, and Rexus is to represent him in the trial.

"Against Plotina?"

"He'll be unarmed in an epic battle of wits." Minem seemed to savor the thought of Rexus being skewered by Hadrian's niece. "Do you understand the philosophical basis of Roman justice, Severus?"

"Justice?" Severus stammered for a second. "Justice is based on truth, laws, evidence ..."

"You see why I'm concerned? We can manufacture plenty of evidence. Witnesses aren't expensive, but the case still doesn't feel solid. There's still something we lack."

"The truth?" Severus had made notable improvements in not blurting out the first thought that flew into his mind, but the stray gaffe still took wing before his mouth could slam shut.

"What we lack is popular support for our defendant," Minem

111

said. "A leader's job is not to be loved—a trait in which Rufius exceeded."

"The audience will want blood even if he's innocent," Severus said. He was relieved that Minem appeared unaware that Rufius was on the lam.

"Charging admission assures a better class of spectator than your usual arena crowd, but you're right, people still want to be entertained." Minem's eyes appeared over the top of his document. "When push comes to shove, they'll want to see the big man go down. I imagine the plebes are still mad that the last governor died in private."

Severus tried to hide his discomfort. If Carbo's allegation was true, Minem had played a starring role in the death of Governor Biberious. He then profited from the rise of Festus Rufius and stood to gain even more from his fall.

"If I were you, I'd lock up Vindex and torture Carbo till he confesses." Minem buried his face in another document. "Let's get back to the business at hand. The Trial of the Century is only days away."

Minem stepped out of the room to request a favor from Tertulia that she obviously resented. The front door slammed as she stormed out of the office to do his bidding.

Minem returned, flustered. Something about Tertulia clearly got under his skin. "Here's where you come in," he said. "We'll need some people in the audience to shout in support for Rufius. A few loud and respectable citizens on our side will neutralize the majority against us. I need you to search the forum, the shops, and taverns for people who still believe that Rufius is a stout fellow."

"I'm not sure I'm cut out for this kind of —"

"Communications role? You're a natural! Get your noisy brother to help."

"Brother?" Severus felt his face flush. Minem seemed to know everything.

"Your brother's got flair. It just needs to be channeled in the right direction before his youthful idealism gets him sent to the lead mines."

Severus could hardly refuse. The reference to Marius seemed more like leverage than a threat, at least for now. The basic request was innocuous enough, and the task would give him an excuse to get closer to Minem's affairs.

"Perhaps you'd like an internship as my assistant. I could use a smart young man around here. Did you know that there's an academy for administration in Rome?"

"A school, sir?"

"An institute. A one-year program to train up-and-coming young pups like yourself in the pomp and process of civic administration."

Severus stopped short of observing that governance in Hispania was all pomp. The province did not follow rhyme, rule, or reason. Administrative posts were reserved for the dimwitted sons of old money. "I would be very interested in bettering myself through advanced training."

"I could write you a recommendation if you're interested." Minem unrolled another document and looked it over. "Hadrian's building a huge villa—an administrative center east of Rome—lots of interesting opportunities for a promising fellow like you."

"I haven't heard of if," Severus said.

"A monstrosity worthy of Nero. They say he's filling it with bric-a-brac and relics from across the empire." Minem tossed aside the document and waved Severus away "On your way now! Spread the word. Remember: Perception is everything."

Severus left on winged feet. His excitement about the possibility of a Roman education was cut short by a large crowd of noisy, impatient people that stretched out onto the docks. Curious why they had gathered, he advanced in spurts until he reached the stern of Plotina's vessel.

The crowd was unusually upscale for the lowbrow neighborhood. Nobility on the docks, refugees in the forum—it was as if Tarraco had tipped sideways and every fish was out of water.

Saturnalia, indeed.

Seventeen
XVII

The crowd shouted her name.

Men in starched togas guided their double-chinned wives over the splintered planks. Dandies slathered in pomade trawled the wharves for lonely prospects. Rich and otherwise respectable citizens pounded on the ship's hull. An orange scarf blew into the air and drifted across the water.

When Lena's face peeked over the top of the boat, people cheered as if the emperor had just declared a new holiday. The crowd pressed forward, and Lena recoiled in surprise.

"Seer! Augur!"

"They think you're a goddess." Zinzin had a new bruise on her bicep, a souvenir from her recent romp across the forum. She squinted down the long queue to see where it ended. "Go figure."

"I told a few fortunes in the tavern," Lena said. "I interpreted some dreams in the villa … but this?"

"City people are so gullible," Zinzin said. "Go ahead and tell some fortunes, girl. Use the money to buy Vindex as a present for me."

"Rexus," Lena muttered. She pushed a lock of hair from her eyes. "Rexus is behind this."

"My husband is crazy," a woman called from somewhere along the wharf. "What should I do?"

"She's probably the real crazy," Zinzin whispered. "Just say anything."

"He thinks he's a grain of wheat," the woman shouted.

The crowd hushed to hear Lena's response.

"Do you think he's a grain of wheat?" Lena asked.

"No." The women thought about this for a second. "But what about the birds?"

"Is December a good month to give birth, or should I wait until spring?" an extremely pregnant woman asked from directly below the ship.

"Will the sun ever return or have the gods forgotten to mind the seasons?"

"They'll believe anything," Zinzin whispered. She noticed Vindex on the wharf and waved to him. "Hey, piglet!"

Vindex ignored her.

She blew him a kiss, but it missed.

"Should I kill my husband?" a woman asked, though she sounded as though she had already made up her mind.

Lena watched a *denarius* spin through the air, hit the deck and roll away. After years of helping her scheming mother bilk the gullible, Lena had come to see money as something dirty. But here was an untainted coin, offered in gratitude, shining in daylight. She could put the money to good use freeing slaves. Offering solace in the open air was far better than auguring for drunks in the sticky darkness of the Gladiator's Goblet. If people were willing to wait in line and pay for advice, where was the harm in that? Still unconvinced, she stepped back from the edge of the boat. "There must be some mistake."

"No mistake," Plotina draped a comforting arm around Lena. Her long sleeves shone like iridescent wings. To the people gathered below, her every gesture fractured into a thousand hues. "People want prophets."

"And Rexus wants profits," Lena said.

"Rexus is my hostage," Plotina said. "Next time I'll just ask for a real goat."

The crowd shoved toward the ship. Well-fed men and their upper-crust women clamored for Lena to interpret their dreams, predict their futures and reassure them that tomorrow would be no worse than today.

"A goddess has emerged from the sea!" The dockside crier ran off to exaggerate the story across town. "The daughter of Neptune has come to bless Tarraco!"

"Prophet! Goddess!" the crowd shouted.

Lena slumped to the deck. The rocking boat and sight of so many people made her dizzy. For a moment she was lost in childhood, unsure of her whereabouts. Had she run this far only to stumble into another circus?

Plotina's long braid touched the deck as she stooped to comfort Lena. Her sleeves shimmered like a sunlit butterfly. "It's a shame to waste a gift, little sister."

"Please get rid of them," Lena whispered.

"The gods of fame and fortune favor you!" Don Rexus appeared smiling and unscathed from any indignities he might have suffered as a hostage. The actor straightened his toga and surveyed the crowd. "These folks are in the mood to spend money."

"You are free to go." Plotina glared at Rexus.

Zinzin ran off in search of a rope ladder.

"I'm not leaving before Lena seizes this opportunity," Rexus protested. "Interpreting dreams in the villa kept her out of the laundry room, but this is the chance of a lifetime. Just look at this crowd!" He gestured widely as if trying to hug a hundred people at once. "*Carpe diem*, girl. I can make you a star."

"A star brings light. You just want to profit from people's misery." Lena said, though the concept was not foreign to her. Rexus and Mum would have cut a fine pair.

"The taxman profits from misery." Rexus turned skyward as if seeking confirmation. "An augur draws reward from hope."

"How is that different from prostitution?"

"Less competition. No middleman."

"You're a pimp!" Lena stood up so quickly that Rexus jumped backward. Many in the crowd cheered, thinking that the two were dancing.

Lena was no stranger to the smell of easy money. It was impossible to deny the melodic appeal of coins landing at her feet. If rich people wanted to pay for cheap advice, who would be hurt by playing along? Perhaps their generosity would dry up if she announced that all proceeds would be spent to free their slaves. Meanwhile, Rexus' oily swagger reminded her that working at the villa was no longer an option. How else was she supposed to earn a living?

As if she needed more evidence that men were trouble, Gaius Severus appeared below looking lost and forlorn. The boy who claimed to love her had also accused her of whoredom. Severus talked a good game, but was he really any different than the rest of his ilk? Men don't want partners, they want slaves with dowries. Once a man hooked a wedding ring through a girl's nose she was expected to scrub tiles, pluck chickens and slap children until it killed her. Why did Lena need a man when she could earn more money in a day than most men in a week? If she did not take charge of her life, who would?

"This crowd could turn ugly," Plotina said. "Believe me; rich people can behave worse than poor folk. If you send these toffs away empty-handed, they'll hire a mob to and burn down the docks."

But for now the crowd was more festive than restive. Men waved their toga sleeves. Women unfurled scarves and waved them in the breeze. The sea of people pulsed like an ocean of fabric and color. Coins sparkled in the air.

"It's winter. People need some of your sunshine." Plotina signaled for the rope ladder to be lowered. "You have the power to make them happy."

"Happiness is overrated," Rexus said. "Money is better." He tried to squeeze Lena's arm but she twisted away.

Preferring the crowd to another minute with Rexus, Lena scrambled down to the wharf, sat on an empty barrel and forced a smile.

"My youngest daughter has nightmares." The first woman in line knelt before Lena.

"Feed her cheese curds before bed," Lena shared the rural remedy against nightmares. Were city folk really so ignorant?

"Bless you." The woman left a silver *denarius* by Lena's feet and went away satisfied. The coin was enough to buy a meal for a homeless family; a thousand more might buy freedom for Vindex.

A bejeweled, well-dressed and very distressed woman crouched in front of Lena. "My husband's being prosecuted for tax evasion. It's not fair that he's being punished while assassins roam free," she whispered.

"Maybe assassins pay taxes," Lena said. Not everyone could be helped.

A pale fellow in a woolen tunic had been waiting patiently for a chance to query Lena. "Not from around here, are you?" he asked.

Lena stiffened. The man had a slight northern accent but she could not place its provenance. She worried that he might recognize her from one of Mum's traveling shows. Nothing in her past was so tainted as to be toxic, but she had no desire to relive the better moments either. "Have we met?"

"Not in this life."

Lena relaxed. This fellow presented no more a threat than any other crazy person. Zinzin nudged him away after he started ranting loudly about the unjust death of Socrates.

"Where can I meet the girl of my dreams?" asked a dandy whose orange zest cologne barely concealed the smell of fawning widows. He reminded Lena of a young Don Rexus and, when the impresario appeared nearby, she considered strangling the young man as a service to the future.

"Lena, Lena, Lena!" Rexus managed to surprise her with an unwanted kiss on the cheek. "From the moment you fought the bull I've been madly in love with you."

Lena pulled away. "If I count to three and you're still here, I'll send you to the sea floor."

Zinzin indicated that his time was up, but Don Rexus ignored the heavily fortified suggestion.

"One," Lena said.

"I can make you a star!"

"Two."

Vindex approached and Rexus waved as if seeing an old friend. "I'll be around when you come to your senses."

Vindex tried to avoid the impresario's advance but found his path blocked by Rexus' outstretched arms and billowing folds. Vindex was too large and the crowd too dense to avoid contact.

"Vindex, Vindex, Vindex!"

Vindex shrugged off an attempted hug. "You've got the wrong fellow."

"Only if you want to die poor."

"Rich or poor doesn't matter when you're dead."

Vindex sidestepped the actor and continued back toward Lena.

"Let me organize your triumphant return to the arena." Rexus followed the gladiator. "Half your weight in gold, the other half in girls."

"I don't want your money or your daughters."

"Wait!" Rexus yanked on Vindex's tunic and ducked when the giant swatted at him. "I've seen you in the arena. You're a natural. It's a crime to hide such raw talent from the world. Besides, if you stay around here, you'll be convicted of murder."

"Murder?" Vindex extracted his tunic from Rexus' grasp. "You want to see murder? If I return to fighting, you'll be my first victim."

"You see?" Rexus clapped his hands in delight. "Killing's in your blood. And I can turn blood to money."

"*Finitus!*" Vindex roared.

"As you wish." Rexus shrugged and swept his arms as if brushstroking the horizon. "But just remember: Across this water, in every town worth its salt, in every rundown arena from Narbo to Sicilia, men pit themselves against the odds, the gods, and each other. Do you know why?"

"Because the gods are sadists."

"Men fight to prove themselves worthy." Rexus took advantage of a gap in the crowd to squeeze in front of the gladiator by nudging a delighted matron aside. "They fight to rise above the fray, to break free from fickle destiny. They slash and claw their way up from forgotten towns and second-rate arenas. They fight for the only goal that matters: Rome."

Vindex glared like an old fire. His fingers crackled like kindling when he balled them into fists. "You would steal the coins from a dead man's eyes."

"Everyone dies, Vindex." Rexus reached for the gladiator's shoulder. "The only question is how."

Vindex shook loose and turned away.

Undeterred, Rexus tightened his sash, inflated his chest, and followed the gladiator. A middle-aged woman swooned when he ran a hand through his silver hair and flashed a smile her way. "You can have immortality in the palm of your hand."

"Enough!" Vindex turned and shoved Rexus backward, into the arms of the delighted widow.

"Don't waste your potential in a backwater like Tarraco," Rexus insisted, though he was having trouble breaking free from the old woman's embrace. "A battle here, a battle there, within no time I can have you back in Rome where you belong."

"I don't belong anywhere."

People protested as Vindex pushed toward Lena, but no one dared offer him a lesson in protocol. Seizing the opportunity, Gaius Severus advanced in the gladiator's wake.

Zinzin was delighted by Vindex's arrival and oblivious to his foul mood. She tried to subject him to a security inspection but he shook off her flirtation. He waited for Lena to finish with a dazzling young woman who did not understand why her bed was empty.

"If everyone cheats on their spouse, how come no one's cheating with me?" she asked.

The woman seemed more interested in talking than listening so Lena said nothing. In her first hour of dockside augury, Lena had learned more about the inner workings of the capital and its confused upper class than she ever needed to know. The poor worried about having enough oil and grain to survive the winter. The rich fretted over fresh oysters for the next banquet. Everyone took credit for their triumphs and blamed the Fates for their setbacks.

"Why the long face, Vindex?" Lena smiled up at her distressed friend from the villa.

"Memories are like prison. I can't break free." The color of his eyes matched the cloudy sky. "The soldiers massacred our mothers. My sister died on the forced march to Rome."

"I'm sorry." Lena knew of his childhood along the Danube, the coming of the Romans, and the subjugation of his tribe. "Your pain runs deep."

"I was just a kid." Tears welled in his tired eyes. He looked like he had not slept in days. "At Rome, in the Colosseum, I watched from a cage as my father and brothers were put to death in Trajan's celebrations. It still feels like yesterday."

"Your sorrow keeps their memory alive."

"I'm at the end of my rope."

"You carry a heavier load than most, my friend. I wish I could lighten it for you." Seeing Vindex defeated by his history brought Lena to tears. He needed so much more than any one person could give. She stood and embraced the vulnerable gladiator. Vindex tried to pull away but she held him tight. Ignoring the crowd, they huddled together in a moment of shared sadness. "I will help to buy your freedom."

"I have no reason to stay here." Vindex turned toward the east. "I want to go home—beyond the sunrise. Over the mountains and back to the big river."

He smiled with gratitude, walked to the end of the dock, and leapt into the water.

Eighteen
XVIII

Lena ran to the end of the dock where Vindex had just jumped into the harbor. "Man overboard!" she shouted. "Vindex is trying to swim home!"

"No one can swim that far!" Zinzin followed with a rope, but Vindex had already moved beyond its reach.

Vindex fought the water. There was no buoyancy in his strokes, no rhythm to his kicks. It was clear that his terrestrial strength as a gladiator did not extend to the sea.

Lena was about to jump off the dock when Gaius ran up beside her. "Can you save him?"

"I'm not a good swimmer," Gaius said, but seeing Lena's distress he swallowed his fear and tore off his sandals. "Then again, I'm not a bad swimmer either."

"Over there. He's going down!" Lena pointed to where Vindex was tangled in clump of sea grass that had drifted into the harbor. "You jump and we'll follow with a boat. Hurry!"

Severus leapt. The cold water stung like a tub full of jellyfish. He surfaced and gasped as if his lungs had been ripped from his chest. The water was rougher than it had been a month earlier when he had been pushed off the dock during the melee surrounding the emperor's visit. That day, Lena had pulled him out. Today he would repay the favor or die trying.

He struggled to move forward, dog-paddling to where he had last sighted Vindex, but his soaked tunic felt like an anchor. Severus was barely able to stay above the chop when he felt an undercurrent reaching for him. A sea vine curled around his ankle and tugged his leg. He sucked a lungful of air and fought to stay above water, but the surface broke like glass and the sky vanished amidst the shards.

Severus fought the downward pull until it felt like his brain was about to leak through his ears. Disoriented but still conscious, he saw bubbles rising but was powerless to follow. A startled cuttlefish sent a blast of ink in his direction, obscuring the already dark water. When the ink cleared, Severus found himself face-to-face with a shriveled old man.

121

"Greetings." The tiny man seemed at home in the water and unaware that Severus might not be comfortable below the surface. His long beard undulated with the current.

Where am I? Severus wondered.

"Underwater. Where did you think?"

Severus was surprised that his thoughts had been heard. He released a bit of stale air from his lungs, closed his eyes and hoped the strange dream would end with a timely rescue. Risking a glance, he was dismayed to find he was still face-to-face with what had to be a drowning man's last delusion. "Are you Neptune?"

"You were expecting Jupiter, maybe? What?—the God of the Sea's not good enough?*"

"I meant no disrespect. It's just that I don't want to die, and you look more like my father than how I imagined Neptune."

"How's this?" The old man transformed into a grinning shark. He swam in a circle and brushed against Severus' leg.

"I liked you better with the beard."

Neptune transformed back into the withered old man. The strands of his beard spread and mingled with the kelp.

"I thought Neptune was a big strong fellow with a gold trident."

"That's Poseidon, you ignoramus." Neptune's anger pulsed through the water. Bubbles boiled off his head. "I wish the Romans and the Greeks would keep their gods straight. Poseidon mostly works the eastern seas, and I don't mind telling you that he's got the better job."

Severus' empty lungs stung as if he had inhaled a beehive. "Where are the fish?"

"Fish are fine if you blow bubbles all day. But I like a little intelligent conversation from time to time."

"What about sirens?"

"*Mare nostrum!* What is it with you humans and the sirens? They're half fish, you know."

Severus was fading into the cold comfort of darkness. One question remained, the only one that mattered. "Am I dead?"

"Dead to the world, but this is the underworld. Dead looks different down here."

"No!" Severus insisted. "I can still blow bubbles."

"Again with the bubbles!" Neptune shook his head as if Gaius Severus was the most disappointing visitor he had ever received.

122

Wavelets rippled off his wrinkled forehead.

Severus looked skyward. What little light remained was lost in watery shadow. Of all the terrible ways one might die, drifting weightlessly from this world to the next now seemed like a decent option. He wondered if Charon the Boatman plied his trade below water. "Listen, I'm not ready for—"

"For death?" Neptune laughed. "Think of it like getting married or having kids—who's ever ready?"

"Still …" A surge and a shadow crossed the surface. For a second, Severus thought he saw a face peering down at him. "Listen, I'd like another shot at life. Can we make some kind of deal?"

"Deal—*pah!* —everyone wants to make a deal. What am I, a shopkeeper?"

"No. You're a god."

"Nice of you to notice. Sea gods don't get a lot of respect these days. The land gods, they get recognition—sacrifices, harvest festivals, you name it. The sky gods are loved, feared even. Apollo gets the sun. Diana gets the moon. What do I get? Bubbles."

"What if I promise to build you a temple?"

"*Pah!* Feathers on a fish."

A cloud of silver sardines pulsed like a liquid mirror and then vanished in the kelp. Severus looked for the face he had seen but it was gone. Perhaps it had never been there. Life was one heartbeat away from over. Perhaps it had already ended. "I'll sing your praises ten times a day."

"Spare me your dying promises." Neptune said. "Your praises won't be heard. Too many new gods are crowding the arena. What's wrong with you people, anyway? Why all these new gods? The old ones aren't good enough? Tell you what—I'll let you live if you promise me one thing."

Gaius Severus nodded weakly. "Anything."

"Go back up there and—"

Interrupted by a splash above them, Neptune turned back into a cuttlefish and vanished in an ink cloud.

Zinzin dove toward Severus. She cut loose the kelp and twisted his body free. Pressing her mouth to his, she blew air into his lungs only to see it bubble from his blue lips. Determined to bring his limp corpse back to the boat, she wrapped one arm around his waist and kicked back toward the surface.

Nineteen
XIX

"Am I dead?" Gaius Severus spat out a lungful of seawater. His throat burned from brine, his eyes stung of salt. Dream and daylight shared a gauzy border. He remembered jumping into the water but the rest was murky.

"Thank God you're awake."

"Thank Neptune." The sound of his brother's voice meant that eternal rest would have to wait. Gaius rubbed seawater from his eyes. Marius came into focus, hair tossed by the wind, no trace of worry on his face. "Neptune didn't want me."

"He must have liked Vindex," Marius said. "Poor sod never surfaced."

Gaius tried to sit up but the warped pier seemed to roll beneath him. He ran a hand along the damp planks, but something did not feel right. This was no wharf. He shivered with cold and confusion. "Where are we?"

"On a boat." Marius pulled his brother upright. "Dry off, you drenched rat. We're going on a trip."

"A boat? How did I end up in a boat?"

"You were unconscious."

"So you just threw me into a boat?"

"You're not that heavy," Marius said. "Lena thought it was a bad idea, but I thought you'd want to help make history."

"I feel sick." Gaius leaned over the edge and confirmed that, indeed, they were passengers aboard a small vessel. The boat was barely big enough to transport the tuna that seemed to be swimming around in his stomach.

"We're going to Judea!" Marius said, triumphantly.

"Are you completely mad? God's take me, this can't be happening."

"Quiet," Marius shot back. "The sailors don't know."

"They don't know where we're going?" Gaius tried to contain his anger at having been kidnapped and dragged along on his brother's craziest scheme ever. "Please tell me this is a joke."

"Don't worry. God is with us."

"As I recall, the last time God put a couple of Jews on a boat, he destroyed the world while they were out sailing."

The brothers had always lived close to the water, but this was the first time either had ventured beyond the coast. Even among the stouthearted, the sea was a harsh mistress. Tarraco was full of fishwives whose husbands had not returned, though some said this was by choice.

The boat bobbed and cut through the water. Gaius turned leeward and saw a silhouette that looked like Lena watching from the wharf. He offered a shy wave that she did not return. She had lost Vindex and now Severus was losing her. No great augury was needed to predict that they would never meet again.

One sailor, a fisherman to judge from his creased face, rowed the vessel beyond the harbor. The other fellow, not as weathered looking, raised the boat's square sail. Other than a net stuffed into the bow, there was no indication that the boat was ready for a long voyage.

Gaius had been unconscious, probably slung over his brother's shoulder, when they boarded. As far as he knew, Marius had no money. How had he negotiated passage? What kind of crew would admit an insolvent rebel with unconscious cargo?

"If this boat sinks, it will be the high point of my day." Gaius slumped down on the worn bench that spanned the midsection. He considered his options, counted his blessings, and quickly concluded that he had neither. His head ached too much to argue with Marius, and he lacked the strength to overpower the sailors. There was no way to turn the boat around. "This piss-poor boat will never make it to Judea."

"Of course not.." Marius' voice dropped to a whisper, barely audible above the wind. "We'll join a whole crew of rebels soon."

"Lunatics, you mean."

"If you consider restoring the Kingdom of God to be lunacy."

"I consider kidnap lunacy. I consider a sea voyage during winter lunacy. How was this trip paid for anyway?"

"You worry too much." Marius glanced at the crew. "No more talk. These sailors aren't in on the secret."

One of the sailors seemed familiar, but exhaustion weighted heavier than memory. Rocked by the water, Gaius drifted off to

125

sleep. The sea soon haunted his dreams. Inky depths swirled with dark green columns rising directly from Hades. Scaly creatures with piercing eyes circled as he drifted downward.

In his dream, the sea gave way to what looked like a temple. Four black cats danced around an altar. One carried a knife in its mouth. The others had sharp teeth and blood-stained claws. They gorged on wet flesh from a defiled sacrifice.

The cats danced faster and faster, swirling into darkness that again became the sea. Convinced he was drowning again, he choked, coughed, and woke up gasping like an old stonecutter.

His head felt full of rags, and it took a moment to shake off the confusion. His stomach rolled up one side of his rib cage only to slide down the other. He gripped the gunwale and choked back a dry heave. The endless expanse of dark water seemed like where the River Styx went to die.

Gaius tried to picture the destination, not the journey, but found comfort in neither. Judea was halfway across the empire, but this boat was inadequate for such a voyage. Perhaps they would hug the coastlines. Maybe the plan was to transfer to a larger, more stable vessel. Either way, the trip was perilous in winter. On a good day the sea could swallow a tiny boat whole, and no one would ever know.

Today was not a good day.

Gaius tried not to imagine how it would end, clinging to a scrap of wood, lost on an infinite sea. Instead, he sought the security of a horizon or the assurance of a gull, but land was nowhere to be seen.

The Mediterranean was known to be deep and dangerous. Creatures like the jagged-toothed monkfish and all manner of eels lurked below. Shellfish oozed around like insects on the seafloor, and Neptune ruled the depths.

Gaius had a sinking sense that the boat and its crew, like everything else he had encountered lately, were not what they seemed. The fisherman working the tiller looked like an honest laborer. The fellow tightening the rigging did not. Unlike the weather-beaten slaves and sailors who frequented the docks, this man's skin seemed untouched by wind and sea water.

"Storm coming," the fisherman said. He struggled to steady the tiller. "We need to turn back."

"No!" The man at the sail spoke with authority. "No turning back."

Gaius' heart dropped into his empty stomach. He had heard this voice before.

"Lower the sail or the wind will rip it away," the fisherman said.

"Nonsense," the other fellow said. "I'll tighten the sail and we'll outrun the storm."

Not happy with the response, the fisherman abandoned the tiller and started toward the mast. "If you want a job done," he muttered, "you have to do it yourself."

"Back to your post." The man at the mast pulled out a knife. "Find some guts or I'll spill yours to the fishes."

The sailor shrugged and returned to the stern.

The man with the knife tightened the sail, and the boat lurched over the wavy sea like a flying fish.

"Marius," Gaius whispered sharply, but his brother seemed hypnotized by the water. Once sure the crewmen were distracted, Gaius gave Marius a sharp nudge in the ribs. "We'll never make it to Judea, Marius."

"Nonsense." Marius yawned and smiled. "We'll be fine. God is with us."

"God is against us … always has been." Gaius shuddered. For every gray cloud above, a darker one was reflected in the sea below. "Have the sailors turn the boat around."

"These men know their craft."

"I recognize the man at the sail," Gaius whispered. "His craft has nothing to do with boats."

"There is still much you don't understand."

"I understand this," Gaius insisted. "That man's an assassin, a praetorian from the night of—"

"Hey you two!" The soldier threw the end of a line at Gaius and indicated where to secure it. "Make yourselves useful and tie down these ropes."

"We're going to need a miracle," the fisherman said. "Pray to your gods, boys."

"Pray I don't silence you!" The praetorian shook a fist. His forearm bore an eagle talon tattoo.

"Maybe we should turn back." Gaius smiled and extended his arms in conciliation. "Tomorrow's another day. Let's try again tomorrow."

"Anyone who craves the shore can swim there." The praetorian waved his knife for emphasis.

"Christo!" The fisherman raised his hands in supplication. "Save us."

"Damn your false god!" the praetorian shouted back. "You'll only make things worse."

"Christo is the true God!"

"Amazing!" Marius said, intrigued. "He's a Christian. This should make for an interesting conversation."

"Probably not the best time to talk philosophy." Gaius fumbled with the rope and monitored the man who had helped kill half a cohort. He racked his brain to understand why the Fates had reunited them on this tiny, wave-tossed vessel. If forty dead soldiers had not satisfied the praetorian's thirst, what would?

A wave hit Gaius but did not dissolve his lingering shame over having not stopped the massacre. Four praetorian guardsmen had punished his cohort for their inept misdeeds. Imperial justice had been cold and quick, but still incomplete. The killer on board was proof that Gaius could never outrun his negligence.

He recalled the dream: Four feral cats, like the four praetorian killers, would not rest until every mouse had been caught. There could be just one interpretation.

The surface of the sea broke into fragments of evening blue and olive gray. Water surged against the hull and foamed like ghosts over the sides of the boat.

"Did you know that Jesus was Jewish?" Marius spoke as if participating in dinner party conversation. "I'll bet it wouldn't take much to convert that sailor."

"I'd convert to anything if it kept this boat from sinking."

"Don't be silly." Marius grabbed the rope and secured it. "The storm will pass before you learn to tie a knot."

The sea rose and fell with greater intensity. Gaius watched the fisherman look up with terror from the tiller and realized that the man was not a willing participant in the adventure. Unlike the praetorian, this fellow's face was creased with worry.

A large wave pitched the boat. Gaius fell and banged his head hard against the gunwale. For a moment, the dark sky appeared to sparkle. He looked down and saw an old man's face ripple across the churning surface of the water.

"Neptune."

The boat was tossed like a toy in the hand of a steel-gray giant. Froth-fingered waves rose from the water and clutched the boat. The sail strained against its rigging.

Gaius heard moaning. The depths seemed alive with the sleepless spirits of tormented souls. Again the *lemures* beckoned. Waves rose in the form of a many-headed serpent whose every face was that of Neptune.

A dark funnel cloud enveloped the boat and set it spinning. Wind beat the strained sail like a drum skin and then ripped it away.

Gaius knew what had to be done. "We must ask Neptune for mercy!"

The fisherman tried to kneel in prayer but the rising water offered no sanctuary. "*Christo* will save us if we pray together."

"Mithras will smite you both," the praetorian hissed.

"Yahweh is older than all three," Marius insisted. "If you're going to pray, at least pray to the right God."

"No more blasphemy!" The praetorian waved his knife. "Calling upon your false gods will only anger Mithras."

Gaius flushed at the mention of Mithras. He remembered the recent ceremony aborted by beast and fire. Was the praetorian here to avenge his comrades lost that night? "I'm not blaspheming. I have met Neptune personally."

"I'm warning you ..." The praetorian turned his face to the wind as if the force of his glare might stop it from pitching the boat like a scrap of tree bark.

For a terrible, silent second, the vessel hung unbalanced between crest and trough. An unsecured sack fell into the water. The praetorian hugged the mast. The Christian wrestled the tiller.

Gaius Severus looked down into the water and saw the old sea god laughing. His fears were confirmed: Neptune was calling. The tempest was personal.

"I can save us. I'm the cause of this storm."

"Nonsense," Marius said. "Water is the cause of this storm."

"Bail!" insisted the praetorian.

In the lull between waves, the sailors fought the remaining oars. The brothers bailed water with their hands.

"I never told you about Neptune!" Gaius shouted to his brother.

129

"I was dead and he revived me. He's come to collect what I promised."

"Don't be a fool. Only our God is real."

An incoming wave filled the boat nearly to the brim. One oar washed away.

"Pray!" the fisherman insisted. The water level forced him to let go of the tiller. He raised his hands skyward. "Calm the sea, oh gentle *Christo*. Jesus, Lamb of Yahweh, Lord of the fisherman—"

"Jesus was a Jew." The boat's predicament seemed to have no effect on Marius. He spoke to the fisherman as if lecturing Socrates on philosophy. "Perhaps you should pray to the God he worshiped. Pray to the God of Abraham, Isaac, and Jacob — the God of Carmel."

"Your God gave us his son. You must accept him if we're to be saved."

The sermon was interrupted by a wall of water rising over the bow. Again, the praetorian clung to the mast. Marius grabbed a rope with one hand and his brother with the other. As the wave crashed it tore the Christian from his tiller and sucked him into the churn.

"We must save him," Marius said. He looked around for a lifeline or a net but even the last oar was gone.

When the sea subsided there was no sign of the fisherman.

"Bail!" the praetorian ordered.

"This is my fault," Gaius shouted to his brother. "I made a promise and didn't keep it."

"Promise to bail water!" the praetorian grumbled.

"Neptune wants me." Gaius lunged for the side and managed to get one leg overboard before Marius intercepted him. "Throw me overboard if you want to save the ship! Offer me to Neptune and you'll be safe."

"It's worth a try." The praetorian considered the proposition. "We don't need the ballast."

"No sacrifices." Marius clutched his brother's tunic and pulled him back into the boat. "No one's going swimming."

"Let me go!" Gaius tried to twist away but could not escape his brother's grip. "I'm the reason for this storm."

"Throw him in," the praetorian shouted.

"Let me jump!" Gaius tried to wrench free from his brother's grip. "Neptune is angry that I broke my promise."

"What did you promise?"

"To build him a temple."

"But you're Jewish! Jews don't build pagan temples." Marius held tight as the boat crested another wave.

The debate gave the praetorian enough time to approach unnoticed. He tore Gaius away from his brother and dragged him toward the bow. "Feeding Neptune is worth a try."

"It's murder." Marius stumbled after them.

"That doesn't bother a murderer," Gaius said. He struggled to break free of the assassin's grip.

"You both should have paid your debts." The praetorian ignored Marius and lifted Gaius overhead like one might a crate of apples.

The boat rolled off a fresh swell and lurched forward with a spar-cracking thud that sent the praetorian stumbling. Gaius hit the deck just short of the bow and looked up just in time to see Marius brandishing their father's missing menorah. The holy artifact from the siege of Jerusalem blessed the praetorian just short of his skull.

"That's our menorah!" Gaius was both surprised to see his father's sacred relic and relieved at how well it worked when used as a blunt instrument.

"It's God's menorah. I'm just returning it."

"You mean stealing it. That's how you paid the boatman." The stunned praetorian rolled to one side, grabbed Marius by the foot, and pulled him down. "Give me that lamp!"

Marius tossed the menorah to his brother. Fists in motion, he let fly but was no match for the trained killer. Within a second, the praetorian had Marius in a headlock and was pressing his face into the flooded deck.

Gaius felt the weight of the menorah in one hand and his brother's life in the other. There was no doubt as to which was heavier.

"You want this?" Gaius dangled the menorah over the side of the boat. It suddenly struck him why the praetorian might have wanted the lamp. The silver was valuable, but the symbolism was priceless. "Let go of my brother or Neptune gets the lamp."

"Do it and I'll kill you both." The praetorian pushed Marius' face deeper into the water.

Gaius lowered the lamp over the edge. He kept his eyes on the praetorian, behind whom a fresh wave was building.

The assassin lunged.

Gaius tossed the lamp into the air. It spun upward, glistening in a slow arc away from the shifting boat.

The praetorian knocked Gaius aside and reached for the airborne lamp. He reached out over the water while trying to keep his feet inside the boat as a wall of water cracked the mast and sent the boat spinning.

Twenty
XX

The boat was lost and listing. An eerie calm had replaced the storm. The fisherman had been swept overboard. The praetorian had followed the menorah to the seafloor. Gaius and Marius were adrift and alone.

Huddled for warmth against his sleeping brother, Gaius contemplated the stars shining through the thinning clouds. Unless someone up there was watching out for them, this night would likely be their last. He fought the exhaustion pulling at his eyelids. Someone needed to keep watch, if only to witness the end.

He sensed motion at the other end of the boat. A shadow had joined them for the final journey.

"It's never as bad as it seems," a voice said.

Lena.

"Am I dreaming?" Gaius pinched his earlobe.

"You're always dreaming," she said.

Gaius had never doubted her magic, but this was hard to fathom. Had her spirit come to say farewell? Perhaps Charon had taken her form to guide the boat upriver.

He considered the possibility that they were both dead. She might have been so distraught about Vindex's drowning that she chose to join him. Whatever the explanation, she was here now and he was glad for it.

"I need some advice," Severus whispered. His words tasted like salt. "Do you know a good augur?"

"I'm not sure you can afford my services."

The starlight was just enough to see that she was smiling.

Severus resisted the urge to leap forward and embrace her, to tell her that he had been a fool and he would give anything to start anew. "I'm in love with this strange, wonderful girl but she doesn't love me."

Lena's gossamer hair caught the light breeze that had replaced the gale. "Maybe she can't love anyone. Maybe she's trying to protect you. I think she would want you to know that."

"I think she's running from something." He whispered so as not to wake his brother. "Sometimes she acts like phantoms are chasing her."

"And now you think she is a phantom."

Gaius did not want to risk saying anything that would scare her away. If there remained even the coldest spark between them, he would try not to douse it. He preferred spending his final hours with her, phantom or not. Still, he sensed that this might be his last opportunity to untangle her story.

"We met in the mountains, but I'm sure she's from somewhere else. She looks northern, unlike anyone I saw in the Pyrenees. Her Latin is nearly perfect—barely an accent, but I've also heard her speak another dialect. If I had to guess, I'd say she was from Britannia or maybe Germania."

Lena nodded in the darkness but did not respond.

"She's got—how should I put this?—unusual skills. She's smart and strong as a mountain lion. She can flatten a man twice her size. But she talks of magic and seems a bit clairvoyant. I wonder if she isn't some kind of rogue priestess."

"I'd like to meet her."

"So would I, but she hides behind secrets and won't let me in. I can understand not being in love with me—most girls aren't, but I can't understand not trusting a friend."

"Perhaps there's something she's trying to escape from." Lena flickered like a dying candle.

"Don't go." A tear rolled freely down his feverish cheek. "Is this the last time …"

"We'll meet again," she said, and vanished.

Gaius listened to the water lapping at the battered boat. The gentle rocking lulled him back to sleep until he was awakened by a change in the breeze. Daylight crawled across the pewter sky.

Lena had left no evidence of her visit.

"Strange," he said, noticing his brother stirring. "I saw Lena last night. We had a full conversation. Did you hear it?"

"It must have been a dream." Marius rubbed sleep from his eyes and twisted stiffness from his neck. "The other night I dreamt Mother was alive. She told me that the way to breathe underwater was to inhale through my nose and exhale through my mouth."

"Trust me, it doesn't work." Gaius tried in vain not to smile. Marius was the only family he had left, but even more true was that bad luck followed him like the tail of a wet dog. This excursion at sea had to be their final venture. If they survived, separate paths awaited.

The weak sunrise offered a cardinal direction and a ray of hope. A slight current nudged the wounded craft westward.

Gaius tried to see into the depths. Somewhere below them Neptune might be dining with Vindex with sinful crustaceans wallowing at their feet. The sea appeared so vast that Hispania and the empire to which it connected might as well be island. What could be more solitary than a small boat drifting on the infinite gray?

"We may not have much time left, so you might as well tell me the truth. After what you've put me through I think I've earned it."

"A stroke of bad luck is all."

"Bad luck is your middle name," Gaius said.

"Most of my bad luck lately has been thanks to you."

Gaius ignored the provocation.

"I suppose you blame me for losing your pagan girlfriend, too."

"You're a lodestone for trouble." Gaius did not want to provoke an outbreak, but Marius was in no position to do more than rock the boat. "You were within striking distance when my legion camp was attacked. You made me swear to kill Hadrian—not exactly a good career move. You were nearby on the night of the Saturnalia fire …"

"I saved your life that night!" Marius protested. "I pulled you from the flames."

Gaius weighed this against all the other misfortune that Marius had wrought, but could not make the scales balance. His brother's reappearance on Saturnalia, seconds before a calamitous blaze, could not have been a coincidence. It was the second incident in a month where Marius was within shouting distance of men being massacred. Men Marius considered enemies. A pang of conscience might have compelled Marius to pull his younger brother from the fire, but it would not be wise to count on a rebel's conscience.

"Were you going to ransom Festus Rufius or just slit his throat that night you hid him at the public baths?"

"Neither! He came in raving like a lunatic. Claimed he was being followed by mercenaries. I wasn't even sure who he was." Marius looked away. "At least I didn't sell my soul to Neptune."

"But you've sold it to someone." Gaius could tell his brother was getting angry but avoiding eye contact and the truth would not make it sting any less. He knew that once spoken, his accusations could not be retracted. Voices may die, but words live forever. So be it. When laid end to end, the evidence was impossible to deny: Marius was more than just an innocent menace. "What about your clever stunts, little riots and rock-throwing parties? Chaining your body to the gates of the villa, painting the town red with slogans. That homeless rampage you tried to provoke could have crushed more than just my bones."

"You shouldn't have nuzzled up to the occupation. Did I force you to join the Romans? You think you're on a ladder to the top, but they've got you sucking hind teat like a runt piglet. Can't you see? You're on an aqueduct to nowhere."

"I've done more good by cooperating with the so-called occupation than you have by fighting it."

"If you knew half the truth, you'd be twice as stupid."

"I'm all ears." Gaius was almost amused that Marius considered him such a sellout, an insider, nearly Roman. The truth was far less flattering. Neither fish nor fowl, he had left one tribe only to be rejected by another. "Suppose you tell me the truth about the menorah, the assassin, and that bogus boat ride to the land of milk and honey?"

Marius shrugged and stared across the water.

"Fine," Gaius said. "I'll tell you what I've figured out."

"I'm all ears."

"I think it starts at the top." The puzzle pieces were still rattling around in Gaius' mind, but thinking out loud helped him to see the bigger picture. "It starts with the emperor."

"Hadrian? All Hadrian cares about is money."

"Among other things." Gaius also found that talking took his mind off their current predicament. "The official story is that he came here to collect Hispania's overdue tribute, and visit his father's birthplace."

Marius lowered his voice as if keeping a secret from the eavesdropping walls. "But in addition to busting Governor Rufius' pudgy balls, you think he came in pursuit of knickknacks?"

"Hadrian is the High Priest of the Temple of Mithras," Gaius said. "He's obsessed with cult objects, strange rituals, and obscure religions. He's building a palace near Rome and plans to fill it with magical relics and curiosities from across the empire."

"Since you're privy to Hadrian's plans, did he explain why Father's menorah is part of his project? Did he mention the part about the Kingdom of God won't arrive until the menorah is returned to Jerusalem? Feel free to keep talking, but pardon me while I drift off to sleep." Marius made a point of snoring loudly for a moment, but then interrupted himself. "Why would Hadrian ransack the empire to fill the world's biggest villa with the world's largest junk collection? Do you really think someone clever enough to be an emperor would be so superstitious?"

"Hadrian may not be superstitious, but his guardsmen are," Gaius said. His thoughts had been churning, washing around randomly, but now he saw how the disparate threads wound together. "Remember how that drowned assassin shouted down any mention of gods other than Mithras?"

"Religious intolerance is not exactly a new phenomenon," Marius said as if lecturing a child. "Our family history is living proof."

"Exactly." Though lost at sea, Gaius felt suddenly rooted. As the picture came into focus, his head felt clear and free of pain. "We may live on shifting soil, but intolerance is in the bedrock."

"I would settle for a handful of shifting soil right now."

Gaius let the moment fade. Being lost at sea meant nothing was urgent. The bow caught an eddy and spun the boat around slowly until a stronger current moved them onward.

"I suspect that the Praetorian Guard is trying to eliminate any trace of faith they don't share. They're trying to restore Mithras before any more new religions take root. They especially fear the Christians."

"An interesting theory," Marius said. "But I don't see how it concerns me. Only your unbounded imagination could connect me to Hadrian's fool quest for relics. The notion that I might be caught up in anything of remote concern to the Divine Roman Emperor is beyond grandiose."

In truth, Gaius had not thought his argument through to a logical conclusion. The faint line leading from Marius to the emperor still had many segments missing. "You're right. I've probably overestimated your significance."

"I wouldn't go that far," Marius said. "I am trying to overthrow Hadrian. My protest movement is more of a threat than you give me credit for. Maybe that's why the praetorian was on the boat."

"Your protests blended in with all the other Saturnalia antics. Frankly, yours were tame in comparison."

"If you had left me in jail, we wouldn't be here now. This entire situation is your fault."

Gaius laughed though he knew Marius was serious. "So, now that I'm responsible for everything, suppose you tell me how you managed to recover our stolen menorah."

"Never underestimate the power of incompetence." Marius squinted toward the west. "There's no greater force in history."

Gaius could not argue the point so he changed direction. "Does incompetence explain why you abandoned our father somewhere north of nowhere?"

"You've got it backward. He abandoned us. He abandoned everything he ever taught us. He let himself be seduced by the enemy."

"How can love ever be the enemy? Don't you think he's entitled to some happiness after pain enough for two lifetimes? I don't care if he shacked up with some pagan widow. Who appointed you the judge? Are you so constipated with self-righteousness that you would abandon your own father?"

Silence descended like a mercy before the argument turned to blows. The boat drifted and turned, seemingly without direction. Gaius noticed his intense thirst and wondered how long it would take to die at sea. He drifted into a waking daze until the distant call of a bird jerked him back into consciousness. "Land!" he shouted as the gull approached. Soon the coastline near Tarraco came into view. "We're saved."

Marius leaned over the edge to splash water on his face. "Now you can have me arrested."

Gaius did not feel strong enough for a fresh argument, but there was little time left to ferret out the truth. Perhaps exhaustion would force Marius to lower his defenses. "I haven't figured out how you got your hands on Father's missing menorah, but I'm pretty sure that the praetorian was willing to kill for it. He wasn't on the boat by accident. I recognized him, but he didn't know me. The only logical explanation is that he was after you."

"Anything's possible."

"What's impossible is you having the money to buy back the lamp from whoever stole it. Even more impossible is you having the cash to book passage to Judea, or anywhere for that matter."

"You're rich, I'm poor. What of it?"

"I don't have a hobnail. Neither do you." Gaius gave Marius a moment to fill in the blanks. When no explanation came, he fit the rough pieces together in the only story that made sense. "You borrowed money from someone to buy back the menorah. Then you went to some other money lender and borrowed against the value of the lamp to book passage to Judea. You planned on skipping town with that cursed relic and never paying your debts."

"How could you possibly know that?"

"What you didn't plan on was that vexed praetorian following you. At first I thought he was after me, but he was after the menorah."

"He got it, didn't he? Honestly, I can't believe we're related. I'm going to put you up for adoption if I don't just kill you first."

Gaius ignored the comment and Marius continued the tirade. "I can't believe you tossed it into the ocean. That was our only link to the past. The sacking of Jerusalem. The destruction of the second temple. The defining moment in our people's history. The menorah could have restored us to our rightful place in history. I still have to go back."

"The menorah had no special power. Neither do you. How many generations need to pass before you stop dwelling in the past? The temple fell sixty years ago. Let it go."

"Our grandfather saw the temple burn."

"That doesn't mean you need to carry its weight on your back." Gaius saw that his argument was being blown off course. It was more important to understand the praetorian's presence and suicidal fervor for the lamp, but he could not let go of the argument. "I loved that menorah as much as you do. It was toss or be tossed."

"That menorah was our only hope to reclaim the land of milk and honey."

"*Vesuvius!* All my life I've heard Father talk about Judea, the bride of the desert, the paradise of fig and pomegranate where prophets rest under ancient cedars and God's presence is everywhere."

"It's true!"

"It's a dream. After so many generations of war and occupation, the milk and honey has run dry. Your promised land is probably nothing more than a dusty strip of scorched earth."

"You bite your tongue," Marius shouted. "You're nothing better than a damned Roman."

"Damned if I am, damned if I'm not."

A lone bird rose as if guarding the border between earth, wind, and sea.

A slight current eased the boat along until it washed up on a rocky beach where fishermen were mending frayed nets. A pair of men ran over to greet the vessel and dragged it ashore.

Gaius was so relieved to be on solid ground that he forgot his anger and exhaustion. The good-riddance speech he had intended to give his brother faded with each new breath. The logic had been simple: if misfortune was the only product of their union, better that they should part. But now that the parting moment had come, Gaius was tongue-tied. He simply could not disown his foolish, reckless brother. Marius was the only family he had. If brothers could not find common ground, there was little hope for humanity.

"What you said about Hadrian's interest in relics was true." Marius looked around to be sure the fishermen were not listening. "The praetorian angle makes sense as well."

"We can talk about it later. I need to get back to my post." Gaius started walking up the beach.

"Remember that dream you had about the four cats?"

"I'm so tired that you seem like a dream." Sensing that Marius was about to come clean, Gaius fought the rising tide of fatigue and tried to pay attention.

"You worked in a stone quarry." Marius' tone was somber as the dawn. "You dreamt of cats dancing on a stone altar. Coincidence?"

"Lena wouldn't think so." The thought of seeing her again filled Gaius with joyful dread. Would she celebrate him home or devastate him with indifference? She was probably more distraught over whatever happened to Vindex than the unlikely fate of two harebrained brothers.

"I think the four deadly cats are the four rogue praetorians who attacked your legionary camp."

"So … two cats died in the Mithras ceremony. The third was lost at sea."

"I can't be sure, but I think the fourth is the dodgy bastard I sold the menorah to."

"Sold? But you had the menorah on the boat."

"You were right." Marius' eyes tightened. He looked down at his feet for much longer than was needed to verify their ongoing attachment to his ankles. "I borrowed money from a questionable antique dealer to buy the menorah from one of the villa slaves. The little one called Carbo."

"Carbo's selling relics?" The surprise was short lived. "Good for him!"

"Your friend Lena is helping him."

"Of course." Lena was consistent in her own unpredictable way. She had resorted to crime in order to free slaves. In her mind, one crime justified another. "They're raising money to buy his freedom."

"Did you know he's a Christian?" Marius began to speak as if racing the sunrise. "The fellow I cut a deal with is a thug who calls himself Monobrow. He approached me in town and offered passage to Judea if I helped him."

"Short man with a boney nose?" Gaius had a sinking feeling that he had dealt with met this man once before. Half a cohort had survived, but for the others the man's terms had been most unfavorable. "Rough voice? Eastern accent?"

Marius nodded. "One thick eyebrow."

Gaius found it hard to breathe given the likelihood that his brother was caught in a deadly web with the remaining assassin, possibly the captain. "So you accepted his offer of passage to Judea and tried to abscond with the menorah."

"He wanted the menorah. I wanted to return it to Jerusalem," Marius said. All contrition had left his voice. "My destiny is to rebuild the temple. The menorah was going to usher in the Kingdom of God."

"Noble cause, I suppose. But then all your causes seem noble

141

until they splatter like a dozen dropped eggs."

"If you hadn't thrown the menorah overboard …"

"We'd be hanging by our fingernails from the hinges of Hades. You underestimated Monobrow. He anticipated your move and put a killer on board to counter it."

"That's why I can't return to Tarraco." Marius extended his hand.

A few minutes earlier, Gaius had wanted to be rid of his brother, but a drop of blood is still thicker than all the water that had flowed under the bridge. He took his brother's hand. "Where will you go?"

"North," Marius said. "I'll try to find Father."

The idea of finding their father warmed Gaius' tired spirit. Until this very second, Gaius had not allowed himself to admit how much he missed him. Perhaps someday they would all be together again.

Be careful in town," Marius said. "Monobrow knows who you are."

Twenty-one
XXI

Gaius Severus wandered up the coast until the arena came into view. Concerned that the restless undead *lemures* might still be awake, he turned into a fisherman's neighborhood and slipped back into Tarraco. Feeling too grimy to face daylight, he headed toward the plebian baths to wash and borrow a clean tunic. The pong of the voyage followed him like a cloud.

After being tossed and lost at sea, nothing sounded better than the prospect of soaking in a hot tub until his skin shriveled. A long bath might soothe his aches and bruises, but he knew there was no time to linger. Once clean, he would need to eat. He planned on returning to the governor's villa in search of scraps but given his absence and poor showing as a security chief, he might now be a *persona non grata*, or worse.

Of all his worries, the threat of Monobrow loomed largest. Would it be better to seek him out in the relative safety of sunlight or gather a gang of pirates to confront him under cover of darkness? Perhaps the remaining praetorian would accept monetary payment for the menorah that Marius had stolen. If so, where would Severus find the cash?

The fact that the menorah had once belonged to his family no longer mattered. He tried not to analyze the logic of raising cash to bail out his brother from having borrowed money to purchase the relic in order to barter with a thug for transit to a revolution against said thug's commanding officer and then absconding with the object in question. Like the minor detail that the menorah was currently on the sea floor, some things were best not examined too closely.

He entered the bath house where his brother once worked, the place where a pair of young Jewish fugitives and a fast-talking ex-governor had once found refuge in the ductwork. Severus undressed and stashed his torn tunic under a pile of used towels. He took little time to savor the warm bathwater and even less to dry off. He stole a tunic from the dressing room and headed toward the marketplace in search of an unguarded food cart. A handful of nuts would sustain him until he could sneak into the kitchen of the governor's mansion.

Perhaps he would find Lena in the spice cabinet and all would be as it was.

And then donkeys would dance.

Back on the street, Severus noticed that the town was flush with dogs. Dogs were everywhere: Roaming the alleys, sleeping under stoops, fighting over scraps barely worthy of the compost heap. Governor Kleptus had reckoned that turning dogs loose would suppress the burgeoning cat population. The call for canines must have been heard in the hinterlands, and now Tarraco had a dog problem far beyond the usual strays. Peasants must have come from miles around to dump their hungry, unwanted mutts, and once the dogs had tasted Tarraco they would never go back to the farm.

A bold splash of graffiti reminded Severus that the Trial of the Century was only days away. The usual verbiage promoting dentists, politicians, and similarly questionable services had been whitewashed over and replaced with Trial of the Century promotions. Every fresh advertisement inspired two scrawled insults that left Severus to wonder if his brother had passed by with a brush. Painting over the graffiti of slurs and lewd images would require a full-time crew.

He wondered if Rufius had resurfaced and shuddered to imagine the scene in the theater if the accused were to forfeit the stage. The cost of having lost the man he was supposed to have been guarding might be to lose the career that had already fizzled.

Severus entered the forum and grabbed a hard-boiled egg from an untended basket. Had it been an August morning, the plaza would have been teeming with people hurrying to avoid the onslaught of midday sun. Today, under December's stoic chill, the plaza was left to a few shivering vendors and a loose pack of stray dogs.

A few men gathered around the snack stands. A couple of old women exchanged gossip A few boys scurried underfoot, but the plaza was otherwise quiet. There were no girls to flirt with. Even the old storyteller who confused one tale with another had traveled south for the winter.

Dried apples, nuts, and sundries were sparse surrogates for spring kale or the plums of August. The colors and smells of the summer market had faded into the dull hues of winter. A scrawny chicken clucked as if longing to be eaten, but the butcher was cautious not to slaughter anything without the promise of a sale. Low prices on coarse fabrics attracted no interest.

Only the dogs looked happy. They slurped dirty water from potholes, marked columns, and growled at any vendor who questioned a canine's right to steal a fallen giblet. In the center of the plaza a large mutt coupled with a smaller one in full view of gods and mortals.

Gaius Severus stopped at an olive cart and tried to blend in while keeping a lookout for Monobrow. It struck him that transporting olives to Tarraco made as much sense as bringing milk to cows. There were olive groves for a hundred miles in each direction and no need to move the fruit more than a hundred paces to find an oil press.

"Nice olives," Severus said. He squeezed one as if inspecting it for firmness. "Where are they from?"

"Here and there." The big-boned man had an inland accent and a northern attitude.

Dust on the olives suggested they had been gathered off the ground long after the harvest. The vendor, too, had a dull sheen about him. He seemed to be an itinerant merchant, selling what others had let fall along the margins.

"A bit late in the season, no?"

"Bumper crop," the man muttered with no enthusiasm for selling his goods.

With a bit of food in his belly, Severus decided to head toward the governor's villa. Halfway across the plaza he heard a familiar voice squeaking nearby.

"Severus!" Winus Minem glided into view and brought the dim light of missed opportunities back into harsh focus. "Where have you been?"

"It's a long story, one disaster after another." As if in confirmation, Severus saw a man who could only be Monobrow emerge from the colonnades. The crook-nosed praetorian looked around for a moment and then glared directly at Severus. The single dark eyebrow made his menace complete.

"Disaster is just another way to say opportunity," Minem insisted.

"In that case, I'm surrounded by opportunity," Severus said, but the opposite was true. He appeared to be surrounded by threats as Monobrow seemed to have multiplied. Instead of one assassin, there

145

were many. For a second, every man, woman, and statue bore his rutted face and distinct brow. By the time Severus blinked his eyes, the forum had returned to normal and the real Monobrow was gone. He swept a flash of fever from his brow.

Was this how death signaled its arrival?

"We've got work to do, kid," Minem said. He pulled a notepad from his sleeve and added a few scribbles in the wax. "I've compiled a list of things I need you to do."

"The town is crawling with assassins," Severus said.

"Second oldest profession." From the beads of sweat forming along the perimeter of Minem's bald spot, it was clear that the little man's mind was racing.

Severus tried to focus, but his heart beat louder than whatever Minem was saying.

"… I also need you to deliver this bottle of wine." Minem's voice cracked with sudden nervousness that appeared to be due to the approach of a large dog rather than the possibility of nearby murderers.

A short-haired Gaulish hound bounded toward Severus. It was the sort of dog once favored by sportsmen and rich idlers. The gray dog leapt forward and parked its paws against Severus' chest. Next to Minem, the hound appeared as large as a horse. Severus pushed the beast away but this only encouraged more playful interest. An eventual compromise was reached when Severus agreed to let the dog nuzzle him immodestly. "You haven't heard tell of any rogue praetorians?"

"Rogues? They're all rogues!" Cleary uncomfortable around canines, Minem took a step back and kept a watchful eye on the hound. "If you don't like rogues, I won't send you to Rome."

"Rome?" Severus perked up. "The sooner the better!"

"Rome: where the gods go for recreation," Minem said, as he turned to leave. "I'll put in a good word for you once you deliver the bottle and complete your errands."

Severus scratched the hound behind its limp ears. He imagined for a moment that they were hunting for stag in a northern forest before he remembered that an assassin might be hunting for him. "What are we going to do with you once the cats are gone?"

The hound ran off as if concerned by the question.

"Sorry. I thought all dogs liked a good scratch behind the ears,"

Severus said. He watched the dog bound away just as Monobrow came into view again. Severus blinked to be certain this was no illusion. As disturbing as his visions were, a waking dream would have been preferable to the fact that a small man in a brown tunic was indeed approaching with his one brow furled. Rather than run, Severus stood his ground, clutching the bottle to keep one hand from shaking.

"Is there something I can help you with, sir?"

"You can kill yourself so I don't have to."

"Hah! Love that Roman humor. So dark, so—"

In less than the blink of an eye, Monobrow grabbed Severus by the tunic and twisted the loose fabric into a knot. The bottle fell but did not break.

"I have no dispute with you," Gaius said.

"I have a dispute with your entire family."

Gaius knew to be careful with what he revealed. It was not clear how much the praetorian captain knew. "I don't have what you're looking for."

"Your brother has it."

Sins of the brothers. "One thing is certain: I clearly have no control or influence over my brother."

"There's no such thing as an innocent bystander. Not when my men are dying." Monobrow shoved Severus backward but remained in his shadow.

"If you'll let go of my tunic, I'm sure we can arrive at a mutually beneficial solution. Besides, it sets a bad example to manhandle the security chief of Tarraco."

"I outrank you on so many fronts it would take all day to list them."

It occurred to Severus that Monobrow might still be ignorant as to recent events. It was too soon to know that the menorah, and the thug he had sent to fetch it, were at the bottom of the Mediterranean. He likely had no idea that the boat had washed ashore or that Severus had been on it. Knowledge was power, but in this case ignorance might be stronger. Before Severus could think of what to say next, Winus Minem reappeared with spring in his step and pluck in his voice.

"Severus! I forgot to give you the tablet."

Monobrow was gone as quickly as he had appeared. The small

praetorian was stronger and faster than he looked. Severus straightened the twisted fabric on the front of his tunic.

"Did you see him?" Severus spun in both directions, but the assassin had vanished into the sparse crowd. "Did you notice someone talking with me just now?"

Minem appeared oblivious to the question. He shoved the tablet into Severus' hand. "All my instructions are written down. Report back once you've finished. Off with you now, vital work to do!"

Severus was just exiting the plaza when the gray dog returned. It was slightly larger than a jackal, though his snout was less angular and his ears more inclined to flop.

"You're like me." Severus gave the dog a playful smack on the rump. "Not sure about your next meal, quick to fall in love with whoever doesn't kick you. I'll call you Nolo if you don't mind."

Nolo seemed pleased with the name. He tagged along until Severus reached the *Via Sacra*, the street that led to the temple of Augustus and Apollo. Perhaps sensing greater acceptance in the plebeian slums, the dog let Severus continue on alone.

The *Via Sacra* was lined with expensive shops, the likes of which Severus had never entered. Only the wealthy could afford the imported fabrics, fine jewelry, and exotic perfumes the street had to offer. One shop was mobbed by slaves jostling to acquire the latest bobble from Rome for their masters. A few looked like they had been waiting since midnight. All were better dressed than Severus had ever been. The tunic he had borrowed from the plebeian baths was barely fit to polish floors in the homes where these slaves served.

Minem's tablet bore a scrawled list of prominent shopkeepers he hoped would provide moral support for Festus Rufius during the trial. If allies turned out to be in short supply, Gaius Severus was still expected to ferret out new evidence to muddy what was expected to be Plotina's clear case for the prosecution.

Severus looked dirt common and cash poor, so most shopkeepers refused to speak to him. Some even refused him entrance to their shops. The few purveyors of imported wine, spices, and fine victuals who did agree to talk were condescending, resentful, and inclined to complain.

Tarraco's upscale merchants believed that government existed only to suck them dry. They especially hated the city inspectors and tax collectors. Many complained about the unreliable street cleaners and garbage collectors who they claimed enjoyed more holidays than the gods. The few merchants who understood that the provincial government was teetering on the brink of default were all too eager to push it off a cliff.

"Having a governor is worse than having a jealous mistress," said a silk shop owner with evident authority. "But at least a mistress is good for something. Government is just legalized robbery."

"But your taxes contribute to roads and bridges."

"What do I want with roads and bridges?"

"How about aqueducts and trash collection?"

"How about getting out of my shop?"

Severus found that nothing was sacred on the *Via Sacra*. The lack of civic-mindedness was universal. If there had ever been a droplet of affection for Festus Rufius, it had evaporated within days of his arrival.

"Help Rufius? I'd rather set fire to my rectum!" said a spice merchant who had the means to do both.

Severus proceeded down the broad avenue, checking shops off the list and watching for evidence of Monobrow. After a few more rejections, he decided to deliver the wine and not bother with the remaining establishments. Minem wanted him to find allies and seed rumors that might undermine Plotina's case, but it was clear that no creditor would support Rufius unless his debts were reimbursed sevenfold.

Severus resisted feeling shame at being part of an institution that was so roundly distrusted. In spite of the obvious benefits—roads, aqueducts, and the *Pax Romana*—these successful merchants insisted that government was the enemy.

Severus was wary about entering the apothecary shop. His father had always regarded the herbalist in the same light as physicians, soothsayers, and other charlatans. The rotund little potion maker also moonlighted as an undertaker, a clear conflict of interest. He was rumored to have killed as many people as he had cured.

Severus intended to deliver the gift and leave quickly. The bottle of imported wine was intended as a fresh down payment on the invisible mountain of unpaid debt.

Shrill chimes tinkled upon his entering the shop, but the red-faced proprietor did not look away from the broad matron commanding his attention. Severus avoided eviction by standing in the woman's shadow. His eyes wandered across the ceramic jugs lining the walls and along the counter to where the matron's gaunt daughter was watching him.

Her wink made Severus lurch like a startled colt. The girl, roughly Severus' age, offered a thin-lipped smile that revealed a collection of yellow teeth that cast about in all directions. She pointed at the bottle and made a drinking gesture with her thumb. Getting no reaction, she waved a handful of boney fingers and winked.

"She's too skinny," her mother insisted. The matron sighed and pulled a too-small wrap tightly around her fleshy shoulders. "No man in his right mind will marry my daughter again. We need to fatten her up."

"I have just the thing." The shopkeeper stepped out from behind his counter and eyed Severus with an air of disapproval.

Severus smiled and held up the wine bottle. "A gift," he whispered.

"This had better work," the woman insisted. "Your last mixture made her thinner."

The small proprietor slid a stepladder over to the far wall and established a tenuous perch on the first rung. He clutched a lower shelf and balanced his bulk before conquering the next step. The air fell still except for the pharmacist's wheezing. Like most practitioners of the Hippocratic arts, the man was woefully unfit to exercise much more than his jaw muscles. Climbing the groaning ladder took an Olympian effort; the top step was a precarious summit.

Severus blocked the door lest a burst of air send the shopkeeper plummeting. Distracted by the man's strained ascent, he had not noticed the skinny girl approaching.

"My name's Egnatia," she whispered into his ear. Her thin voice whistled through her narrow nostrils. "Who's the bottle for?"

Hoping to restore a comfortable distance, Severus stepped back and accidentally bumped into the entry bell just as the shopkeeper reached for a high jar. Startled by the ringing, he teetered and the ladder moaned. Severus dashed across the shop just in time to wedge a shoulder beneath the man's ample bottom.

"Bravo," Egnatia cried. She clapped her hands like bundles of sticks.

Severus was stuck bracing the heavy fellow who could not balance or descend. The strain of supporting the man's weight would have been too much if Egnatia had not intervened with surprising strength. They negotiated the shopkeeper back to his feet and finished nose to nose, too close even by Mediterranean standards.

"Do you believe in love at first sight?" She batted her eyelashes, revealing that one of her eyes was brown and the other dusty blue. Uncooperative curls tumbled from a head that was too large for her transparent, blue-veined neck. She seemed to have been assembled from bits and pieces of defeated tribes from across the empire.

"Allow me, sir." Severus maneuvered away from Egnatia and handed him the wine bottle. "I'm tall enough to reach the top shelf."

"Tall indeed." The apothecary looked at the bottle with approval and Severus with disdain. "Your mother must have used my willow root and boar blood poultice. There's no better way to assure a tall child."

Severus pushed the stepladder aside and grabbed a container from the top shelf. The jars were numbered but not otherwise labeled, presumably to protect trade secrets from the worse shops and quack physicians. It occurred to him that the hundred odd pots might all contain the same substance. Before handing the vessel to the shopkeeper, he opened the lid to sniff at the contents and immediately regretted his curiosity. Scrapings from a pig sty would have smelled better.

The pharmacist had already opened the wine bottle and poured himself a glass. Offering none to his guests, he grabbed the herb jar and padded over to his work table. He measured a few spoons of carbonaceous flakes into a small container. "If you mix this with pig fat and pound it with an iron-free pestle, she'll be plump and pleasing in no time."

"Or dead." The matron took the powder, clucked her disapproval, and swept her swooning daughter out the door.

The girl's thin arm lingered, waving from the doorway until her mother yanked the rest of her away.

"That's a real problem," the shopkeeper muttered between gulps of wine. "I can cure thin, but there's no fix for ugly."

"The wine is a gift from the governor," Severus improvised. "A rare bottle from his personal collection offered in friendship."

151

"Friendship I probably paid for ten times in taxes."

"Falernian, I believe. Good wine, I'm told. No need to dilute it."

"I never dilute anything." The shopkeeper filled another glass and unloaded a lung full of complaints. Like every other business in town, his shop was a favorite target for government officials demanding favors and bribes to overlook invented irregularities and obscure violations.

"The governor owes me a small fortune." The fuming apothecary fumbled around in a drawer and pulled out a scroll covered with notes and numbers. "I've kept detailed records and can prove every claim. Normally, I maintain strict confidentiality about my clients and their peculiarities but, seeing as though justice is at stake, I might be convinced to reveal something interesting if promised immunity from your greedy inspectors."

Severus wondered if the man's story was any more trustworthy than his powders. Selling aphrodisiacs to cheating husbands might render the apothecary privy to the town's secrets, but it did not make him a credible witness. More than likely, the fellow was just trying to negotiate a tax holiday in exchange for divulging a baseless rumor.

The door chimes rang just as Severus was about to ask if there existed a cure for one-sided love. A well-appointed slave slipped into the shop to see if his master's gout balm was ready. Severus remembered what Carbo had said and lingered by the door until the transaction was complete. "I forgot to ask you something."

"You're still here?" The pharmacist looked up from the wine glass he had just drained.

"Why would someone need dogroot?"

"Useful against mildew," the apothecary muttered without hesitation.

Severus watched for even the slightest reaction but there was none. If the pharmacist was a co-conspirator in the death of Biberious, he hid it well. "I'm told it can make your lips turn green."

"Don't know about that, but it turns blue in milk."

Severus left the shop, satisfied that there was no flaming arrow to be found. If, as Carbo had insisted, former Governor Biberious had died from dogroot, it only mattered who administered, not who sold it. So far, the governor's murder was a perfect crime.

Severus had last visited the *Via Sacra* six weeks prior on the day of Governor Biberious' funeral procession. He had abandoned his legion post and gone in search of his recently arrested brother and father. Instead, he saw the ex-governor's body lying stiff on an open bier. Makeup had obscured the possibility of green lips. Either way, the man's widow had not appeared particularly distraught, and the paid tears of professional mourners evoked no sorrow as the parade inched along the great avenue.

Back then, Severus had been nothing more than a scrawny fugitive. He had never seen death and never known love. He had now experienced both but felt none the wiser.

He continued along the posh avenue, lost in thought, weaving between the shoppers and dandies who came to spend and be seen along Tarraco's finest avenue. Severus felt alone in the crowd, a stranger in his own hometown. Even Nolo had disappeared.

Weren't dogs supposed to be loyal?

Severus opened Minem's small tablet and rubbed the remaining shop names from the wax. He wondered why Minem had bothered to send him on this mission given the predictable results. Hatred toward governors past, present, and future was universal. Based on the hostility encountered so far, there was no point in continuing.

He angled the tablet's two leaves into the light to see if they concealed any erased secrets, but there was no way to tell what might once have been scratched into the wax. Severus warmed his thumb against his fingers and rubbed both writing surfaces until they were soft and bare. The smooth olive-wood case balanced lightly in his palm. His finger fit perfectly through the leather hinge loops. The stylus rested firmly in the slotted cover. The tablet's simple elegance was almost unbearable.

The disorderly queue he had seen earlier was gone. Where slaves had spent the night to reserve a place in line, a few of their masters remained to brag about their latest acquisitions.

A short young man in a finely stitched tunic pointed at Severus' wooden tablet. "Still using the old model?" He gestured toward the people lingering by a nearby shop and lowered his voice. "I've got a trade-in deal if you want to upgrade to the S-IV."

"The what?"

"The new and improved fourth edition slate. It's the latest, straight from Rome." The young man flashed an inauthentic smile. He was barely older than Gaius but seemed to come from a different world. "Once you try the S-IV you'll never turn back. Writing on your old tablet will seem like chiseling stone."

"No thanks," Gaius said. "I like my old tablet and really must be going."

"Not until you try this." The fellow pulled a polished brass object out of his pouch and shoved it into Severus' hand.

"Where's the wax?"

"None needed!"

The S-IV appeared to be nothing more than a brass plate with rounded edges. It was heavier and larger and, unlike Minem's wooden tablet, required two hands to balance.

"Where's the stylus?"

"Obsolete!" The salesman pulled a piece of cut papyrus from his tote bag and clipped the page to the top edge of the slate. He then produced a writing instrument and a small ink pot. "Try this little wonder."

Gaius dipped the pen in ink and traced a few squiggles on the page. "Nice," he said. "But I ..."

"Of course you can afford it!" The salesman reached up and gripped Gaius by the shoulder. "Admit it: Writing on this tablet is an erotic experience."

"Have you ever had an erotic experience?" Gaius tried to hand the device back, but the salesmen refused to take it.

"Face it: Your current device is one misery after another. I know you're probably wondering how you've tolerated that clunky old wooden tablet for so long. You know that terrible feeling when you press too hard and your stylus scratches through the wax? Gone!"

"That really wasn't a problem."

"Gone, gone, gone are the write, melt, and replace cycles. The S-IV works equally well in bright sunlight as it does in the dark. Trust me, friend, with the S-IV you'll be the envy of your friends and I'm prepared to offer you quite a deal if you act now."

"No thanks. This metal slate weighs a ton and it's too big for my pocket." Gaius tried to shove the device back into the salesman's hands. "I prefer my old tablet."

"Old indeed! That tablet, like the tree it came from, belongs in the dirt. Each wasteful wooden tablet represents another tree that will never bear fruit or provide shade to our children. Metal is a much more socially responsible material."

"You wouldn't say that if I hit you over the head with it! Now take your S-whatever back and let me pass."

"I appreciate your passion. In this age of rampant indifference it's good to meet someone who actually cares."

"All I actually care about is ending this conversation." Having heard enough, and unable to return the S-IV to the insistent salesman, Gaius turned and began walking away with it.

"Here's something you haven't considered: In the time it takes for some old, half-blind craftsman to make a wooden tablet, my modern facility can produce twenty identical units!"

"And putting some old tablet maker out of work is a good thing?"

"Progress, my friend. We can't stand in the way of progress."

"But I can stand in your way." Severus wanted to arrest the salesman, but hucksterism was not against the law. Stealing a hardboiled egg was illegal, but claiming a false article was the greatest thing since the bread oven was how half the empire did business.

"We sell tablet covers in five unique colors so you can truly express yourself! Imperial Red. Forest Green. Aqua—"

"Not interested."

"We also sell papyrus refill kits, tote bags, and ink pots."

"Not interested." Gaius put the slate on the ground. "My old wooden tablet suits me fine. Now, if you'll excuse me—"

"Honestly, I'm a bit disappointed. I expected a young fellow like you would lean more toward the future. Everyone in Rome is using the S-IV, but I guess you're just not interested in progress." The salesmen followed Severus and tugged at his sash.

Severus whirled around, grabbed the short fellow by the tunic and lifted him into the air. "I have a wooden tablet and I'm happy. It fits in one hand and it's as lightweight as you are. Maybe I replace the wax from time to time, but that costs next to nothing. You hear me? Next to nothing!"

"Yes ... but ..."

"But according to you, 'progress' means I buy your shiny object and forever feed it expensive sheets of papyrus and bottomless containers of ink. My old tablet is always ready to write. What if your nasty slate runs out of papyrus in the middle of the night?"

"Who writes in the middle of the night?" The salesmen's feet dangled and few inches above the cobblestone. "Anyway, I'd expect a smart fellow like you would plan ahead."

Severus drew the man upward and inward until they were face to face. "S-IV? Was there ever an S-III or an S-II or did you just make this whole thing up? The latest from Rome? I'll travel to Rome someday. Nobody will have one of your stupid slates."

Severus put the salesmen down with intentional force. He fought the desire to thrash the young huckster, beat him in retribution for every small-time con man that ever slunk around in sandals.

"If you don't want one, just say so." The salesmen picked his slate off the ground and ran back to the shop he had sprung from.

Twenty-two
XXII

Remembering that Monobrow was at large and dangerous, Gaius Severus decided to see if he could rally a few of Plotina's pirates to help capture the little thug. As he snuck along the western edge of the forum, he heard a ruckus rising from the other side. Women were shouting in the distance, and Lena's angry voice rose above the din. A dustup sounded imminent.

A crowd was gathering, drawn in by the possibility that a catfight would liven up the otherwise drab day. Severus ran across the plaza expecting to find Plotina's pirates in the thick of a brawl, but none was present. He took advantage of the confusion to grab a piece of charred meat from a smoking brazier as he ran by.

He swallowed the morsel without chewing.

"I can practice where I please!" Lena was shouting.

"Not in the forum." An insistent older woman produced a fist from under her robe and shook it. "This is our territory."

Severus understood immediately that Lena was making large waves in the wrong small pond. Augury was not unlike other trades, and Lena's sudden popularity had threatened the soothsayers who normally haunted the city center. The forum belonged to the Goddess Guild, a loose group of crones who worked the talisman and spirit circuit around the plaza. A few, like the old oracle almost lost in a flowing dress, were legitimate priestesses. The others had no such credibility, but they paid their dues to the organization for the right to sell solace and predictions.

Severus wove through the eager spectators and pulled Lena away from the priestess she was about to strangle. A fight would have been no contest, but defeating the town's most influential sage would be a pyrrhic victory.

"What are you doing?" It took Lena a second to acknowledge that he had returned to Tarraco but she was too full of vinegar to welcome him home. "I thought you were sailing into the sunrise."

"I'll explain later." He tugged at her elbow and tried to pierce her with an insistent glare. "Please come with me."

"I'm not going anywhere." Lena dug in her heels. "This is a public plaza. I have a right to be here."

"Maybe, but this is a bad time and the wrong place to practice your augury," Gaius insisted. He nodded his head and rolled his eyes toward the hostile guild members "Can't you see they are ready to pounce?"

"These old witches?" Lena spoke loud enough to be heard by the indignant gaggle. She slammed her fists into her thighs. "They don't scare me."

"Of course not," Severus said. "But you'll win a battle and lose the war if you challenge them like this. I promise I know a better way."

"They called me worthless." She spat out the word as if it were coated in sour milk.

"You're worth more than the lot of them." Severus tried to take her hand, but her fist remained clenched.

"I've been called worthless my whole life." The rage in Lena's eyes faded just enough to bring the broader scene into teary-eyed focus. These were not the attentive truth seekers from the docklands; this poor mob was more interested in violence than prophecy.

Lena shrugged and ceded the territory. The head priestess scowled and her associates jeered. The crowd first complained loudly at seeing the tension diffused and then dispersed in frustration. Calm returned to the cold marketplace.

"There are still a few things about Tarraco you don't understand, and the Goddess Guild is one of them." Severus caught up and walked beside her, trying to assemble the pieces of who Lena really was. She was very smart, very strong, very pretty, and thoroughly unimpressed with civilization. She had a gift for prophecy, but her true story still lay shrouded. "Right or wrong, the forum is their turf. They're like the carpenters or the tanners. You can't ply their craft without giving them a cut."

"But they're phonies," Lena said. "Complete frauds."

"The Romans have a god for phonies."

"I don't believe in him."

"There's even a god for nonbelievers. He rewards his followers for not bothering him."

"Are you mocking me?" Lena glanced back at the forum. "Do you think I'm no better than they are?"

"They were here before you." Severus swept an arm across the architecture. "This is their storefront. They've got a lock on the goddess business—"

"The goddess business? You think it's all quackery?"

"No," Severus said. "At least, you seem like the real thing."

"Seem like?"

"Don't take it the wrong way. It obviously works on some—"

"What are you trying to say?"

"It's just that ..." Severus tried to reverse the direction of the hole his tongue was digging." If you're so good at predicting things, why didn't you foresee the last few disasters that hit me?"

"So it's about you?"

"I nearly died three times since I saw you last. Why didn't you give me a hint if you saw any of this coming?"

"Because I can't see into your future. Some people are cloudier than others. With others, I can sense the next moment before it arrives. It's as if time tilts me forward, slightly ahead of them. It doesn't work with you."

"Maybe I should be thankful."

"If I could see your future, you probably wouldn't listen. If I told you a stone was about to land on your head right now, would you believe me?"

Severus made a point of scanning the sky for incoming meteors. "I don't believe in magic, but I believe you have a gift. You were doing fine at the docks, why not practice there and leave the forum to the crones?"

"Because," Lena exhaled with frustration, "life is short and I need cash to free as many slaves as I can." Lena shook her head as if there were no point in trying to explain.

"Is that why you and Carbo sold a lamp to my brother?"

Lena blushed. "We gave him a good deal."

"But it already belonged to him! Did you know what he planned to do with that lamp—who he got the money from?"

"You're not going to arrest me, are you? "

Severus was happy to see that she had calmed down about the Goddess Guild. Sensing her evasion, he saw no point in antagonizing her about the menorah. "Carbo will be in huge trouble if he gets caught. Isn't there a safer way to buy his freedom?"

Lena shook her head. "Prophecy doesn't pay."

"Neither does crime."

"Silly." Lena laughed. "Of course it does."

"In that case, Rufius will be found innocent." Severus pointed to some Trial of the Century graffiti painted around a column. "He'll probably walk away without a scratch."

"Maybe he's not the real criminal." Lena almost lost her balance when a wide matron barreled past her. "The real criminals are on this street, spending their unearned money on nonsense like silk and perfume. What they waste in a day could feed the homeless for a month."

"Probably right." Severus pointed to the apothecary shop. "The bottle of wine I just delivered to the apothecary was probably worth a fortune."

"I'll bet your apothecary doesn't even know what half his herbs are good for." Lena looked back toward the shop. "I know more than he does. Too bad women can't work as pharmacists."

"I'll add that to my list of wrongs to right," Severus said.

"Does he sell dogroot?"

"Funny that you mention dogroot." Severus tried not to sound suspicious.

"I know that Carbo has confided in you. For what it's worth, I believe him."

"I don't disbelieve him," Severus whispered, "but a slave's accusation isn't enough to tip the scale."

"Do you know where dogroot comes from?"

"Dogs? Roots? Dogwood trees?"

"Idiot!" Lena smacked Severus on the shoulder. "It comes from Macedonia just like your little boss."

Severus looked around nervously. "We shouldn't discuss this in public. Have you ever seen the aqueduct? I feel like taking a walk and it's not far."

"Not today, lightning boy. I have to pick up a few supplies and get back to the ship. Plotina's preparing for the trial."

"Lightning boy?"

"That's what Zinzin calls you."

Severus was struck with a renewed sense of just how romantically finished things were between them. He fought back a rising river of loneliness lest it drown him on the spot. Losing Marius was tolerable. Losing Lena felt like all the light had been sucked out of the world. With no friends, no family, and no Lena he was navigating without a star, drifting on a dark sea of failures.

Lena was his most glorious failure to date. Not only did she not love him, but she had now turned to crime. Freeing slaves was a noble cause, so was freeing Judea, but neither warranted lawlessness unless the law applied only to those without a noble cause.

It took a moment before he noticed the large hound nuzzling his limp hand.

"Who's that?" Lena asked.

"Nolo. My new best friend."

Lena knelt and held the dog's head between her hands. The dog licked her face and then crouched onto his front paws and shook his head as if daring her to play. Lena stopped abruptly and turned around.

"Isn't that your little sidekick?"

Limbo was running toward them shouting, "Murder! There's been a murder!"

Twenty-three
XXIII

A crowd had gathered at the far end of the avenue, in front of the apothecary shop. One of the criers was shouting something about a corpse. The other had already left to spread fresh rumors.

"He's dead?" Gaius Severus followed Limbo through the crowd.

"Expired. Joined the majority." Limbo now appeared resentful that a dead man had torn him from more lively pursuits. "Should I round up your brother and the usual suspects?"

Severus and Lena entered the shop to examine the crime scene but found little to see beyond the simple story told by the broken goblet on the floor. Minem's wine bottle was half empty.

"Green lips," Severus noticed after a quick glance at the former apothecary. "Dogroot, no doubt."

"Just like Governor Biberious." Lena looked around the shop for other evidence.

"Can I leave now?" Limbo peered in from the doorway.

Severus ordered him to disperse the crowd. Happy to apply one of his few talents, Limbo slammed the door and started yelling at people to leave.

"Seems your wine was poisoned," Lena said.

"One more death and the day's only half over," Severus muttered. He steadied himself against the counter to hide his shaking knees. The praetorian's death at sea had been an act of self-defense, but the wine-stained shop tiles told a different story. This was murder. The knot in his stomach had a new neighbor. "The wine was a gift from Winus Minem."

"Seems that your job was to cover his little tracks."

"And take the fall." Severus gathered the broken shards into a towel he found behind the counter. He removed a small scroll from the drawer behind the counter and gave it to Lena along with the wine bottle. "If you're right, we'd better hurry. Can you fetch Plotina and get this evidence to the magistrate? I'll meet you at the courthouse."

"What about the dead man?"

"He's not going anywhere." Peering into the wine bottle, Gaius recalled something the apothecary had said. "One more thing: Bring some milk."

He silenced the door chimes as Lena slipped away. A moment later, Winus Minem's voice pierced the air, shrill as breaking glass.

"Arrest him," Minem shouted. He pointed at Severus.

"But he's my boss," Limbo said with reluctance born more of sloth than loyalty.

"Not anymore." The low ceiling made Minem looked taller than usual. "Gaius Severus is accused with the murder of our town's beloved apothecary."

Severus did not fight the accusation or the rope that Limbo used to bind his wrists. "A little less enthusiasm would be appreciated, Limbo."

"We've caught the killer," Minem announced as he shoved Severus outside.

"Is it true the apothecary was killed by one of his own aphrodisiacs?" the remaining town crier asked.

"Shut up," Limbo said.

"That means yes!" The crier ran off to spread the rumor across Tarraco. "Apothecary killed by his own potion!"

"Tarraco can rest easier now that the killer has been apprehended." Minem led a procession toward the courthouse.

Severus knew that creating a spectacle would just add heat to the pot he had landed in. He understood how Vindex must have felt when falsely blamed for the death of Governor Biberious. Now that Vindex was gone, Minem needed a new scapegoat. If Minem was behind both killings—and who else could it have been?—he had been clever enough to assure that all evidence pointed elsewhere.

A swirl of blue fabric swept into the courthouse shortly after Severus arrived. Plotina had let her hem down.

"I had no idea the wine was poison," Severus whispered.

Plotina seemed to float in a sea of folds and rippling creases the color of water. "Can you prove your ignorance?"

"I prove it every day, *domina*."

The bailiff finished his sweet roll and quieted the courtroom before the sullen magistrate could express more than his usual impatience to be somewhere else.

"What do we have here—criminals accusing each other?" Judge Soranus glared at Minem and Plotina with evident displeasure. "The Trial of the Century is tomorrow, but you couldn't wait to get started?"

"I'm here to accuse *Minus* Minem of two murders," Plotina said.

"Never fear, Minem. I'm here to defend you." Don Rexus made a dramatic entrance and shook a few hands as he sailed up the aisle. His perfectly draped toga left no threads to chance.

"Have you two been drinking henbane?" Minem asked and then muttered something in his native tongue that needed no translation. "I'm here to accuse young what's-his-name of the same two murders."

"That makes four murders," the bailiff offered before intercepting the magistrate's glare. "Perhaps I should order in some food."

"Winus Minem was in the villa the night of the murder," Plotina said. "He dined with Governor Biberious and spiked his wine with poison."

"This is absurd," Minem protested. "Why rehash an old murder when a fresh corpse demands justice?"

People had profited from the bailiff's distraction to fill the room beyond capacity. The unsolved murder of the unloved Governor Biberious had been a source of gossip for weeks, and the fresh allegations were titillating enough to inspire fresh interest in the old case.

"You dined with the governor that night," Plotina said. "He retired early, complaining of heartburn and palpitations, did he not?"

"I don't remember!" Minem insisted. "What if he did? How is this relevant to the dead apothecary?"

"So you admit you were there!"

"Judge, will you please reassert control over your courtroom? I am not the accused here."

"Actually, you are." Don Rexus put his arm around Minem and drew the little adviser close. "Don't worry, bear cub. You've been so good to me. This is the least I can do."

"I wish you'd do less."

"Dogroot," Plotina continued, "is well known in Macedonia, where Winus Minem comes from. It's an excellent remedy against mold. Did you not instruct the villa's staff to use dogroot for cleaning?"

"Seriously?" Minem pointed at Severus and turned to the crowd. "We're talking about cleaning supplies while this young killer laughs behind our backs."

"Answer the question," the judge insisted.

"Those barbarians were using diluted urine to clean the governor's kitchen and you have the nerve to accuse *my* client?" Rexus said. He winked at Minem and whispered, "This is my dress rehearsal for the Trial of the Century."

"Dogroot is not illegal," Minem said. He tried to distance himself from the actor, but Rexus clung like a shadow. "Since the judge appears to be interested, I'll point out that dogroot is available from Tarraco's finest apothecary."

"Interestingly enough, dogroot was available in Tarraco because Winus Minem imported it. He consigned a considerable quantity of this practical herb to the chemist a week before the murder." Plotina produced the apothecary's scroll and handed it to the judge. I have the documentation right here."

"Commerce was legal in Hispania the last time I checked," Rexus insisted.

Minem tried to push past Rexus. "It seems impossible, but you're worse at law than you are at theater."

"Commerce is legal, murder is not," Plotina continued. "Dogroot's a great bane against mold when dissolved with water, and it's a deadly poison when mixed with wine."

"That's as irrelevant as an Etruscan horse," Minem insisted. "Everyone knows that the governor was stabbed. Stabbed by Vindex."

"So your story is that Biberious was stabbed by Vindex and killed by Severus?" Rexus expressed confusion. "I need a minute to help my client get his alibi straight."

"Severus was nowhere near the governor's villa that night." Plotina spoke over the arguing men. "The fact is that Vindex was discovered bound and unconscious, incapacitated by the tainted wine you gave him. Once Vindex was out of the way, it was easy for Minem to stab the already dead governor and place the weapon in Vindex's hand."

"This is insane!" Minem shouted. "Why didn't this imaginary tainted wine kill Vindex?"

"He probably needed a bigger dose," Rexus said. "Vindex was bigger than Hercules."

"Hercules was a hero. Vindex was a killer," Minem insisted.

"He knifed the governor right through the heart."

Plotina smiled and waited for the bailiff to silence the murmuring crowd. "Would you say that Vindex knows how to kill a man?"

"Of course." Minem shrugged like a seagull. "He was a gladiator. Murder was his profession."

"Do you think he knew how to use a dagger?"

"His specialty!" Minem insisted. "Judge, I think we've heard enough."

"Then he would know which side of the body the heart is on?"

"All I know is you don't have one."

Plotina waited for the crowd to stop laughing. "The stab wound did not kill Biberious. In fact, the knife missed his heart entirely. To pierce his heart, the knife would have had to penetrate the sternum— or enter from underneath the breast bone." Plotina poked Minem in the sternum hard enough to make the impact felt across the room. "Biberious was stabbed on the far right side of his chest, through the ribs. His personal physician is willing to testify that this was not a lethal wound."

"Physicians? Now we're letting *physicians* testify?" Minem's composure had clearly left the courtroom. "Can you find anyone less credible than a doctor to impugn my integrity? Why not let a slave take the stand?"

"Fine. If you don't want to confront the governor's physician, perhaps I'll invite our town's apothecary to take the witness stand?"

"What? That quack?" Rexus intervened. "I can say from personal experience that his aphrodisiacs are worthless!" Minem tugged at the actor's toga, but Rexus was a one-man show. "How much have you paid him to impugn my client?"

"Would you please shut up?" Minem shouted. "Everyone in town knows that the apothecary is dead."

"You're calling a dead witness?" Rexus' surprise was stage-worthy. He milked his incredulity for all it was worth. "A dead witness? Is that legal? Either way, I consider a dead man more credible than a physician."

"Perhaps Minem can shed some light on the matter. He gave the apothecary an interesting gift just before the old man crossed the river." Plotina reached for the open bottle that had been sitting on the bailiff's table.

"Pish posh," Minem shouted. "Security Chief Severus gave him the wine."

Gaius Severus held his breath. He and Lena had provided Plotina with all the evidence and hearsay they could gather, but the link to Minem still felt circumstantial. If Minem managed to wriggle free from the charges, he would marinate Severus in fish brine and roast him on a spit

"Severus delivered the gift, but you prepared it." Plotina placed the bottle on the judge's table. He sniffed it and raised an eyebrow in approval. "Don't drink it, your honor. "

"Hey! You gave me one of these, too." Rexus said after inspecting the bottle. "I was going to invite you to drink it with me."

"Go drink with Socrates!" Minem climbed on a chair to get the judge's attention. "Can I make it clear that I have not asked this windbag to defend me?"

"Windbag?" Rexus let out a huge sigh. "Everyone's a critic."

Plotina continued to build her case in spite of the distractions. "An hour later, one of my girls found the poor fellow dead on the tile."

"Won't be the last time one of your so-called girls kills a man." Minem said. "Besides, people die every day."

"With green lips?" Plotina paused to make sure everyone heard her. "Green lips. There is one detail about dogroot that I neglected to mention: The kiss of death by dogroot is green. Governor Biberious had green lips when he was found dead."

The crowd remained silent enough to hear the judge thinking.

"She just made that up!" Minem turned to the crowd. "Are we going to let some overdressed Roman import fool us? Plotina may think I'm stupid, but now she's accusing you people of being stupid. Plotina, are you saying the judge is stupid, too?"

"Don't answer that," Soranus muttered.

"Since you seem to enjoy rhetorical questions, I'll ask you one." Plotina lifted the half-filled bottle for the crowd to see. "Would you like to taste a glass of this fine imported *vino*, Minem?"

"No, thank you." Minem recoiled as Plotina waved the open bottle under his nose. "I never drink before noon."

Plotina snapped her fingers and a nearby pirate delivered a pitcher to the stage. "Another fascinating thing about dogroot is that it turns a gray-blue color in milk. What do you think will happen when I mix milk with your wine, Minem?"

The crowd pressed forward. Plotina poured. Minem scowled. Severus watched with relief.

"Baseless alchemy!" Minem shouted. "Don't be bamboozled by this cheap trick."

Plotina held up the glass of grey-blue liquid. "Would anyone like to taste this delightful concoction? I'm told that milk is an antidote. Would you like to test the theory, Minem?"

Two of Plotina's most imposing pirates approached Minem from either side to prevent his escape.

"No further questions or evidence, your honor." Plotina turned to the audience which, like Minem, was hanging on her every word. "Tarraco, I rest my case, but you must never relax your vigilance."

"And if you liked this trial, we still have tickets left for tomorrow's Trial of the Century," Rexus added. "Purchase two tickets now and we'll throw in a full skin of poison-free wine. Satisfaction guaranteed!"

"The charges against the Imperial Associates adviser, Winus Minem, are serious enough to warrant condemnation." Soranus turned to the ashen-faced Macedonian. "Security Chief Severus will deliver you to hard labor where you will live out the rest of your days."

Cheering erupted. Most of the crowd had never seen nor heard of Winus Minem, but it was still gratifying to watch a little man fall from a high place. The bailiff nodded with approval and tied Minem's wrists.

"You can't do this!" Minem shouted. "I'm an important member of Imperial Associates."

"There is no Imperial Associates," Plotina said. "Imperial Associates is a big idea that exists only in your little head. It was a great scam while it lasted."

"Hadrian will have your head, and you'll live to regret it," Minem growled.

"That reminds me," the judge added. "All the assets you stole from our province—the port, the temple, the land—all of that reverts back to its previous owners." He waved his hands to indicate that the proceedings had finished and then retired to his chambers.

"My sincere thanks Domina Plotina," Severus said.

"Job well done, kid." She patted his shoulder and swept out of the courtroom.

Twenty-four
XXIV

After the quick trial and abrupt sentence, Gaius Severus and Limbo set off for the mines with their reluctant prisoner in tow. Because of Minem's complaints and foot dragging, the trip consumed much of the day's remaining light.

The shameless cawing of crows and distant howling of jackals added urgency to the mission. Severus and Limbo were both armed with knives against the possibility that a determined individual might try to free Minem. What mattered most was getting to the mines and back before nightfall.

The mines had been a rich source of silver in the storied times of the Divine Augustus, but all that remained now were a few weak lead veins that provided Hispania's convicts an opportunity to die slowly. On summer days when the wind shifted out to sea, acrid smoke from the smelters drifted across Tarraco.

Nolo returned from one of his many excursions with what looked like squirrel fur pasted to his black gums. Severus had just enough time to scratch him behind the ears before the half-feral hound disappeared into the underbrush again.

"Fifty Caesars," Minem increased his earlier bribe and refused to get off the ground. "Each, including the dog."

Limbo pretended to consider the offer before tugging on the rope tied around Minem's waist. "Perhaps a bit of hard labor will set you straight."

"You don't understand," Minem protested. "I'm very important."

"Not anymore," Limbo said.

"We've got less than two hours before nightfall." Severus picked up the pace. He did not want to return in the dark, not tonight. Saturnalia week was ending. The twenty-fifth day of December was also the birthday of Mithras—not an auspicious day to meet Monobrow and the unmoored ghosts of three dead praetorians.

The rogue praetorians were gone, but mercenaries were a *denarius* a dozen. Severus wondered if Minem had any allies who might rally and stage a rescue. Festus Rufius was still loose. Limbo was hardly trustworthy. Knowing that ambush would be an easy prospect anywhere along the narrow path, Severus picked up a solid walking stick and hoped Nolo was still nearby.

Minem's once firm cheeks now hung in folds over his slack jaws. His tiny eyes were red as a rat's. He sat down on a stump and refused to move. "I should be banished to an island, not sent to the mines—that is, if I were guilty, which I'm not, so in fact, I should be set free."

"Stop talking, start walking." Limbo jerked Minem upright and gave him a shove. He broke a thick switch off a low branch and slapped Minem's bare leg. "March!"

"A hundred gold coins!" Minem shuffled forward but kept turning back to engage his former disciple. "Come on, kid. Cut me loose and I'll induct you into Imperial Associates. Just imagine it! Within a few years you could be just like me."

"Just like you? Are you driving a one-wheeled chariot?" Severus tried to avoid eye contact with Minem lest he succumb once again to the tiny man's magnetic sway. Given his persuasive powers, Minem would probably be running the mines in a week. "You tried to frame me for murder and now you want my help?"

"You're making a grave mistake. I'm known in high circles." Minem slouched to his knees and again refused to move. "If the emperor were here, your head would be rolling downhill."

"Your head's too flat to roll." Limbo poked his stick into Minem's shoulder and looked back at Severus. "How much am I allowed to beat him?"

Severus yanked the bantam prisoner up by the scruff of his dirty tunic. It took surprisingly little strength to lift the dead weight that hundreds of taxpayers had once supported. He shoved Minem forward and resisted the urge to deliver a heartfelt kick.

"You boys are too young to understand." Minem raised his bound wrists as if summoning the gods. "Without me, Hispania's prosperity will sink below the seafloor."

"Hispania is prosperous?" Limbo asked with uncharacteristic curiosity.

"Hadrian won't take lightly to this offense. If you boys let me go, I'll make it worth your while." Minem sweetened his tone and focused on Severus. "Think about it, kid. You can sleep in that guard shack for the next five years or you can be successful like me."

"Like you?" Severus kicked a stone into the underbrush. He felt stupid for having ever believed in Minem. "You call this success? How can you not see this as anything but failure?"

"What you call failure is really just a new form of opportunity." In spite of his predicament, Minem grew animated. "This isn't defeat, it's a transformational moment!"

"I'll transform you if you don't stop talking." Limbo shook his stick in Minem's face.

"Such misguided passion." Minem struck a Socratic tone. "Since when is it a crime to be smarter than everyone else? Perhaps I've misread you boys. I thought you were foxes, but you're just sheep."

"Enough chatter!" Limbo poked his stick into Minem's bare arm. "What's your freedom worth to you? Best offer. No negotiating."

"Five hundred each."

"Where will you steal that from?" Limbo asked. "You don't have a coin left for the boatman."

"You dumb, narrow-minded milk pup. Don't you see how the world really works?"

"How the world really works?" Severus pursed his lips so tight that his forehead creased. "You killed a governor, poisoned a pharmacist and tried to take down the emperor along the way."

"Wrong again, Plato. Vindex killed Biberious. Rufius wanted to depose the emperor but I stopped him. That quack herbalist poisoned himself just to get me in trouble."

Limbo waved his stick in Minem's face. "Are you drunk?"

"I'm drunk with patriotism. I'm a model citizen. If you fools hadn't been palling around with Plotina, we'd all be heading to Rome right now."

"No roads lead to Rome," Severus muttered. "Any chance you have a friend called Monobrow?"

Minem averted his eyes.

"I thought so."

The fact that Monobrow had not struck yet offered no solace. If they had been in cahoots, perhaps he benefitted from having Minem disposed of. Severus considered the possibility that he was both doing Monobrow's dirty work and hastening his own demise.

The end of the trail was marked by a low-hanging dust cloud where the entrance to the mine fed a series of tunnels that many believed led directly to Hades. Carts full of blue-gray powder to be used as glazing were parked by the shaft's dark opening. A few lead ingots lay in rough piles as if waiting to plumb the empire. On a good day, an ounce of silver might still emerge from a ton of slag, but this was a place where good days were few.

A grinning supervisor emerged, his dirty arms extended in greeting. A "SlavePower" logo was embroidered across the fellow's right sleeve, barely visible on his grimy tunic. His dust-encrusted teeth were as dark as the mine shaft. "The Honorable Winus Minem," he said, "how wonderful to see you again."

Minem groaned as if Atlas had just dumped a load on his shoulders.

"Palo Polo, sir." The enthusiastic young man was barely older than Gaius Severus. He extended a filthy hand before noticing Minem's wrists were bound. "Remember me?"

"Like a beating."

"We met a few weeks ago," Polo said. "I was supervising a crew on the *Via Augusta*, getting the province ready for the emperor's entourage."

"Instead of filling potholes and pulling weeds, you spent a pile of my money to move bricks halfway across the province." Minem made no attempt to be diplomatic with his new jailor.

"Time was of the essence," Polo said. "We beat the deadline."

"And left Hispania's roads worse than before," Minem sneered. "I thought I banished you from Hispania forever."

"But I'm not *in* Hispania," Polo laughed, "I'm *under* her. When Governor Rufius signed Hispania's mineral rights over to Imperial Associates, you hired SlavePower to run the operation. That's how I became your man underground."

"Unfortunately for you, I won't be staying here." Minem tried to clear his throat but the dust had already coated it. "There's been a minor misunderstanding. I'll be leaving soon."

"Sorry, old man, but the orders are very clear." Polo smiled. "Don't worry, though, we'll have a grand time together. Permit me to say how delighted I am to work with you again."

"If you ever want to join Imperial Associates, you'll cut the charade and remove these ropes." Minem shook his bound wrists at Palo Polo. "I outrank you in every possible way."

"Except one." The glint in Palo's eyes shone through the dirt on his face. There was no doubt that he was enjoying Minem's comeuppance. "The good news is that we're doing some truly breakthrough work in these mines."

Minem could barely balance on his own two feet. His neck sagged beneath the weight of his head.

The brief silence was broken when the overseer, a sadistic-looking southerner, emerged from the mine shaft and limped forward to inspect his newest worker. "Let's see our new girl." He inspected Minem's hands with obvious disappointment. "Not used to doing real work, are we sweetheart?"

Minem grimaced as the overseer pinched him in soft places where muscle should have been. "You'd be wise to treat me well. I've still got powerful friends in high places."

"Now you have powerful friends in low places," the overseer said.

"It's really not so bad here, sir." Palo Polo grew animated. "Under my guidance, we've increased productivity and decreased mortality. You'll be happy to learn that I've got the three mine shafts divided into rival teams. Competition gives the men something to live for, and the sense of camaraderie has cut the murder rate in half."

"Spare me the details," Minem said. "I'd rather die in the arena."

"Mine shaft Alpha is our traditional arrangement where the overseer reigns supreme with harsh words and stiff whips." Polo began to pace and wave his hands. "High productivity and minimal downtime make them a tough team to beat."

The overseer acknowledged the compliment with a brutish grunt.

"In mine shaft Beta we're testing the possibility that compassion and justice might not be mutually exclusive." Polo kicked up a gray-blue dust cloud as he paced faster. "Though convicted and fated to die, we allow the Beta prisoners to maintain some dignity. The results are fascinating! With each passing day, the Beta miners enter the shaft with increasingly higher levels of self-esteem and a greater will to live."

"How nice! If it works, I'd like to try it in our prisons," Severus said.

"Unfortunately, the increased food expenses are eating up the profits." Polo smiled at Severus as one might a future client. "I've been thinking that the compassionate treatment of prisoners, if implemented correctly, might extend life expectancy on your arena floor. If a prisoner lasts even five minutes longer against a beast or gladiator, the uptick in concession sales could represent a windfall."

The scarred overseer spat out a mouthful of lead dust and left to attend to a sudden outbreak of shouting from below. "See you in the hole," he said to Minem before disappearing.

"I'm so happy to finally have someone intelligent to chat with," Polo continued. "I know you'll be fascinated to learn about my most daring experiment: mine shaft Gamma. We're studying what happens when you take the most distasteful two-legged riffraff and let them self-govern."

"No whips? No bosses?" Limbo choked on dust and disbelief.

Polo nodded with evident pride. "This could revolutionize prison camps across the empire!"

Severus had been watching two crows fight on the slag heap. "Won't they just kill each other?"

"Of course," Polo smiled as if encountering a long-lost twin. "Gamma shaft isn't very productive, but the lower costs help me fund my more expensive operations. I'm still playing with the formula, but it's coming along nicely."

Severus nodded his head slowly and backed away from the mine shaft.

"You're a smart chap," Polo said. "What's your name?"

"Gaius Severus." He looked up at the dim sky. "Sorry we can't stay any longer. We need to get back before dark."

"Always dark in the mines!" Polo slapped Minem on the shoulder. He took the rope and dragged his former superior to the mouth of the mine. "Come back and visit when you want to talk prison reform, Severus. I've got some great ideas."

"No!" Minem dropped to his knees. He looked skyward and begged the Fates to reconsider. "Please don't leave me with him!"

"Relax," Polo said. His tarnished smile twisted with hints of cruelty at the corners. "Time in the mines passes like no time at all."

Coastal fog blew into the narrow canyon that cut back toward Tarraco. Nolo ran ahead, never distancing himself too far along the trail. In spite of the dog's urging, Severus and Limbo proceeded slowly through the fallen rock and debris dislodged by the recent downpours.

"Ten days since the Ides," Severus said after what had been a long silence. "Some would call this fog an omen."

"Fog is fog, nothing more," Limbo said.

"Remember the bull ceremony a week ago?" Severus advanced the topic with caution as one never quite knew with Limbo. "Do you have any idea what that was?"

"Some dumb soldier cult." Limbo laughed to himself. "A lot of good it did them. If their god is real, why did he let them die in a fire?"

"Maybe he wanted us to survive," Severus said, and then thought better of discussing anything more complicated than water with his slow-witted subordinate. He stepped up the pace as the fog thinned and the dim fires of Tarraco came into view. Stragglers could be seen rushing home along the wider streets. Shopkeepers would be locking their storefronts and throwing the day's trash into the alleys where first the poor and then the dogs would pick through the remains. "We need to hurry. Before long, the hills will be safer than the streets."

"What's so special about the twenty-fifth day of December, anyway?" Limbo walked at double-stride to keep up.

"The last night of Saturnalia is also the birthday of Mithras."

"The god of soldiers?"

"The god of Hadrian. Mithras." Severus invoked a dramatic, Don Rexus baritone that would have echoed nicely off the canyon walls a few moments earlier. "Born of a virgin mother. Mithras redeemed the earth, died and rose again."

"Who would believe anything so preposterous?"

Severus stopped and stared out toward the dark sea beyond the port—east toward the world of Mithras. "Tonight in dark caves and cellars across the empire, new initiates are brought further into the mysteries than we ever traveled."

"Is that why we were dragged into the cellar? To be initiated?"

"Our superiors intended for us to join the fold."

"Looks like the fold joined them." Impatient to get back to town, Limbo ran ahead. "I'll stick with Bacchus, thank you very much. See you later, boss."

Severus gave an involuntary laugh. He could barely believe in his own invisible god, let alone all the others who lined up to torment humanity. Was there a shred of evidence anywhere to support any of it? Had anyone ever checked to see if the claims of every sect, cult, and temple added up to anything more than one big bathtub full of contradictions? Perhaps Limbo was wiser than he appeared. Given the options, Bacchus might be the best choice of all.

"The trial's tomorrow," Severus called after Limbo, but the boy did not acknowledge him. "Be there bright and early."

Twenty-five
XXV

As he meandered home, Gaius Severus realized that he had never returned Minem's tablet. He took it from his pocket, slid the knurled stylus from the tablet's leather hinge and rolled it between his fingers. It felt eager and articulate. Minem would not be needing it in the mines, so Severus opened the cover and drew one spiral and then another. The stylus seemed to propel itself. The nib slid effortlessly through the wax until the tail of the spiral turned into a word. "Move beyond Marius," it wrote.

Surprised, Severus rubbed a few letters away but stopped when he realized that the stylus had offered sound advice. Marius never suffered the consequences of his mistakes and missteps. That honor fell to Gaius. Why continue to chase bad ideas and worse luck down a dead-end road? Establishing a healthy distance was the right thing to do.

It was good to feel free and disconnected, to walk beyond the din and rattle of town. He twirled the stylus between his fingers until it felt warm.

"Forgive Father," it wrote, but this was the opposite of what Severus felt. Wherever his father was—Judea, the seafloor, or rolling in some widow's arms—did the old man give a donkey tail about how his boys had fared? He had raised them in a fantasy world of legends, prayers, and impossible ideals. Father had not prepared them to live in the real world; he had not even tried. It was no wonder that Marius was such a dreamer. But resentment would not bring either of them back. The stylus was right. It made more sense to forgive than it did to stay angry.

Severus cut across a sparse grove where the air smelled of wet earth. Droplets collected by the pines fell like yesterday's rain. He paused under an ancient hemlock and let the stylus drift again over the wax.

"Love thy Mother," it wrote.

Memories of his mother were shrouded by half a lifetime spent without her. Father spoke of her with reverence, Marius with resentment. It occurred to Gaius that part of his father might have died with her passing. If the brothers struggled to find light in her gauzy shadow, only God knew their father's true grief.

Severus picked up a long, straight stick and used it to bat stones into the brush. The path sloped upward through the scrub. He continued, deep in thought, oblivious to his surroundings until he came within full view of the enormous aqueduct.

The great bridge was five hundred feet long and stood eighty feet high at midspan. It rose above the canyon as if placed there by the hand of Zeus. Severus wondered how many men had been sacrificed to build the stone marvel. Structures such as this were the real reason Rome ruled the world. A race that could divert rivers and vanquish thirst could conquer anything.

He rolled the stylus between his fingers and set the point to wax.

"Forget the Titans," it wrote.

This advice rang true. Lena might call it fate, but only coincidence and tragedy had landed Severus in the service of an accidental governor and his conniving associates. Cassius Kleptus would auction off his last testicle if the price were right. Don Rexus could barely take his eyes off the mirror. Winus Minem could sell turd for gemstone and now would be mining for both.

Saturated with advice and not hungry for more, Severus slipped the stylus firmly in its slot and dropped the tablet into his pocket.

The great bridge now consumed the canyon. Mankind might be unpredictable, brutal at times, but accomplishments like this immense aqueduct gave Severus reason to remain hopeful as he stepped onto the covered channel. Advancing slowly at first, he tapped his walking stick like a blind man feeling his way forward. Once assured that the cover stones could hold his weight, he proceeded with confidence.

Giddy with altitude, he felt as if he were gliding where no bird had flown. A quarter of the way across the bridge he stopped to watch water flowing through a rare gap between the thin cover stones. At mid-span, high above the rock and scrub, he looked down and saw a gray-backed jackal working to dig up a root or rabbit warren.

"That's what I do every day," he said. A superstitious Roman would have seen the jackal as a portent of something evil, but Severus had lost count of omens amidst the recent torrent of assassins, slavers, and sea gods. The darkening sky heralded a fresh storm coming in from the sea, but, like the jackal below, Severus chose to ignore it.

The sound of water flowing underfoot reminded him of his debt to Neptune. He felt a wave of compassion for the old sea god, confined to saltwater, forgotten by all but a few drunken mariners. Did Neptune's dominion over the sea also extend to wild rivers and man-made channels? The subtleties of salt and sweet water were not worth debating. Severus had promised a shrine and the aqueduct seemed appropriate. He raised his hands in benediction and turned toward the east. "I dedicate this bridge to Neptune, God of the Sea. Thus I pay my debt."

Halfway across the bridge, hunger rendered moot any further contemplation of Neptune's reach. The sound of flowing water was no substitute for a bowl of porridge or a rump of cheese.

Fresh fog washed into the canyon. Severus needed to return to Tarraco before further darkness fell.

He noticed a man approaching. Though still a silhouette in the mist, this was no phantom. There was no doubt as to who it was. High above the valley, the shadow of death had arrived. Though visions of Monobrow had haunted his days and crowded his sleep, Severus felt strangely calm now that the moment was nigh. He was weary of playing mouse to Monobrow's cat. It was time to end this game.

Monobrow pulled a knife from his sash and advanced patiently.

There was no doubt as to the man's intentions. The assassin had not come to negotiate.

Severus glanced sideways over the edge. If death was imminent, was jumping the better alternative? If he leapt, how long would it take to hit bottom? Would the impact kill him instantly or would he be forced to die twice? Romans considered suicide honorable, but the God of Abraham frowned on taking one's own life. Was that why he had sent Monobrow to do the deed?

Perhaps anticipating a meal, the jackal had climbed the canyon and now waited at the end of the bridge. Severus knew that jackals typically hunted in packs. They were not known to attack men. The scavenger had only come to clean up the mess and feed on the misfortune of others.

Severus clutched his stick. He felt more alert, more in the moment than he ever had before. Every heartbeat mattered as the last

179

drop in his water clock seemed suspended in midair. In less time than it would take for Severus' short life to pass before his eyes, Monobrow drew within range.

The praetorian chief palmed his dagger.

Severus' veins pulsed with the lost opportunity of a life foreshortened like a shadow at noon. He missed the mother he had barely known. He longed to hear his father chant one more Sabbath blessing. He ached to hold Lena one last time. He even missed Marius.

"We meet again, and once again you have the wrong man."

"Then the wrong man survived." Monobrow's rough voice and eastern accent were unmistakable. "And loyal servants of Mithras perished."

"Perhaps their passing, like my survival, was God's will." Severus gambled that doubt might be the best weapon against a true believer.

"So you admit to having been there."

"Today is the twenty-fifth of December, the day of His birth." Severus felt strangely calm playing his gambit. Any possible reason for timidity had vanished. "What better day to die?"

"You should have died in the legion camp."

"I did." In the absence of fatal doubt, a shred of confusion would suffice. Instead of striking, Severus tossed his stick into the air. It spun skyward in a slow arc and seemed to hang at apogee for a prolonged instant.

The weight in his pocket reminded him of Minem's tablet, and Severus seized upon Monobrow's brief distraction to hurl the object into the side of his head. The unexpected projectile disoriented the assassin just long enough for both Severus and the approaching jackal to strike. Severus dove for his ankles to avoid the downward sweeping knife. The jackal leapt for the back of Monobrow's neck. The effect of Severus tackling Monobrow at the knees at the same instant the jackal crashed into his backside sent the assassin twisting.

The jackal landed on Severus and the two rolled sideways, knocking Monobrow into the foggy canyon.

The praetorian fell without a cry. A dull thud from below served as his unspoken last word. The fourth cat did not land on its feet. The water flowing through the aqueduct was not from the Styx. Not this time.

Severus pulled into a fetal crouch to fend off the beast. When no teeth slashed his flesh, Severus looked up and saw it was Nolo.

Trembling, Severus wrapped grateful arms around the dog's gray neck and offered thanks to any and all gods that might be listening.

Twenty-six
XXVI

The morning of the trial coincided with a freak, freezing rain that rendered the streets of Tarraco as slippery as fishtails. It felt cold enough for the sea itself to ice over. Starved for entertainment and hungry for vengeance, people gathered early and braved the chill.

An enterprising group of young street musicians, two of whom Gaius Severus recognized from the Gladiator's Goblet, demanded payment to stop playing their peculiar blend of loud and dissonant music. The band was soon upstaged by a troupe of amateur acrobats who could not gain purchase on the icy cobblestone. The gymnasts did more falling than tumbling. Spectators were more generous with derision than tips.

The security bottleneck frustrated the impatient crowd, but the inspections and pat-downs proved invaluable at extracting sharp objects and potential projectiles.

Plotina's pirates patrolled the alleys and colonnades. Ever since their rough handling of the homeless camp, the capital had been calm and crime-free. People had found them intimidating enough in blue tunics, but today they wore fearsome dark trousers. Simply sighting one of Plotina's crew dressed as a northern barbarian was enough to render a thief respectable. The plummeting crime rate suggested that Gaius Severus' accidental approach to public safety had borne fruit. Unfortunately, the one prize Severus needed most continued to elude him.

Festus Rufius had yet to surface.

Conveying the ex-governor to trial was the only job Severus was supposed to be doing though it did not require a great juror to predict that the scales of justice would never tip against a nobleman, but Severus wondered if the opportunity to defend himself in court might still bring Rufius forward. Perhaps he would sneak into the theater just to watch the spectacle.

Pretrial scuttlebutt circulated like chariots at the circus. Earlier in the week, a rumor spread that Rufius had purchased half the tickets in order to turn a quick profit scalping them. Another rumor had Rufius placing large wagers on his own condemnation. At the front of the line, the docklands crier insisted that Rufius had sired half the newborns in Tarraco though all were conceived before his arrival. Midway along the colonnades, the forum crier claimed that Rufius had a legion poised to storm the gates and declare independence from Rome should the verdict turn against him.

Gaius Severus stood by the door and watched every person enter. People filed into the auditorium and fought over choice spots from which they hoped to see Rufius skewered like the overcooked brochettes that were for sale in the lobby. People who had queued early were angry to learn that the front rows had been promised to Tarraco's elite and Don Rexus' swelling entourage of lonely matrons and aspiring actresses.

Plotina's trouser-clad pirates clung to the shadows. They stood guard but did nothing to stop the minor brawls that rose like dust storms across the auditorium. People eventually made the best of the tight arrangements.

The covered theater had once offered an upscale alternative to the plebeian amphitheater. In better times, a local troupe staged performances for wealthy patrons who feigned interest in Greek drama. But the salad days had long passed, and the majority of today's crowd had never seen an indoor production. Culturally illiterate parvenus tossed sausage casings onto the floor and stood on the benches to wave and shout at friends across the hall. Wealthy patrons in the front rows were appalled by those who did not understand that uncouth arena conduct was inappropriate in a house of high society.

When the proceedings started and it was clear that Rufius would not show up, Severus snuck backstage to implement his hastily conceived backup plan. He changed clothes quickly and listened for his cue.

Appearing larger by half than he had a week earlier, Governor Cassius Kleptus waddled forward and was met with hisses and catcalls. A few scattered drunks cheered, but others who recognized the former taxman threw whatever was handy. The dull yellow bunting wrapping the stage proved to have been a bad choice of color for hiding stains.

"Barbarians!" The matron from the apothecary shop stood and shouted at the crowd behind her. She took it upon herself to defend the governor and the well-heeled front rows against the vulgar masses. Her gangly daughter Egnatia slumped with embarrassment.

At Kleptus' insistence, the hall eventually fell silent except for the seasonal coughing.

"Welcome to the way we do business in the new Hispania," Kleptus boomed. He had not looked so happy since the increase in export taxes. "Since we owe Rome a small fortune and you all cheat on your taxes, I am proud to introduce a new approach to paying off the province's debts."

"Snack gouging?" a man shouted from the middle rows. His half-eaten projectile hit the podium. "This sausage tastes worse than sawdust."

Kleptus ignored the heckler and introduced the attorneys for the defense and prosecution. People were shocked when Plotina appeared wearing a perfectly starched and draped man's toga. Her unspoken message that she was not to be trifled with was reinforced by her strong, bare shoulder. It took a moment for the audience to digest and reject the notion of a woman wearing traditional male garb. With the exception of stage makeup, Don Rexus was dressed much the same as she.

People groaned when the unpopular Judge Soranus hobbled over to his central position. Hardly anyone lacked a relative not scorched by the flames of his justice.

"I'm sure you'll enjoy today's trial." Kleptus smiled as if already counting his cut of the proceeds. Between the admissions, the concessions, and the oversold seats he stood to do very well. "After covering our expenses, profits from today's performance will pay nearly half the interest on Hispania's overdue debt to the empire."

The shopkeepers in the audience understood this to mean that Hadrian would be the only creditor to see any relief. Tarraco's economy would continue to run on smoke, bluster, and the hope of an early spring.

"Now without further ado, I give you The Trial of the Century!" Kleptus waved and exited the stage.

A hush settled over the room until someone shouted, "Where's Rufius?"

Gaius Severus heard his cue. He drew a deep breath and bounded onto stage wearing a prisoner's tunic and a pointed felt cap of the kind sported by recently freed slaves. A pillow strapped around his waist gave the appearance of soft bulk. He raised his bound wrists in victory and shouted, "Friends! Romans! Spaniards!"

The light was so dim that even those who had seen the real Rufius now claimed to recognize his impersonator. Some cheered, but most booed with enough disdain to confirm that the public had fallen for the disguise.

Severus took his seat.

"What are you trying to pull?" Plotina maintained her poise, but her cobra braid looked ready to strike. "You're not Rufius."

"It was too dangerous to expose Rufius to this crowd, *domina*," Severus whispered. "Since we can't guarantee his safety, we'll try him *in absentia*."

"You don't really have him, do you?" Plotina was livid.

"Our rendition of Rufius will be far more entertaining than his could ever be," Rexus said. He had not been in on the ruse but was quick on the uptake. "I only wish we had found a better thespian to play your part."

Judge Soranus was too deaf and nearsighted to recognize that the defendant was an imposter. He drained his wine goblet and signaled his impatience with a flip of the hand. Everyone knew that the trial had to resolve before his nap time or he would become irritable enough to condemn the entire audience.

Severus looked out across the crowd in search of Lena but saw only Egnatia fluttering her hands like palm fronds. The sparsely placed oil lamps made it hard to be sure, but she appeared to have six fingers on each hand.

"Procedural objection!" Don Rexus lodged a protest before the formal arguments could start. His thundering voice silenced the chattering crowd. "The prosecutor is the defendant's wife."

"Overruled." Praetor Soranus struggled to swallow a pork rind. "Who better to prosecute a husband than his wife?"

People were packed together like garlic cloves, but the atmosphere was festive. Snack vendors touted wineskins, finger sausages, and honeyed almonds. The ceramic Plotina figurine with the exaggerated cobra braid proved a popular souvenir.

The real Plotina stood stern as granite. Her braid glistened as if anointed by Zeus. She waited at the rostrum, but the crowd showed no intent to hush. Unperturbed, she took a sip of water and straightened her sash. Plotina had helped her father prepare and litigate enough cases to know that the last refuge of an unprepared

solicitor was to badger his betters. She knew better than to get
flustered by cheap provocations. "As I was saying, the ex-governor
of Hispania left you worse off than you were two months ago. He
took office with a surplus and burdened you with a deficit. Festus
Rufius could not be bothered with governing so he delegated day-to-
day management of the province to his little Greek adviser."

"Objection!" Rexus slammed his fist on the lectern so hard it
startled the sleepy judge. "Minem was not a Greek."

"Sustained," Soranus muttered. He filled his goblet and glared at
Plotina. "Stick to the facts."

"Nothing wrong with being Greek." Plotina smiled, apparently
pleased with how easy it was to get under Rexus' skin. "Festus
Rufius signed contract after contract, none of which he read, the sum
of which gave Imperial Associates near total control over Hispania's
resources. As if such negligence and dereliction weren't enough,
Rufius drained the treasury even more with his lavish spending."

A few spectators who had benefitted from Rufius' largesse
cheered and woke those who had already nodded off.

"You're dull, Plotina, boring as bricks," Rexus whispered.
"Punch it up a bit, before you lose the rest of the audience."

"When it became clear that Hadrian was coming to collect
missing taxes and tribute, Rufius changed course." Plotina walked
over to where Severus was seated and pointed an accusing finger at
his nose. "Festus Rufius plotted to assassinate the emperor. He
intended to seize imperial power."

The criers took inaccurate notes on their new S-IV slates. One
wrote that Plotina's cobra braid had come to life and attacked the
judge. The other was having trouble keeping his inkpot level.

"Objection! Speculation! Indemnification!" Don Rexus shouted.
Experience had taught him that audiences appreciated drama more
than veracity. A feisty performance atoned for many sins. "By the
way, can we get a few more oil lamps on stage? This dim light is
most unfavorable."

"Overruled." Soranus snorted loudly and waved his hand in a
gesture the bailiff understood to mean the wine had run out again.

"Even as a would-be murderer, Rufius proved hopeless," Plotina
continued undaunted. "In spite of the fortune Rufius squandered on
expensive preparations, Hadrian never set one divine toe in
Hispania. Alerted to the inept assassination attempt, the emperor's

boat never docked. Between the reckless spending, the gross incompetence, and the generous contracts to Winus Minem and Imperial Associates, Rufius has left Hispania barefoot, bankrupt, and pregnant."

"Objection!" Rexus shouted. "Hispania was pregnant long before Rufius arrived."

"Enough!" Soranus shredded a document, sending fragments of papyrus flying in frustration. "If you two don't stop bickering I'll declare you married."

"No further statements." Plotina had laid out a logical case, but Don Rexus had upstaged her in the courtroom of public opinion. Plotina shuffled her scrolls while Rexus prowled the edge of the stage blowing kisses to star-struck adolescent girls.

"For those of you who couldn't follow Plotina's logic," Rexus said, launching into his defense, "I will summarize: What wife believes her husband innocent of anything? Plotina came all the way from Rome to avenge herself on a husband who had understandably neglected her. If that cobra on her head were alive, it would strike Rufius dead out of sheer mercy."

"Objection!" Plotina shouted from stage right. "I'm not on trial, Rufius is."

"Sustained." The judge smiled. "Calm your cobra, Plotina."

Plotina pursed her lips. She knew that the only reason the judge had permitted her to prosecute was to slam the profession's portals shut on the smarter half of humanity. But despite Soranus, she had donned a toga, wedged one foot in the courthouse door and so far resisted the urge to plant the other one in his chest. Someday, women everywhere would thank her. Someday, women would rule the empire.

"Your honor," Rexus continued, "the citizens of Hispania are too smart to fall for the pathetic agenda of a woman scorned."

"Objection!" Plotina shouted so loud that the judge tipped his wine glass.

"Overruled," the judge moaned. "Let this poor man finish a sentence."

"My friends," Rexus said, "this trial isn't about Festus Rufius, it's about Plotina. No woman in the empire is hungrier for power than she. Isn't it obvious that all Plotina wants is to ruin a good man and impugn his name forever? Is this how we reward our selfless public servants? I hope not!"

Applause rolled like summer thunder. Murmurs circulated as people debated who had argued the better case so far. The general consensus was that Plotina had demonstrated far more diligence than Rexus. She had demonstrated far more competence than the pompous actor. She was smarter, more articulate, and better prepared, but because she was unpleasant, overdressed, and female, popular opinion favored her opponent.

Gaius Severus was seated upstage when he heard Egnatia's voice from behind the rear curtain.

"I forgot your name," she said.

"Never told you," he whispered.

"That's a funny name. I recognized you right away." She reached through the gap and poked him in the ribs. "Let's get out of here. Mum and Daddy are busy. The villa's empty and the wine's warm."

Severus heard her words, but was slow on their meaning. "Sorry, I'm working."

"I can see that. You're doing a great job occupying that chair." Egnatia parted the curtain so that only he could see her. She was wearing a tight-fitting dress with a neckline that plunged to nowhere.

"Don't you have anything better to do?"

Egnatia stomped away like a wounded giraffe.

Judge Soranus swallowed a yawn. His tired eyes struggled to remain afloat in their wrinkled sockets; his forehead drooped like a wet tent. He had barely enough stamina to bang his fist on the table. "I hereby—"

The judge's decree was lost to sudden disruption.

"Traitor! Blasphemer! Republican!"

All heads turned as a poor likeness of Hadrian ran into the hall. Draped in red and purple rags with a scrub brush tied to his head, the mock emperor marched down the center aisle waving a toy sword and wooden shield. He pointed directly at the poor facsimile of Festus Rufius.

"You can't kill me because I'm immortal!"

The crowd rose to their feet faster than Gaius Severus could shrink into his chair. For a second, he regretted not having left with Egnatia. His brother's timing could not have been more embarrassing.

Furious at having his luncheon delayed, Soranus pounded a

pitcher on the table. Wine sprayed over the starched white togas in the front rows, and even the normally reserved noble folk began shouting.

People swarmed the imperial pretender hoping, perhaps, that some of his self-proclaimed divinity might rub off on them. Benches were overturned. Food trays were knocked from vendors' hands. Plotina's pirates tried but were unable to break through the hubbub swirling around the ragamuffin imposter.

Gaius Severus cradled his forehead. Saturnalia was over, but his brother's world was as upside down as ever.

"I hereby dissolve the empire," Marius shouted. He tried in vain to force his way down the aisle, but his wooden sword could not cut through the excited crowd. It seemed that everyone wanted to touch his ragged toga. "Long live the Republic. Long live freedom!"

"Long live freedom!" Happy for the chance to shout about something, the common people joined in the chant. Arms waved like wheat in the wind. The proper women in the front rows hid jewelry in their cleavage. They pressed against the stage where the stained bunting now hung in tatters.

The bailiff pushed toward Marius.

"What son of a scorpion dares confront his emperor?" Marius pointed his wooden sword at the bailiff. "I am divine and you, sir, are but a toad."

"Do you know the penalty for impersonating the emperor?" The bailiff reached for Marius.

"Another century of occupation? Return to your honey pot, you flabby equestrian!"

In a surprising show of strength from one so fond of sweet bread, the bailiff knocked Marius' shield aside and wrestled him to the floor. The two remained locked in mutual inertia until Zinzin arrived and hoisted Marius over her shoulder. Two determined pirates cleared a path and Zinzin lugged Marius kicking and shouting toward the exit.

"Power to the plebes!" Marius yelled, but the crowd's interest had waned. Taking advantage of the turmoil, many snuck forward into better seats.

Judge Soranus pounded his table, but the audience paid him scant attention. By this point the greasy snacks had wound through their collective intestines and the contents of now-discarded wine bladders added to their general discomfort. With the exception of an old woman who had been sneaking forward throughout the proceedings, the audience was mainly interested in taking what was left of the law into their own hands.

Rexus climbed to the rostrum to face the rising tide of impatience and invoked all the volume his voice could muster. "The defense calls Governor Festus Rufius to the witness stand."

Gaius Severus walked forward into a hailstorm of abuse and half-eaten debris.

"*Absolvo!* Innocent!" a paid spectator shouted, but one call for clemency was overruled by many shouts for blood.

"*Condemno, condemno, condemno!*"

Rexus had prepared a soliloquy worthy of Cicero. He expanded his chest and drew a deep breath, but when a hard-boiled egg hit him in the forehead he aborted the performance.

"No questions, Your Honor. I rest my case."

"What?" Severus hissed. "You're not even going to defend your client?"

"It would be lost on this crowd." Rexus wiped the egg from his brows.

At this, Plotina jumped up like a rabbit from a basket. It barely mattered that only the front rows could hear her. The time had come to skewer the brash, false, and flirtatious actor whom she appeared to hate almost as much as her estranged husband. "Typically in a case like this, the court is flooded with *amicus* briefs from influential citizens and legal scholars hoping to sway the judge's opinion."

"Time to kiss and make up!" the old, white-powdered woman in the third row shouted.

Plotina ignored the heckler. She crossed her arms, glared at Rexus, and turned her full fury on Severus. "Festus Rufius, how do you explain the fact that no one, not even your own father, has come to your defense?"

"My poor father ..." Severus slumped with feigned sorrow.

The crowd showed their dislike for Plotina by applauding for Severus, even though everyone knew that Rufius' father was a rich senator. Many had seen the old patrician standing in the imperial entourage during Hadrian's ill-fated visit to Tarraco. The obvious lie about his health bothered no one. If witnesses told the truth, there would be no need for judges.

"I have a receipt in my hand." Plotina waved a document, but only the mascara-smeared matron in the third row took a squinting interest in the details. "A receipt that bears your seal. Can you identify it?"

"Let me see that!" Rexus grabbed the note and winked at a young actress with a hide-and-seek scarf whom he had recently auditioned for a supporting role. He beamed his wide smile across the audience. Even in the dim light his teeth shone like the Pillars of Hercules.

"I must admit that I found the governor's tastes to be quite, er, extraordinary," Plotina confided to those in the front rows. "I wasn't aware that peafowl were edible, and his interest in large women seems excessive."

Rexus unrolled the document, turned it sideways and rotated it in both directions. He examined the stained papyrus up close and then held it at arm's length. "*Vesuvius!* Just listen to this menu: oyster pasties, boar's blood sausages, and grilled baby leeks."

"You lie!" The frumpy old matron in the third row shook her head so violently that her hair uncurled.

"That's enough." Plotina retrieved the document from Rexus and handed it to Severus. "Would you care to tell the people of Tarraco why you were spending their tax money on such lavish fare?"

"Would the people of Tarraco care to tell me why they never paid taxes?" Severus found that he enjoyed being in character and wondered if it ran in the family.

The din of a hundred tax evasions filled the hall. Even people who had enjoyed Rufius' parties shook their indignant fists against the possibility of having to pay for them.

"The list is endless." Plotina droned like a philosopher in a bath house, placing great emphasis on every syllable as if it might aid in comprehension. "Sow's udder, rooster combs, urchin roe, sea hedgehogs—"

"Dog sausage!" The boisterous old woman in the third row threw her empty wine skin at Plotina and shouted, "Rufius doesn't even like sea hedgehogs."

Something about the increasingly irritated, pasty-faced old woman shook Severus from his performance. He made eye contact with two of Plotina's nearby pirates and pointed toward the rowdy old matron.

191

Instead of coming forward to investigate, the pirates left the room.

Plotina had lost the crowd, but still she forged on. "All of these documents bear the imprint of your little friend Winus Minem, the Imperial Associates vulture who plundered the province while you feasted, vomited, rinsed and repeated."

"Fish feathers!" The woman's voice crackled. Her sash had fallen and her rumpled *stola* now hung loose. "You're the real criminal!"

Plotina ignored the outburst. "Endless remodeling of a perfectly good villa … immodest piles of delicacies … overflowing flesh pots … do you not feel the slightest remorse for your behavior?"

"Being governor means never having to say you're sorry," Severus said. He stood up to get a better look at the agitated old woman. "Your last governor was murdered in his sleep and now you're trying to kill me in broad daylight. I didn't ask to lead this province. What am I on trial for here, being a patriot? Answering the call of duty? Is this the thanks I get for giving my life in service to the empire?"

A few people applauded while others clogged the crowded exits to demand a refund. Plotina glared at Rexus, the judge stared into the bottom of his goblet, and Vindex appeared at the back of the hall.

Vindex. Back from the bottom of the sea. Severus was so happy to see the ex-gladiator that he almost leapt off the stage. It was all he could do to stay in character because he knew that Rufius hated Vindex.

"Long live Rufius," shouted the old woman. She was inebriated and restless, disheveled and disorderly. *"Absolvo! Absolvo!"*

Vindex had no trouble parting the crowd as he crept toward her.

"Don't be fooled by his sad soliloquies," Plotina insisted. "Festus Rufius curses the Fates like a rooster curses sunrise, but he alone is to blame. Did a grand conspiracy really bring him down? No! Rufius brought this upon himself."

"Go to Hades!" shouted the old woman, now in the front row. Her face was a patchwork of rough skin and white powder. She picked up an apple core and threw it at Plotina, but like the entire trial so far, it veered off course.

"Plotina, I find you guilty!" Rexus tried to get the show back on script. He could not hide his disappointment in Plotina's performance. The show was nothing short of a debacle. In spite of her serpentine coiffure, superior intelligence, and smart Roman attire, her performance had lacked flair. Rexus had written many dramatic lines for her, but Plotina insisted on hiding behind dull fact and legal precedent. She was the worst leading lady he had ever shared a stage with. For a second, his rich baritone seemed to cause the incoming debris to hang in midair. "You are guilty of injustice to all who paid for an afternoon of enjoyable entertainment," he shouted at her.

Of all the minor roles he had ever played for every unruly audience in every sagging, two-*sesterce* theater across the empire, this was the worst. The best he could hope for was to avoid the projectiles today and return to Rome tomorrow.

The traffic toward the exits slowed as people stopped to enjoy the complete breakdown of decorum. Even the rich people hurled insults.

"Rufius alone is responsible for the debt that will burden your children long after you've crossed the Styx." Plotina refused to be cowed. She paced the stage, dodged insults and closed her case. "He should have read the fine print in all those contracts, but he was either too lazy or too dumb to sweat the details. Someday the entire province will be thrown into slavery to pay for his deeds. In spite of every portent, every warning, and every messenger from Rome, Rufius continued his reckless pursuit of pleasure, avoiding anything that smelled like work except for trying to murder the emperor."

"Blasphemy!" the old woman shouted. Her sagging scarf revealed a double chin and a chubby neck. She grabbed a half-eaten sandwich and threw it at the stage. "Rufius regrets that he only has one life to give in defense of the Roman Empire."

Plotina refused to yield. "Rufius wanted Hadrian dead. He was plotting regicide, the worst form of murder. Judge Soranus, there is only one possible sentence you can render. Festus Rufius must die."

"Objection!" The old woman shouted. "*Argumentum ad naseum!* You're to blame! You weren't happy with half! You wanted it all!" Dark stubble was now visible above her lip. Many local women had moustaches, but hers went beyond the pale. Her dress had shifted enough to expose a hairy shoulder. A tuft of dark hair bristling up the back of her neck did not match the brown curls cascading off her forehead. She climbed upon her seat, too agitated to notice that

Vindex had pinched a lock of her hair. As she pulled away from him, the wig came loose in his hand.

Rexus laughed like Bacchus on holiday. The word spread like a tenement fire: Festus Rufius had returned. Gaius Severus felt a warm twinge of relief that no one cared about his charade and the secret of his incompetence was safe for another day.

"Give me that!" Rufius swatted at Vindex and reached for the wig. His bloodshot eyes bulged like cracked eggs. His once-cherubic cheeks hung limp with defeat.

"What a pleasant surprise to see you again," Vindex said. He lifted the ex-governor overhead and displayed him for the crowd to jeer at.

"Court's adjourned," Soranus shouted, but nobody heard him.

"Help!" Rufius squirmed but could not wiggle free "This monster is a murderer! Put me down, you overgrown slave! I thought you were dead." Rufius flopped around like a beached fish.

"Sorry to disappoint you."

"Wait!" the judge shouted. "I haven't rendered a verdict!"

Plotina and her pirates had already left when a tipped lamp ignited the last swatch of dry bunting. Smoke inspired some people to exit, while others threw fresh debris into the growing fire.

"You're my hero!" Egnatia extended a hand to Severus as he left the stage. She yanked him into a hug and planted a wet kiss on each of his cheeks.

Severus lingered in her grip for a moment. It felt good to be appreciated, even by the strangest patchwork of a girl he had ever seen. If she thought him a hero, there was no reason to argue.

Egnatia wanted to stay and feed the fire, but she allowed Severus to drag her swooning and fawning toward the exit.

Looking back through the smoke, Severus thought he saw Don Rexus dancing in the flames.

Twenty-seven
XXVII

People fled from the smoking theater and spilled out into the central plaza. Unable to afford tickets, most of Tarraco had been loitering along the colonnades, waiting for a verdict and hoping for an execution.

The town criers had done a reliable job of keeping the people outside the theater as confused as those within. Neither crier had waited until the flaming finale, but this didn't stop one from claiming that Festus Rufius was fated to die in the arena, or prevent the other from announcing that he had been acquitted and reinstated as governor. The contradictory reports assured that misinformation would swirl and multiply for days to come. Hoping to extend Saturnalia one more night, the crowd overflowed into taverns and snack shops to consume rumors and squander their few remaining coins.

Gaius Severus deposited Egnatia with her mother and ran back to help stragglers escape from the smoking theater. Once certain that the bucket brigade had the flames under control, he returned to the plaza and wiped the smoke and exhaustion from his eyes. For the first time in recent memory, things appeared to have worked out. Monobrow was gone. Winus Minem had been arrested. Marius would land on his feet. Though no verdict had been read, it was clear that Festus Rufius' Spanish rampage was finally over.

In between wheezes, Severus remembered having left his hungover deputy guarding the door to the treasury. He hurried across the plaza and caught up with Governor Kleptus padding toward the basilica as fast as his overtaxed legs could bear. Don Rexus shuffled alongside the governor, stopping frequently to allow the big man to rest his fallen arches.

"What a dismal event." Rexus shook his head. "Really, some days I don't know why I bother with the theater. It's just not what it used to be."

"Nonsense! The people who stayed until the end got double their money's worth." Kleptus scolded the tired actor as he might a reluctant taxpayer. "You're just mad that Rufius stole the show."

"Stole the show? He may have stolen everything else in this

blighted province, but that show was mine from start to finish."

"At least the emperor will be happy," Severus said.

"If Hadrian's happy, I'm happy. Anyway, he's off our backs for now." Kleptus had been supervising the flow of ticket money and upfront payments from vendors and concessionaires all week long. He put a heavy arm around Rexus and smiled broadly. "And what's good for the emperor is good for Hispania. We've replenished the treasury and now we're entitled to a share of the spoils."

Gaius Severus ran ahead of the slow-moving duo to verify that Limbo was still on duty. Guarding the locked door to the treasury was a job only a fool could make a hash of, hence the concern.

Limbo was snoring against a column outside the basilica with a stray dog curled beside him. The dog fled when nudged but Limbo just rolled over and mashed his rosy face into the fluted stone. Unable to rouse him, Severus grabbed the boy's ankles and dragged him away before the governor and Rexus came into view.

"I can't wait to count the winnings." Kleptus padded toward the once gilded door and braced himself with the bronze handle. He reached inside his sweat-stained toga, extracted a leather lanyard and struggled to pull the tight loop over his head. "Let's take off our sandals and wiggle our toes in gold!"

"More gold than the gods!" Rexus seemed giddy. "Hadrian doesn't need all of it, does he?"

"We're certainly entitled to a commission." Kleptus fumbled with a second key. He squeezed through the inner door and then stopped abruptly. *"Vesuvius!"* The big man staggered backward, crumbling in what promised to be a slow, hard fall.

Rexus strained against the collapsing weight of the stunned taxman. Severus jumped forward to help stabilize the governor and push his trembling bulk forward into the domed room.

Drawers hung open. Strongboxes had been emptied and now lay scattered. Nothing remained except one tarnished coin and a fragment of papyrus. The room had been ransacked.

"Romulus and Remus!" Rexus muttered. "We've been robbed."

"Where's the money?" Kleptus ran his finger along the edge of an open drawer and inspected another to verify that indeed, the treasury had been drained. A great wave of worry broke across his damp forehead. He clutched his heart with a fleshy fist. "Not one *sesterce* is left!"

Severus picked the papyrus fragment off the floor. He struggled to find his voice. "Hadrian thanks Hispania," he read.

"This happened to me once in Narbo," Rexus said. "A stage manager stole the proceeds and disappeared with one of the actors."

Kleptus slumped to his knees with a dull, chubby thud. He crawled along the intricate tile floor, seeking either a clue to open an investigation or a knife to open his wrists. Finding no sharp insights or implements, he lay face down on the floor and heaved like an expectant volcano. "I'll be crucified."

"Don't worry, sir," Severus said. "I'm pretty sure you exceed the weight limit."

"This is your fault, Severus," Kleptus moaned without looking up from the mosaic. "You're even dressed like a criminal."

"The prisoner's tunic is my stage costume," Severus said. He decided that it was better to scour the room for evidence than further explain his attire. A quick once-over revealed no holes in the walls or cracks in the skylight. The impenetrable sanctum was as Kleptus had left it, minus any sign as to how the money might have been removed.

"How could this happen?" Kleptus asked. "I have the only keys."

"Which makes you the prime suspect," Rexus said. "Say, if it's time for another governor, I'd be willing to fill in, but I'd require payment in advance."

"Don't be daft," Kleptus snapped. "I didn't rob myself. Besides, I was at your stupid show all day long."

"My stupid show?" Rexus flinched as if struck. Genuine indignation shone from under his faded stage makeup. He stomped out of the treasury with his toga swirling.

Defeated and too weak-kneed to stand, Kleptus propped himself against the wall. For all the firm trappings of power, the governor appeared to be melting like lard in a pan. He flipped the treasury's lone coin and watched it spin through the air. The serrated edge hit the tile with a dull ping. Hadrian's bearded profile on one side danced with the maiden holding a stalk of wheat on the other. The coin wobbled, fell and landed on Hadrian's face.

"Don't worry, Governor," Severus whispered. "Hispania may be in dire straits, but that's nothing new. Think of this as a new opportunity to demonstrate your leadership."

"You sound like that viper, Winus Minem. Are you still working

197

for him?"

"No, that is, I never really worked for him. In fact, I was kind of working against him. I'm just a natural optimist, sir."

"Only an optimist would assign a drunken kid to guard the treasury." Kleptus wiped a hairy forearm across his drooping eyes.

Severus said nothing. There was no point in mentioning that even sober, Limbo lacked the cunning to have staged such a clever robbery. "Let's get you back to the villa."

"No! Run down to the docks and stop Plotina from leaving. Search her vexed boat. Tear out every plank and nail. I don't care if it sinks with her on it. I want that money back."

"Yes, sir." Severus saluted as if still in the legion. "No one can hide a treasure like this for long."

"I've had enough frustration for one lifetime," the governor moaned. "I'm fed up with greedy Spaniards and thieving Romans."

Severus edged toward the exit only to find Egnatia blocking the doorway. He tried to slip past her but she thwarted his attempt to leave.

"Relax, Daddy," Egnatia said. "You've had a bad day, but now I'm here."

"Daddy? He's your father?" Severus almost choked on his words. "You're the governor's daughter?"

Egnatia nodded playfully and breezed into the room. She crouched down and kissed her exhausted father on the cheek, then stroked his head and purred. "Poor Daddy, you're exhausted."

"Exhausted? Let me tell you about exhausted." Kleptus slumped like limp bread dough. "I'm so exhausted, even my exhaustion is exhausted."

"There, there," Egnatia murmured. "It's always darkest before the dawn."

"I quit!" Kleptus closed his eyes. "I quit. I quit. I quit!" he muttered as if hoping to fall asleep by counting resignations.

"You don't mean that, Daddy. It's been a rough day, but things can only get better from here." Egnatia then whispered something to her father that no one else heard.

"Severus?" Kleptus opened his eyes as if trying to banish a bad dream. "You want to marry Severus?"

Egnatia looked up and smiled at Gaius. "Sounds like we have Daddy's blessing."

Severus dashed away, leaving the big man with his unleavened biscuit of a daughter. He ran into the plaza and tried to purge the ringing sound of Egnatia's voice from his head. As much as he wanted to dismiss her, he could not deny her strange charm. She was as sweet and gentle as she was ugly and awkward. Unlike most rich girls, she truly cared for her father, something Severus wished he could still do.

A disturbing notion hit Severus as he wound toward the port. For a young man harboring dreams of rising to his full potential, an alliance with Egnatia might offer the fastest ship in the fleet. Perhaps it was time to wake up and smell the fish brine. The glaring truth was that Lena harbored no romantic notions toward him and never would.

Severus tried to shake Egnatia from his mind and focus on the mission at hand. He had to reach the port and stop Plotina before the Trial of the Century begat the Crime of the Century.

Where Lena was an impossible dream, Egnatia was real and had certainly signaled her interest. Severus shuddered at the thought. Had he really sold out to the point of considering the governor's odd daughter? Why not? She was lively, attentive, and interested—all qualities that would outlast beauty. It was not as if a gaggle of other girls were waiting in line. Sharing a bed with Egnatia could not possibly be worse than sleeping in the guard shack.

It dawned on Severus that he might have no choice in the matter. If he shunned Egnatia, Kleptus would blame him for the robbery. The treasury heist had to have been an inside job, so, naturally, the governor would punish an outsider. Never mind that Severus had no key or that he had been in court all day. Every thief had an alibi and who better than the chief of security to take the fall? If slighted, Egnatia might implicate him just to avenge her broken heart.

Either way, he was finished as a civil servant. His clever notion of having Plotina's women patrol the town had barely skirted disaster. Rufius had escaped and evaded custody until betrayed by his own hubris. Plotina had played Tarraco like Nero's harp and had stolen the entire Spanish treasury from under his not insubstantial nose. Severus' only true victory had been to expose Winus Minem as a murderer, but this minor triumph had cost the apothecary his life.

He thought of Monobrow for the first time since the aqueduct. In the end, the difference between life and death had been barely a second's distraction. The harsh justice of kill or be killed still left him jittery. Severus reviewed the praetorian body count: Two dead in the fire, one lost at sea, their leader knocked off a bridge. The danger had passed, but Severus still felt under siege. It was hard to believe the cloud of the four cats had lifted.

The docklands pulsed with people celebrating increasingly inaccurate versions of the trial. Severus pushed through the drunks and revelers pouring in and out of the taverns and snack shops. From what little he could overhear, Rufius rumors were spawning and spreading. Emerging from the slums above the waterfront, he was just in time to see a sail tracing a line across horizon.

Plotina was gone. Her unwashed pirates had vanished like a bad vapor. Lena had departed with them on the rising breeze. Severus bit his lower lip to stop it from trembling. Each step toward the edge of the dock left him feeling worse.

Once again Neptune beckoned.

Ripples trailing from Plotina's wake lapped against the pylons. A pair of gulls traced white streaks across the fading sky. As the crowd thinned, Severus noticed a familiar figure sitting at the end of the dock.

Lena.

Severus sat down beside her. He felt as flushed and tongue-tied as the day they first met. He was uncertain as to what he still felt for her, but the sense of loss he had been feeling now lifted like a sunrise.

"You're still here?"

"Keen observation." She smiled.

"I've always had a gift for the obvious."

They sat side by side, making and breaking eye contact until both laughed at their mutual unease. Severus wondered what was left to say when things were so obviously over. What they had shared was never meant to last.

"I thought you left with Plotina."

"Can you imagine me in Rome?" Lena untied the end of her long braid and gave her head a shake.

"You would be a sensation in Rome. Your knack for augury would—"

"—get me arrested? I can't imagine tangling with Rome's version of your local goddess girls."

"You're better than all of them combined." Severus was relieved to find that talking with her was still easy. "So you're really going to stay here?"

"People think I'm some kind of psychic here—how bad is that? Besides … Plotina's girls are a rough lot. I wouldn't be surprised if they end up in an arena."

"I wouldn't be surprised if Plotina rules the empire someday."

They laughed more comfortably. The bond was weak, but Severus sensed it was still there. Was it too much to imagine that by pursuing their separate destinies, they might still find one together? Worried she might be a mind reader, he tried to suppress the thought.

"I admire you." Severus felt buoyant and out of Neptune's reach. "You came here with nothing and made a go of it. You've conquered a tough town."

"Flattering me?"

"You deserve every word of it. I've lived here my whole life and still can't carve out more than a toehold. You've got a real gift."

"You barely know the half of it."

"Then I'm halfway there."

"We're both halfway to nowhere." Lena shifted as if getting ready to stand. "I liked your stage act. What are you going to do for an encore?"

"Avoid the theater." Severus tried to look into her eyes, but she hid behind a nervous shake of hair. "I didn't really like the security job, but it did open some doors."

"Like the door to the treasury?"

"Someone smarter than me opened that door."

"But you are smart enough to know that Rufius was living on Plotina's boat the whole time you were looking for him."

"Sure." Severus felt the familiar sting of stupidity in his stomach. The fact that it stood to reason explained why he had never considered it. "I knew that all along."

"They were working together," Lena said. "It's the oldest trick in the world. Pretend to be enemies and play both sides of the game. You saw that, of course."

"Of course. Fit right into my plans." Severus felt like he was blushing from the inside out. *The oldest trick in the world!* It was hard to imagine having been more clueless. "Rufius must have copied the keys to the treasury when he was still governor."

"While your friends were putting on a show trial, Plotina's girls were emptying the vault."

"Plotina played Tarraco like a hooked fish."

Lena lowered her eyes to the water and then looked sideways with a twinkle. "Of course you saw all this coming."

"Of course, I saw none of it." Severus smiled. Lena was showing just enough spark to remind him why he had never really fallen out of love with her. As long as she stayed in Tarraco, he might have a chance to win her back.

"Did you also guess what Vindex was up to?"

"I never guessed he'd return from the dead. Maybe now I don't need to apologize for never expressing my condolences for his passing."

"When he couldn't buy his freedom with the money I'd raised, he just faked his own death."

"I nearly died trying to save him." Severus felt his stomach churn like a kicked beehive. "I was happy to see him today, but you could have saved me a lot of misery by including me in the plan."

"It was a surprise to me, too. He dove under the ship and came up on the far side," Lena said. "He holed up in Zinzin's quarters for a day, and then Carbo hid him at the villa."

Severus' mind raced so fast that his thoughts whistled like the wind. In the end, the story was simple: Plotina and Rufius were accomplices, Lena and Vindex were not. "So ..."

"So we trust the magic." Lena's hair caught an updraft from the sea. "I'll see you around?"

"I'd like that." Severus extended a hand.

"Me too." Lena pulled him upright into a warm hug.

Severus did not want to let go. He felt closer to her than anyone on earth, yet she remained a mystery, one he still hoped to unravel. He watched her disappear into the darkness at the end of the dock and wondered who she really was.

----- *fin* -----

About the Author

R.S. Gompertz grew up in Southern California inasmuch as growing up is possible so close to Disneyland. He has lived and worked in France, Spain, and the West Coast of the USA.

Also by RS Gompertz:

Fiction: No Roads Lead to Rome

Memoir: The Expat's Pajamas: Barcelona

Acknowledgments

Writing a book is a solitary activity, but it takes a village to produce the final result. I would like to thank my small but mighty critique circle of writers and friends, my two sons, and my patient and loving wife for their insights and encouragement.

I appreciate the readers, reviewers, tweeters and Facebook friends who helped make the first book, "No Roads Lead to Rome," an indie success. I hope the sequel was worth waiting for. My characters and the odd world they inhabit have taken on a life of their own so, yes, a third book is in the works.

If you like my work, tell a friend and please post a review online.

Facebook: www.facebook.com/noroadsleadtorome
Website: www.noroadsleadtorome.com
Blog: http://noroadsleadtorome.blogspot.com/
Twitter: @NoRoadsToRome